ASCENSION

A novel

STEVEN GALLOWAY

VINTAGE CANADA

VINTAGE CANADA EDITION, 2004

National Library of Canada Cataloguing in Publication

Galloway, Steven, 1975–
Ascension: a novel / Steven Galloway.

ISBN 0-676-97460-0

I. Title.

PS8563.A454A82 2004   C813'.6   C2003-905691-0

www.randomhouse.ca

Text design: Daniel Cullen
Cover design by CS Richardson

Printed and bound in Canada

2 4 6 8 9 7 5 3 1

FOR LARA

ONE

There is a steady wind, and it blows cold on Salvo Ursari's face and hands but does not deter him. He dips a hand in the pouch he wears at his waist, pinching out a clump of baby powder that he rubs onto both of his hands. Beyond the practical purpose of preventing the slippage of the seventy-pound pole he carries for balance, the powder has a distinctive odour that reminds Salvo of the past, of walks done half a lifetime ago, of his twin daughters when they had been tiny, shrieking infants, of his wife after bathing.

Salvo smiles as one such moment floods into his consciousness. It is nearly forty years earlier, his daughters barely two years old, and his wife has just put them down for the night. Salvo is lying on his back, trying to stretch out a hamstring he has needlessly overexerted. Through a wince of pain he sees his wife's legs as she glides by him, pale, ghostly apparitions, and his eyes follow her as she moves across the room and sits on the ledge of the window. The streetlight outside illuminates her from behind, makes her glow, and Salvo is reminded how breathtakingly beautiful his wife can be.

A gust of wind brings him back to reality. Now is not the time, he tells himself. You are not a young man and you had better keep your mind on the task at hand.

At sixty-six, Salvo has been told he's out of his mind to attempt a skywalk between the twin towers of Manhattan's World Trade Center. Salvo partly agrees with this assessment, but it makes no difference. Of course he's afraid, of course he knows the danger—few have suffered more than he as a result of walks gone bad—but that is of no consequence. It is his fear that lets him know he's sane; the day he's not afraid is the day he won't go out on the wire. He knows he can do this walk.

Salvo is standing nearly fourteen hundred feet above solid ground. It is the highest walk Salvo has ever done, but height is unimportant; you're just as dead if you fall from forty feet as you are from fourteen hundred. Distance-wise, Salvo has walked two and even three times as far, which is tricky because the longer the wire, the greater the danger that it will snap. A very long wire will sag in the middle, and there are few things more difficult than walking the downhill slope of a wire. At least Salvo has the comfort of this being a solo walk. He alone is responsible for the outcome of today's endeavour.

For his efforts Salvo will receive a sum of twenty thousand dollars, but the promoter's insurance company has steadfastly refused to extend coverage to Salvo himself; the policy only covers damage caused should Salvo fall onto someone or something below.

The area beneath the wire has been cleared. From where Salvo stands with his toes curled over the edge of the building, the mounted crowd-control policemen are barely visible, the crowd itself nothing more than a dusty smear. He dislikes that the audience is such a distant entity. Without the immediacy of the audience, without their energy to feed on, the wire can be a lonely place. The only consolation Salvo has is that he has performed so many times he instinctively knows how the crowd will react, can picture the people far below as clearly as if they were fifty feet away.

Salvo receives the signal to begin. He takes a deep breath, collecting himself, and offers up a silent prayer. He's seen enough on the wire over the years to know that skill and luck are not enough to get across. To survive he needs God on his side. At the very least he requires Him to be a benign presence; the last thing he wants is to have God against him.

Hoping that he'll have only earthly challenges to deal with, Salvo picks up his balancing pole. The wind moving across the wire creates a sound not unlike that of the highest string on a violin. As he steps onto the wire, the weight of his body momentarily silences it, before it resumes its singing. Each step Salvo takes interrupts this one-note song, but between steps it always begins again. It is as if this wire is trying to play me a death march, he thinks, and each step I take forces it to start over. As long as I keep taking steps, it can't complete its song, and everything will be okay.

The wire digs into his feet through the ballet-style slippers he wears, and he can feel the wind go right through the cotton of his jumpsuit. Salvo doesn't wear conventional, tight-fitting costumes. He doesn't mind them when performing under a roof, but on a walk like this one he prefers slightly looser clothing, the folds of his snow-white jumpsuit acting like antennae, a way to feel the wind's strength and direction.

For a man his age, indeed even for a man half his age, Salvo is in exceptional shape. He is thin and lithe and undeniably strong, his slight form belying a muscularity that is rare for his body type. His hair has turned from the darkest brown to a peppery silver with the utmost dignity, even if his hairline has slipped back a little. Thick, leathery lips lie on top of a set of teeth that, despite a minimal regimen of oral hygiene, are almost unnaturally bright. His face, still handsome after being weathered and beaten by sixty-six years of hard living, is quietly inviting, trustworthy. A person would, if they were to meet him on the street, be inclined to like him. But the most striking thing about Salvo is his eyes. Set deep in their sockets and veiled behind thick, dark eyebrows, they are the colour of an emerald forest, capable of being cold and piercing one moment, calm and soothing the next. They can speak kindness or anger more loudly than words. Whenever people think about Salvo, they think first of his eyes.

The sky is grey, gloomy, not at all the sort of weather that is good for a Fourth of July, let alone a wire walk, but Salvo would rather have this kind of weather than the bright sun and swelter-ing heat the forecasters had predicted. Hot air rising off the streets can create nasty updrafts, which are considerably more dangerous than a slight breeze. Still, he would not want to be up here in a thunderstorm.

You old fool, he reprimands himself, here you are 110 storeys in the air and you're worried about getting struck by lightning. He pushes such thoughts out of his head, ignores the fact that here, almost fourteen hundred feet above the ground, carrying a large, conductive pole and walking on a steel wire, he is the human equivalent of a lightning rod. He takes another step forward, again silencing the wire.

Salvo settles into a state of intense concentration. He is barely a quarter of the way across, and the most difficult part of the walk is yet to come. The balancing pole is getting heavier with every passing second, but instead of becoming fatigued he makes it an extension of his body, its weight holding him steady. The fabric on the left leg of his jumpsuit snaps taut as he is buffeted by an unusu-ally strong gust of wind. He uses the pole to correct his balance and makes a mental note to pay closer attention to these gusts. There is a fierce way the wind whips between these buildings that both frightens and invigorates him.

Once, a newspaper man asked him what it felt like to walk high above the crowd, with death looming beneath him and success a long way off on the other platform. Not knowing how to answer, he had told the man that it was like being a bird, an eagle, but he knew that wasn't true at all. An eagle has wings. When an eagle flies, it knows it will not fall. He is a man, nothing more, but he is a man who dares do things other men merely watch and admire and envy. He used to walk for these people as much as for himself. Today, however, he is walking only for his own fulfillment. That is the difference with these solo walks. All the past successes and failures and problems of the world below are erased from memory. When he is among people, he is one of them, with hopes and fears and memories of things gone wrong. Here he is timeless, one man on a wire far above it all, in a separate place. He is not free, but he is as free as he will ever be.

Salvo is nearly halfway across now, making good time but not hurrying, and things are going very well. The wire is holding tight, and the wind isn't bad. At the halfway point there will be a piece of red tape marking the place where Salvo has agreed to do a handstand, a special bonus for the crowd below. The promoters had also asked him to unfurl an American flag from his leg. He refused. Not only is such a stunt unnecessarily dangerous, but Salvo is a performer, not a politician. Besides, he isn't even American.

For Salvo, a handstand on a wire isn't that difficult, and the height of this wire will actually work to his advantage. Because the audience is so far away, he has decided not to bother to "sell" the trick. Ordinarily, if he were working at a lesser height, he would waver and wobble his handstand slightly, not so much that he would lose control but enough that the audience would wonder if he were about to topple. At this height, however, there's no point in such theatrics, which is too bad. The selling of the trick

5

is the real essence of it, but from a safety standpoint, at fourteen hundred feet, it's a good thing he doesn't have to bother.

Salvo lowers his body to the wire, bending at the knees and placing the pole perpendicular to his path. He bows his head and thrusts his legs skyward. His hands hold the pole on either side of his head, allowing him to correct his balance from side to side and to use his inverted legs to control his back-and-forth movements. Only the slightest of corrections is possible: if he over- or under-corrects he will fall. That gets most people, he knows. Once you over-correct, you have to compensate on the other side for your mistake, and more often than not that gets you wobbling from side to side until you lose it and you're gone.

When his legs reach their apex he arches his back, and the hand-stand is complete. There follows a brief moment when the wind catches his body at an unfortunate angle, and he's not sure if he will be able to right himself. His arms tighten, and his stomach and thighs strain to halt his momentum. A streak of pain shoots through his hip, but he ignores it and struggles to undo the dam-age. His torso has twisted slightly and he rotates it back into alignment, almost going too far, barely saving it. His left arm, exerted to its fullest capacity, begins to shake, but he continues to struggle, pushing his body so that it screams in protest, then pushing it still further, until he is balanced again and the danger has passed. He holds the handstand for several more seconds, partially to make sure he has fully regained his equilibrium before attempting to dismount, and partially to assert his control over the wind, to show it that it can't blow him over that easily.

Satisfied that he has conquered the handstand, Salvo gingerly returns his feet to the wire. He pauses and lets the blood rush through the capillaries emptied by his inversion, feeling his flesh tingle as sensation returns, his face hot and red. When he has recovered completely, he stands, heaving up the balancing pole and continuing his journey. Salvo knows that what has just happened would have caused most wire walkers to crumple. He has seen others in less trouble give up, and if they hadn't fallen they'd held on tight to the wire and either dropped into makeshift nets or were forced to traverse the rest of the way hand over fist. No matter which, the walk ended in defeat and disgrace. The difference between Salvo and other wire walkers is that Salvo has long ago learned to tell his body to keep going, even when it seems that he has reached the end of his endurance.

He imagines what it must be like on the ground, how the street would be so quiet that you could hear the person next to you breathing, except during his handstand, when some would have been unable to stop themselves from gasping. When he'd teetered to the side it must have seemed like something had burst; the whole crowd would have erupted into shouts and cries. After he'd righted himself and returned his feet to the wire, people would have applauded without reserve, smiling at the stranger beside them as if to say they'd known all along that this was how it would turn out.

His confidence and strength renewed, Salvo steps forward, glad to feel the wind across his face, glad for the cool freshness of the air, glad for the busy smell of the city and the solid, steady beating of his heart. Salvo knows that if he were to fall he would stand absolutely no chance of survival. After only one second he would be over 160 feet from the wire, travelling at a speed of twenty miles an hour. After five seconds he would be four hundred feet down, going nearly 110 miles an hour. At this point he would reach terminal velocity, the highest speed at which a human body can fall. That he would hit the ground a mere seven seconds later, twelve seconds after leaving the wire, he knows because he read it in the paper this very morning, a not so encouraging piece about today's skywalk.

Salvo has long maintained that most people do not want to see him fall. Perhaps one in twenty do, and perhaps nine in twenty come so that they are present if he should fall. The other half of the audience is there to see him face death and make it. It is for these people that Salvo has spent a lifetime performing. He has fear, but he's not afraid. He likes to think that if people see him face his fear, they will in some small way be able to do so as well. That's what he thinks when he's being most optimistic. Newspaper articles like the one that ran today do much to deflate him.

It doesn't matter now, however, because he is advancing steadily and feels certain he will not fall. He is three-quarters of the way across and moving at a good pace. The wind has died down, stopping the wire's singing. Sweat covers his face, and he licks his lips, savouring the salty taste of his hard work. His hip is throbbing a little, but Salvo doesn't mind the pain, having grown used to it long ago. He pictures the crowd below grinning with anticipation; he has completed the handstand and, he believes, even managed inadvertently to sell it. He has visions of his wife, Anna, down on the ground below, pouring rye whisky over ice—one for her, two for him. He always drinks two ryes after a walk; to him, the smell of whisky has become the smell of success.

With his next step he feels the wire slacken. Not a lot, but a little, and that's how trouble starts. He is not overly concerned; his crew can tighten the guy lines and winch up his wire, and everything will be fine. But as he takes another step the slackening grows, and for the next three steps it continues to worsen. He is now more than a little worried and contemplates stopping to wait for the wire to tighten. Just as he is weighing his options the wire does begin to pull taut. He breathes a sigh of relief and picks up his pace.

There is still a little slack in the wire when Salvo is hit hard from the side by a gust of wind, the strongest yet. He strains against the force of the blow, dipping his pole precariously low to one side, legs and arms and stomach fighting for equilibrium. A split second later the wire beneath his feet drops at least three inches. Salvo drops with it, aware that the worst is happening.

Because of their massive height, at their summit the twin towers of the World Trade Center can sway as much as four feet in any direction when confronted with a hard wind. Although Salvo had no intention of walking in any wind capable of blowing an entire building four feet to the side, even a slight movement could threaten him. To compensate, the wire has been mounted onto large, stiff springs at either end. The springs are strong enough that it would take a fair amount of force to move them, only barely less than it would take to snap the wire in two.

He knows that the wind that just hit him has caused one of the towers to sway towards the other, slackening the wire. He instantly prepares himself for the wire's imminent tightening. He bends his knees and drops his arms, lowering his centre of gravity: there is a great danger of his being tossed into the air, which would be very difficult to recover from. Of course, there is also the danger that the wire might snap, but if that happened there'd be nothing Salvo could do. It would be over.

The wire comes taut with a crack that cuts through the air. As much as he tries to hold to the wire, he can't. He doesn't panic when he feels the air under his feet. With honed reflexes he straightens his body and feels his upward momentum halt. For the tiniest part of a moment he is motionless, hanging in mid-air six inches above the wire, nearly fourteen hundred feet above the ground. Then he is moving downward and his feet connect with the wire. He bends at the knees, and every part of his body—from his toes up through his ankles, shins, thighs, into his stomach and chest, arms, neck and head—works to buoy his balance and keep him upright. Even his breathing plays a part in his struggle.

All Salvo is aware of is his muscles tensing and relaxing, and the only sound he hears is the coursing of his blood. There is no past, no future, only this fraction of a second, and then this one and then this one. In four seconds Salvo lives more than many people do in a lifetime, with a singular purpose few can comprehend. He does not think; he does not even start to think. His survival depends on reflex, training and luck.

Reflex and training he has. Luck, however, does not seem to be on his side today. Just as he feels his balance returning, just as it seems as though the situation is once again under control, his left foot slips off the wire. He is fast to act, and he manages to recover somewhat but not completely. His right leg is bent impossibly at the knee; his left hangs orphaned in the air.

He freezes, considering his options. Just don't move, he tells himself. There are things that can be done. He can try and lower himself even more, rest his pole on the wire and lift his left leg. Or he can try to stand, using all his strength to force his right leg to straighten.

Neither option offers any guarantees. If he tries to stand up and doesn't have the strength, he will topple. If he tries to lower himself onto the wire and a stong gust of wind comes before he is ready, he will be blown off. Better to go to the wire, he decides. At least that way if he fails, he can always grab the wire.

Slowly, with great care, Salvo lowers his body. His right leg feels as though it is being burned with a torch. He can hardly keep his grip on his pole. His jaws are clenched so tightly he can hear his teeth grinding against each other, and his vision begins to blur. The pressure in his arms is relieved as the pole comes to rest on the wire, and as his left knee rises to the wire, the pain in his right leg lessens. For the next few seconds he rests. Do not stay here too long, he thinks, knowing that his right leg will cramp if he doesn't stand up soon.

He exhales, feels his lungs burn as the air escapes, and breathes in deeply, summoning all his remaining strength. There's not much left, he knows. Better make good on what's there. If I can stand up, I'll be fine, he thinks. Just stand.

And so he stands. It isn't as hard as he expected; the wire has become solid under his feet, and the wind is gone. High above, the clouds have parted slightly, and a weak beam of sunlight streams down onto the wire in front of him. He confidently steps into the light, scanning the horizon. He is so far above the skyline of New York City, it seems small and insignificant from where he stands. Steel and bricks and concrete are reduced to lumps in a child's sandbox.

Salvo takes a step, then another. The wire feels good, like a familiar warm coat, and he is glad to be where he is. Fear has left him completely. He has faced the worst and has not fallen. That's good, but don't get too happy, a voice inside him says. You're not on the other side yet.

He pushes the euphoria to the back of his mind. There will be plenty of time for celebration later. He won't think of it again until he's down in the trailer with Anna, drinking a rye whisky.

He pauses on the wire, centring his balance, adjusting his grip on the balancing pole. He catches a whiff of baby powder but ignores it, stopping memory from invading his focus. He takes a slow step forward, settles himself and lifts his foot to step again. At that precise moment, the wire drops once more. As he follows the wire downward, the wind hits him like a wave, more than he can handle. When the wire springs up he does not go with it. He pitches to the side, his left leg completely off the wire. He feels the wire snap into the back of his right knee and buttock, and his pole twists far to the side. He can hardly hold it and then his fingers release and the pole is no longer in his hands. His hands reach blindly for the wire, and somehow he manages to clutch it and capture the falling pole between his forearms. Whatever happens, he believes he must not lose the pole. His belief is pure instinct; at this point the pole is irrelevant, but Salvo has been walking the wire for so long that reflex overrides logic. He can hold onto the wire or hold onto the pole, but not both.

His body corkscrews further to the side, and now only his right calf is on the wire, now only his ankle. Salvo is off the wire. He is falling. In his arms he still clutches the balancing pole.

He knows instantly that he's falling, he's dead. He isn't shocked and he isn't afraid. Yet as he falls, he remains focused on one final task. He twists and writhes, hands still tight around his balancing pole, manoeuvring his feet so that they are beneath him, fighting to stay vertical. In the many still photographs that are taken of him as he falls, it appears almost as though he is still on the wire.

He remembers a Romany proverb his father would mutter in times of hardship: *Bury me standing. I've spent my whole life on my knees.* Salvo has a different idea, though, one he has kept in the back of his mind nearly his whole life, one which will be his last earthly thought.

Bury me however you do. I will die standing.

TWO

Salvo wiped the dust from his eyes and stepped quickly, trying to keep up with his father. It had been a hot summer, and the fields were as dry as the dusty road they were travelling. It was 1919, less than a year since the war had ended and the Romanian army had claimed this formerly Hungarian province. If four years of war hadn't been hardship enough, now there was drought. The people of this rural section of Transylvania would have to go without for yet another winter.

Salvo's father seemed unconcerned at the prospect of things going from bad to worse. Miksa Ursari was a thin, gaunt man, with callused hands and scars on his back from having been beaten as a youth with a piece of barbed wire for stealing a chicken. He had indeed stolen the chicken, and hundreds more like it, and when the owners beat him he did not fight back, nor did he cry out. When they finally stopped, he got up and stole a horse and moved on to the next town. Revenge never even occurred to him. What would be the point? He was a Rom, a gypsy, and for a Rom the best way to get revenge was to live another day.

All throughout Europe the Roma were scattered, some having settled into towns and villages, most remaining wanderers. Since the beginning of the war, more and more people had been displaced, more Roma found themselves refugees from battlefields, starvation and conscription. But now there were non-Roma fleeing as well. These *gadje* did not readily take to a life of transience. Miksa felt sorry for some of them. He had no idea what it was to live your whole life in one place and then to be cast out. Old women with appled faces and a lifetime of belongings behind them in ox carts—he felt worst for them. There were others, though, spiteful men with lowered eyebrows, whom he did not feel sorry for. Wherever he went there were *gadje* who would try to lay blame on those who had nothing to do with anything, and nearly always it fell upon the Roma. But while the Roma undoubtedly lied and stole, it was never on such a scale as to do any real harm, and they were certainly not the ones who had brought the war, any more than they were the ones who had lost it. Miksa Ursari knew that there were many people who were looking for an excuse to make scapegoats of the Roma, and he tried hard not to think about what might happen if there were too many of these people and they got too loud.

So if Miksa seemed indifferent towards the drought, it was because he had other preoccupations. Still, he was far less concerned with the things on his mind than others were about the things on theirs. Life had always been hard; why should now be any different? There was no point in becoming obsessed with troubles. Even if life was mostly bad, there were still times that were not. And if you were to spend all your days worrying about the bad parts, you would miss the fleeting moments of good. Whether this was completely true Miksa was not sure, but he had learned that a man had to have a way of looking at things, and at twenty-seven, he thought his was as good as any.

Nine-year-old Salvo tugged at his sleeve. Miksa knew he was walking fast, too fast for the boy to keep up, but he had pressing business waiting and could not afford to slow his pace.

"Step quickly, Salvo, and I'll tell you a story," he said, knowing that his son would run to keep up before he would turn down the offer of a story.

His father had judged correctly. Salvo picked up his pace, eager for one of his father's tales. His father told the best stories of any Rom he knew, and the Roma told the best stories of anyone in the whole world. On clear evenings his father would often gather the family around a fire and tell them stories until Salvo had to fight to stay awake, and when he finally did slip into sleep, they continued in his dreams.

Miksa Ursari swallowed, pushing the grit and dust down out of his mouth. He moistened his tongue and scratched at the stubble prickling his neck, racking his brain for a story to tell his son. He knew a lot of stories, but not all of them were good to tell an impressionable boy like Salvo, especially one who listened so intently and took every word as the truth. For a Rom, his son was ridiculously gullible. Miksa worried for the boy's future.

"Do you know why there are so many Roma in Hungary?" he asked the boy.

"No," Salvo answered.

"Well then, I will tell you." The tone of Miksa's voice shifted from that of normal speech to that of a man who is telling a tale and doesn't want to be interrupted. If there was one thing Miksa would not tolerate, it was being interrupted while telling a story. It caused him to lose his place and ruined any effect he was trying to create. There would be plenty of time for questions after the story was finished.

"A long time ago, maybe before my great-great-grandfather was born, there were no Roma in Hungary. They passed through but they never stayed, finding themselves unwelcome. Then it came that one day a husband and wife and their baby were travelling through Hungary. Now, the husband, he was a great thief. He was so great a thief that it was said he could steal the tongue from your mouth while you were talking with him, and you would never even know it. That is what was said.

"Well, he was a great thief all right, but not so great that he did not get caught. And the Hungarians who caught him took him to prison, leaving the young wife and her baby on their own in this strange land, with no horse and no ox and no mule. The wife walked for many days in the direction the Hungarians had taken her husband, the thief, hoping that if she could find the prison he was in, she could plead for his release.

"On the third day of her walking she came to a village that was deserted. She was tired and her baby was hungry, so she went into a stable and sat on the straw floor and put the child to her breast to suckle. The wife was very beautiful, having had only this one child, and she had long, thick hair that she wore loose about her shoulders, where it fell down to the end of her back. She knew that it was dangerous for a beautiful young woman to travel alone, but she had a small knife and her husband had shown her how to use it, so she was not worried too much for her safety.

"She was just falling into sleep when she heard a noise outside, and not wanting her child to cry and alert whatever was there, she put the child to her breast again. There was no noise for a very long time, and the young wife thought that maybe whatever it was had gone away. And then she saw a snake, a huge snake, slither through the door of the stable and right up to her.

"This snake was enormous, long and wide as the forest's oldest tree, long and wide and fat, with skin so tough and thick that an arrow could not pierce it. It had such an appetite that it had devoured everything in the village, the people and the livestock and the feed. Only a few lucky souls had managed to escape.

"Most wives would shriek at the sight of such a beast, but this young woman was a Rom and the wife of a great thief, so she did no such thing. The snake slithered closer still, smelling her milk, wondering if it tasted as good as it smelled. The young wife recognized the look in the snake's black eyes, and she knew what it was thinking, so she gently took the snake's head and brought it to her breast, side by side with her own child's.

"There the snake suckled, so hard and furiously that the young wife thought it would pull the heart out of her, but she did not pull back. She gently stroked the snake's head, caressing the scaly hide as if it were her own baby's soft flesh.

"After a time the snake fell asleep, and as he slept she reached into her skirts for her knife. She knew that her knife couldn't cut into the snake's strong skin, but she wasn't deterred. She was the wife of a cunning man, and she thought of a plan. Taking great care that the snake did not stir from her breast, she took the knife and she cut off all of her beautiful, long hair. She braided the hair into a good strong rope. At her feet was a fetter used to secure the horses, which had all been eaten by the snake. She tied one end of the rope to the fetter, then took the other end and put it around the snake's neck, tying the rope into a hangman's noose.

"In the morning the snake awoke, and he was hungry, and he drank from the young wife's milk with an appetite suited to such a voracious creature. So intent was he on his breakfast that he did not feel the rope around his neck. The young wife stroked his head and did not flinch. She allowed the snake to drink its fill, knowing it would grow careless with its hunger satiated. After what was a long time to the young wife, the snake grew full and ceased to suckle.

"In one quick motion the young wife gathered up her baby, pushed the snake from her breast and darted towards the back wall. The snake lunged at her, fangs bared, but it was not fast enough to catch her, its belly full of milk. When it reached the end of the rope, the hangman's noose pulled tight around its neck. The beast thrashed wildly to free itself, and the young wife was afraid the rope of her hair would break. But the rope held, and the harder the snake struggled, the tighter the noose became. Slowly the snake began to die, his air choked out of him. At last, his tail grew still and his eyes bulged out, and he was dead.

"When the *gadje* who had escaped from the snake found out what had happened, they were grateful, and they immediately found the prison where the young wife's husband was being held and had him freed. They welcomed the Romany couple and their child into their village and told them they were welcome there always. But the husband, he was a thief, and he didn't want to steal from people who had treated him and his wife and baby so well, so the family left the village.

"When other Roma heard how well the people of Hungary had treated the great thief and his young wife, they wanted to go to that village. The thief, not wishing to see anything bad happen to the village, did not say exactly where it was, but still the Roma went to Hungary. And a great many of them are still looking for the village where the thief and his young wife had been treated so well, as it has been said that if that village could be found again, the Roma would cease to wander."

Miksa continued walking at his brisk pace, and Salvo was half walking, half running to keep up with him. All that could be heard was their feet thumping in the dust and a faint wind rustling in the brittle branches of the trees.

When he was sure that the story was over, Salvo spoke, his breath laboured by the pace his father had set. "Did her hair grow back?"

"What?" Miksa's mind had drifted to other matters.

"The young wife. Did her hair grow back?"

"Oh, yes. It grew back longer and thicker and darker than ever, and she was even more beautiful than before."

"What about the baby?"

"He grew up to be a great thief, like his father."

"Did he ever go back to the village?"

"No. Like his father, he was grateful to the people of the village and didn't want to steal from them. Besides, he was only a baby when he had been there, and he didn't know where the village was."

Salvo thought about this for a moment. He was sure that, as a baby, he had been places he could no longer remember. He had been many places, even as far as his aunt and uncle's house in Budapest, which he could recall, but also into eastern Romania and Bulgaria, which he could not. So it made sense.

"Do you know where the village is?"

Miksa looked at the boy. Why did he have to take everything so literally? "No, I don't."

"It isn't where we live?"

"No," Miksa said. "It isn't."

They continued down the road, past a ditch that had a dead goat half sticking out of it, its rotting legs grotesquely splayed.

"What about the snake?"

"It was dead. It was no more."

"Were there any more snakes like that?"

"I don't think so. If there were, they probably all got killed in the war."

Salvo was relieved. He did not like the thought of such a beast.

SALVO WAS THE SECOND OLDEST of the three living children in his family; his older brother, András, was eleven years old and very strong for his age, able to lift a large wash basin full of water. There was also a baby girl, Etel. There would have been six children, but three had died when they were very small. Salvo had not known them at all, really, so he hadn't been saddened by their deaths, but he heard the keening of his mother at night and he was sad for her. He also heard words like *influenza* and *diphtheria*, and he wondered if he too would die. He kept himself awake, afraid that when he woke up he would be dead, but he always went to sleep and he always woke up very much alive, so lately he worried less.

Before the war had started, Salvo's family had owned a tame bear. Their family name, *Ursari*, meant "bear" in Romany, and the family had made a living from the animal, who could do several tricks and was very smart. The bear's name had been *Bella*, which someone told them meant "good" in Italian. *Bella Ursari* the Bear, or "Good Bear the Bear," supported Salvo's family for seven years, but when the war started there was not enough food, and even though he ate better than anyone else, Good Bear the Bear got sick and, after a while, he was dead. Salvo had not seen his father cry when his younger sisters and brother died, but when Good Bear the Bear finally died, his father had buried his face in the creature's fur and cried like a young widow at her own husband's funeral.

For a long time after that Salvo's father refused to go out. He sat cross-legged on the floor and drank strong coffee and smoked cheap cigarettes, eating little, rarely sleeping, and never, ever telling stories. Then, in the spring, Salvo's mother's stomach began to swell, and three days before the war ended she gave birth to a girl.

After that Salvo's father seemed to forget about Good Bear the Bear and set to work providing for his family. He knew how to work as a blacksmith, and he made a little money shoeing horses and doing the odd repair job. The war had brought a shortage of skilled labour, but as more men returned from military service there was less demand for his work. Most people would rather go to a Hungarian smith or a Romanian smith than a Romany smith, even if the Rom did a much better job. The only jobs Salvo's father got lately were those that were either too difficult or too dangerous for anyone else.

THE ROAD CURVED TO THE LEFT, and as father and son rounded the corner, a church came into view. It was still half a mile away, but its steeple was tremendously high, so high as to be seen from a long way off. It was a very old church, at least four hundred years old—remarkable given the amount of fighting this land had seen in that time and the fact that the church was made out of wood. Rarely did a wooden structure see such an age in a place where people were prone to setting torches to buildings during times of upheaval.

The church was not particularly large, but it did not have to be. There had never been more than six or seven hundred people living in the vicinity, and of that number perhaps only two people in five were regular Catholic churchgoers. The main part of the building was two storeys high, with a steeply sloped roof designed to withstand the large amount of rain that usually fell there. Its white paint had long ago peeled away. Though the church was well maintained by the new priest and his helpers, there was simply no paint to be had.

On the west side of the church, directly above the entrance, was the steeple Salvo had seen from half a mile down the road. It stretched from the roof up towards the sky for eighty feet—square for the first fifty, then tapered for the last thirty and peaked with a flattened knob less than four inches across. What was most remarkable about the steeple, however, was the lack of a cross upon its summit.

The church did possess a cross for the steeple, the cross itself perhaps more valuable and remarkable than the actual church. It was said to be over nine hundred years old, made from an iron that had been forged in Rome and sent from a pope to celebrate the coronation of Saint Stephen, the king who had brought Christianity to Hungary. The cross was on its way to Budapest when the knight sent to accompany it had become ill and died, as luck would have it, in this very village. Since then it had consistently graced the steeples of a succession of churches built on this spot.

When the war came the old priest was worried that the church might be burned, and he had the cross taken down. Exactly how he had done it no one knew; he had died soon after. There had been a succession of temporary priests, but none of them much cared for the place, and they had left one by one. It wasn't until a year ago that a new priest had finally come and stayed. He did not mind this place so much, he said, but he did not like that the cross was not upon the steeple.

While it was decided that the cross should be restored to its proper place, no one knew how it could be done. Various people from the church had tried, but none had even succeeded in climbing the steeple, let alone in getting the hundred-pound cross to the top. Finally the priest had put up a small reward for anyone who could figure out a way to raise the cross. Knowing the inventiveness of the Roma, he made sure that the news of the reward would reach them, and that is how Miksa heard of the problem.

He immediately volunteered for the job, telling the priest that all he would require was a strong rope twice the length needed to reach the top of the steeple. The priest was puzzled, wondering how he hoped to climb the steeple, but Miksa remained tight-lipped. He told the priest he would have to wait and see and that he would come the following day to do the job.

A crowd of about forty people had gathered to watch, not all of them happy about the prospect of a Rom being the one to restore the cross. As he and his father edged through the crowd, Salvo heard the mutterings of an old Bible legend, often told by people who saw the Roma as descendants of Cain, and told by Roma who appreciated it as a good story. Salvo remembered his father telling it to him and his elder brother, András.

"When it came that the Romans decided they would crucify Jesus, they sent two soldiers to buy nails to do the job. The soldiers were given money to buy four nails. But instead of going out and buying the nails, they spent some of the money on drink and food and women. After they had had their fill, they realized that they must have nails for that morning's work, so they went and found a blacksmith, a Jew.

"'Make us four nails, quickly, man,' they said to him, and they lit his beard on fire to make him hurry.

"The man screamed from his beard being on fire, and the soldiers stuck his head in a water trough. 'Hurry! We must have four strong nails so that we can crucify Jesus this morning,' they said.

"The man, knowing who Jesus was and not wanting to have a part in killing him, refused to make the nails. The soldiers stuck their swords into him and spilled out his guts. Then they went to another blacksmith, a Serb, and they said the same thing to him, and he refused, and they killed him.

"Then they came to a Rom, who was hard at work in his forge. 'Make us four nails,' they said, 'or you are dead where you stand.' The Rom hesitated, and one of the soldiers took out a little money, a very small amount, the little that was left in his pocket from the night before. 'I will give you this coin for the nails.'

"Well, the Rom did not want to be killed, so he took the money and put it into his pocket and set about making the nails. When the first nail was finished, the soldiers took it and put it in their bag. When the second was finished they did the same, and again they took the third nail as soon as it was finished. The Rom had just started to forge the fourth nail when the soldiers said to him, 'Thank you, gypsy, for soon we'll have four nails with which to crucify Jesus.'

"At that moment the souls of the men the soldiers had killed appeared and began to plead with the Rom not to make nails that would kill Jesus. The soldiers became afraid and they ran off, leaving the Rom with the fourth nail still hot in his forge. Not wanting to waste good iron, the Rom finished the nail, but when he poured water on it, the metal would not cool; it remained glowing hot. All day long he poured water on it, but the nail never ceased to glow red, like a burning body with fire for blood.

"Terrified, the Rom packed his wagon and moved on. He pitched his tent again only after he had travelled several days, but when he did a man brought in a wagon's wheel for mending. The Rom took the fourth nail and fixed the wheel with it, and the man took the wheel away with the nail imbedded within it. The Rom again moved on, fearful that the man with the nail would return.

Months later, he was many miles away when a different man brought him a sword to be repaired, and when he touched the sword he saw the nail in the hilt, glowing red. He fled again but wherever he went the nail would eventually find him, and he would have to flee. So it went for that man and all his descendants, and that is why the Roma always have to keep moving on, and that is also why Jesus was crucified using only three nails."

The people around them knew this story well, and they knew versions of it where the Rom was not such an unwilling victim of circumstance. Salvo could feel their eyes upon him, and he knew that they were not friendly eyes. This was surely not the village the great thief's wife had saved from the snake.

They made their way to the front of the crowd, where the priest was waiting, the cross lying on the ground at his feet. He shook Salvo's father's hand and spoke to him in a hushed tone that Salvo could not quite hear. And the priest gave Miksa the longest rope Salvo had ever seen.

"You go wait over by that tree," Miksa told his son, pointing to what was once a flourishing tree, standing dead at the edge of the clearing in front of the church. The boy reluctantly obeyed, making his way back through the crowd. Miksa didn't want his son to wait with the Hungarian Christians. There were a lot of bad feelings going around, on account of the war and the revolution and Romania's troops going in and out of the area, and he didn't want the boy to become the object of anyone looking to vent a little frustration.

When he saw Salvo reach the tree, Miksa went inside and climbed a narrow, twisting staircase to a catwalk that traversed the length of the church's interior. It ran to the very back of the building, made a turn and spanned the width. In the middle of the rear catwalk, there was a window, very small, just large enough for a man to squeeze through. Looping the coiled rope over his shoulder so his hands would be free, Miksa pushed open the window and, headfirst but facing the church, climbed out. He stood on the narrow sill, up on the tips of his toes, and was only barely able to reach the lip of the roof. With all the strength in his bony fingers he pulled himself up, as if doing a chin-up, until his chest was touching the edge of the roof. Because it was so severely sloped, he was able to swing one foot, and then the other, over to the side and onto the roof. He walked along the ridge towards the front, where the steeple began. There he saw the crowd of people below, and beyond that he saw Salvo perched in the crook of the dead tree.

It was at this point that the others had failed in their attempts. The steeple was nearly straight up, and there was nothing but smooth wood to hold onto. Miksa adjusted the rope slung over his shoulder and spit on his hands. His foot stepped into the air and outward towards the far edge of the steeple. As he reached the top arc of his stride, his foot landed on a nail, no more than three inches long and less than half an inch thick, nearly invisible to the eye, certainly invisible to the crowd below. Even those who had been up here before had missed the nail, but Miksa had known about it and the others that pierced the steeple, and was relieved when it held his weight.

Miksa Ursari knew about the nails because he was the one who had put them there. In fact, he was the one who had helped the old priest remove the cross in the first place. The old priest had been something of a friend to Miksa, and when he asked him for his help Miksa had agreed without hesitating. They'd taken the cross down early one morning, in secret, and hid it in the forest to prevent it from being stolen. After the old priest died, Miksa wondered if he should go and tell someone where it was, but he hadn't trusted any of the successive priests. They never lasted long enough anyway. Apparently it didn't matter; the old priest had written down where it was, fearful that something might happen to Miksa or that in his old age he would forget where he had hidden it. The new priest found the paper and recovered the cross, but had no idea how the old priest had got it down. When Miksa offered to put it back up, he thought it best not to mention that he had been the one to remove it. Nowadays, he did not volunteer any more information than was absolutely necessary.

At its base, the steeple was about five feet wide for the first fifty feet, and Miksa had placed the nails in an upward spiral, each two and a half feet up and over from the previous one, leaving a nail in each corner and one in between. When he was on the corner he was relatively safe—it was easier to hold on and to switch his feet on the nail—but when he was on the middle nail, he had to stretch his arms out all the way, barely able to wrap his fingertips around each corner of the steeple. The wood occasionally splintered into his hands, but he dared not wear gloves for fear of losing his grip. There would be a brief moment at each nail when he had to switch feet, and here he was most vulnerable. Very quickly, using all the strength in his thickly skinned fingers to clutch the edges of the spire, he would pull his body up, just slightly, lifting one foot off the nail and replacing it with the other.

As Miksa ascended in this manner, he discovered something he was not prepared for. The last time he had climbed the steeple, it had been early in the morning, before the sun had risen. Now, however, in the heat of the afternoon sun, the wood of the steeple had been heated to a temperature that made holding on to it much more difficult. He could feel its heat on his cheek, which he'd pressed roughly against the siding, and his fingers protested vehemently, though he was sure they weren't actually burning. At any rate, it was not their decision whether to hold on or not, so he kept climbing. He wound his way around the spire, rising five feet on each side, making two and a half full revolutions. He reached the top of the square section, fifty feet from the roof of the church, pulled himself over the lip of an eight-inch ledge, and there Miksa Ursari rested.

To the people below it appeared as though Miksa was able to stick to the side of the steeple like a fly to a wall, although there were some who guessed that there were nails. Salvo didn't need to figure the nails out; he had known about them all along. His father had sworn him to secrecy, a secret that Salvo would keep if it cost him his very life. As he watched his father climb the spire that stretched towards the sky like a holy finger, Salvo's heart swelled with joy, and a little envy.

His father rested on the edge of the upper part of the towering steeple for several minutes before continuing. The final thirty-foot portion was triangular in shape, so instead of circling the structure as he had done in the lower section, Salvo's father shimmied straight up. As the steeple narrowed he was able to move faster, and to Salvo it didn't feel like very long at all until his father had reached the top. From where he sat in the crook of the dead tree, Salvo thought his father seemed a long way off, almost in another world. Salvo wondered what it must feel like to be up there, where no one else had been able to go, and as he saw the jealous faces of the *gadje* in the crowd, he was glad that Miksa Ursari was his father.

Miksa did not look down to see the admiration on his son's face. Though he had never told anyone, he was slightly afraid of heights. Sometimes it bothered him and sometimes it did not, and that day it did. He continued, drawing in a sharp breath and digging his fingertips into the hot wood. His face was slick with sweat, and his heart was beating so loudly that for a moment he wondered if the people below could hear it. He glanced down to confirm his suspicion, and the ground swayed and twisted, and he felt his chest tighten up and his stomach flip, but still he made himself keep looking. Face it, and you will either fall or you will get past it, he told himself. So he kept focusing on the ground, and just when he thought he might not be able to control his fear any more, it vanished, and he was as comfortable up on the top of the steeple as he would have been standing on the top of a fence post.

He reached into his pocket and removed an iron ring, four inches in diameter, and hooked this ring over an iron peg that protruded from the top of the spire. The peg was intended to bolt onto the bottom of the cross. Then he untied the rope from around his neck and shoulder, glad to be free of its oppressive weight. Through the iron ring, he strung one end of the rope, lowering its length to the ground. When the one end was on the ground, he dropped the other.

On the ground, one end of the rope was attached to the cross, and three men pulled at the other end. Slowly the cross rose to the top of the steeple. Miksa saw the new priest smiling to himself down below as he watched its ascent. The old priest would never have seen a symbol of resurrection here. All he would have seen was a cross going up on a rope.

When the cross reached him Miksa moved down slightly, resting his feet on two nails that were about eighteen inches below the apex of the structure. He flexed his knees together and removed his hands from the steeple. He supported the weight of the cross with one hand and unhooked the iron ring with the other. Then, with all of his strength, he lifted the cross to rest its base on the edge of the steeple. The peg that held the cross in place protruded six inches upwards, and the base of the cross had a hole to receive it, but a great deal of effort was required to lift the hundred-pound cross that extra six inches and then guide the peg into its sheath.

Miksa braced his knees more tightly than ever and took a deep breath. With a hand on each arm of the cross he lifted it up and over, shifting the base back and forth until he felt it meet the peg. He rested the cross on top of the peg for a moment and attempted to force it down. He managed to get two inches through, but the peg was rusted from its recent exposure and wouldn't go in any more. Slowly, tentatively, Miksa removed one hand and then the other from the cross, prepared to quickly grab it should it move, but it didn't. He tested its stability with a shake, first light and gradually harder, and still it held. Satisfied that it wouldn't fall on him, Miksa turned his attention to the rusted portion of the peg, which was about twice as thick as his thumb. With one hand he rubbed at the rust, feeling it crumble roughly under his ministrations. He jerked his hand back as the cross settled an inch further on the peg. Then he took the cross by the base and twisted it from side to side, feeling it move downward a little at a time.

When there were only two inches left Miksa felt the cross drop suddenly, colliding with the iron skirting around the base of the peg with a metallic clang. A shower of reddish grit skidded down the spire, and out of the corner of his eye he thought he saw a piece of the peg, perhaps half an inch wide, break loose and fall to the ground. The sight concerned him, but there was little he could do about it, as he didn't have the strength left to raise the cross and inspect the damage. Miksa untied the rope from the cross, returned the iron ring to his pocket and prepared for his descent. The last time, when there had been only him and the old priest, he had looped the rope around the cross and, after the priest tied one end to a tree, had rappelled down the steeple. This time, however, there were too many spectators that he simply didn't trust. There was no way he was going to risk having some *gadjo* cut the rope as he came down.

Miksa dropped the rope and began to climb down. The triangular section was easy enough, like walking down a ladder, but the square part of the steeple was far more difficult. Each step had to be aimed correctly or else he would be stepping into thin air with little means of correcting himself. At this point, Miksa could almost feel the ground beneath his feet, and even though it took less time to climb down the steeple than it had to climb up, it felt like forever to him. Instead of traversing the roof of the church and swinging back through the second-storey window as he had done before, Miksa sat and slid down the steeply pitched roof. When he neared the edge he used his feet as brakes, slowing enough to allow him to sit up and halt his momentum.

Beside the church stood a tree, and Miksa leapt into its branches. He was on the ground in a matter of seconds, immediately beginning to look for the priest, not wanting to hang around any longer than necessary.

Miksa could see the disdain in the eyes of the onlookers. He imagined that they must be upset because none of them had been able to restore the cross. They'd come today to see him fail at it too, and now they were disappointed because he had not failed. Their situation was no doubt confused by the fact that some part of them knew they should be happy that the cross was back where it should be, and they were not, which also made them angry, more with themselves than him. But Miksa knew that people seldom take out anger on themselves. He began to wonder if he had been wise to do this job.

The priest, seeing Miksa approaching, stepped forward with his hands outstretched. Unlike the rest of the onlookers, he felt no animosity. In his eyes all he saw was the man who had restored the cross to the top of his church. If he knew what others were seeing in Miksa, he gave no indication.

Miksa forced a smile and grasped the priest's hands. They were smooth and soft, while Miksa's were rough with calluses and scarred by this and other days' work. Even Salvo, only nine years old, had more world-weary hands than the new priest, who had come from a seminary in Budapest just before the Romanians had marched into Transylvania and claimed the territory as their own.

The new priest had worried that the Romanians would take away his church, but they hadn't so much as spoken to him, and since it was well attended, he assumed that he was safe enough in his position. His only regret had been the lack of a cross on the church, and he had for a long while been distressed as to whether he would ever be able to place a cross on top of the mammoth steeple. He had even considered having the steeple torn down and another, shorter structure erected in its place, one with a cross, but he had been discouraged from this course of action by the people of the town. He had been in a state of utter despair until Miksa Ursari had volunteered.

Now, as the new priest looked at the cross—which he did not believe was a waylaid gift for Saint Stephen for the simple reason that this town was nowhere near the road from Rome to Budapest—his heart swelled. He would not allow himself the luxury of joyous tears in public. He thrust a leather pouch containing coins into Miksa's hand, wishing he had more with which to reward this Rom.

As soon as the coins were in his possession, Miksa turned and moved towards the tree where Salvo waited, only to find his son momentarily distracted by a butterfly that had landed only inches from his hand. Salvo watched its wings twitch as it settled in and appeared to assess its surroundings. The butterfly seemed intent on spending some time in the tree, unconcerned with Salvo's presence. A sudden boyish instinct seized Salvo, and slowly he pinched his thumb and index finger around one of the butterfly's wings. The butterfly, to Salvo's surprise, did not protest or struggle. It remained calm as Salvo gently plucked it off its branch. He felt moved by the butterfly's courage and released it just as his father reached him.

Miksa lifted Salvo down from the fork of the dead tree. Without speaking, they started quickly down the road back home. The crowd had not grown any more hostile, but Miksa saw no reason to test their resolve.

Behind them, the new priest was blessing the cross. He stood in front of the church, arms raised to God, as the more-or-less faithful kneeled before him. It was apparent to all how happy the priest was, and his elation was beginning to rub off on some of them.

When Miksa and Salvo were about a quarter-mile from the church they heard a scream. They stopped and turned back in the direction they had come.

There was no way to tell who had looked up. The people kneeling in prayer were supposed to have had their eyes closed, or at least cast downwards, and the new priest had been facing away from the church, towards Salvo and his father. But everybody had heard the scream, so it was obvious that someone had looked up. And at that moment, when the scream pierced the priest's prayer, nearly everyone opened their eyes to see what had caused it.

The priest was somewhat irked; he was just getting to the end of the blessing, and now he would have to start over. It was a hot day, the heat all the worse for him in his black robes, and he did not want to spend any more time standing in the sweltering after-noon sun than necessary. He scanned the devotees for the source of the disturbance, and in a split second he came to the realization that the crowd's attention seemed to be shifting skyward, and the air was filled with more cries. He turned to see what the people were looking at, expecting to see some sort of holy miracle on the summit of his ancient wooden church. Of course these people would receive a miracle fearfully; they were a rural, superstitious bunch, and miracles had historically inspired fear in even the most worldly of souls, but he was not afraid. He would accept this miracle with open arms, and he would help these people see it for what it was. Today was indeed a joyous day.

The new priest had not yet completed his turn when the falling cross landed squarely upon him, striking him on the head. It was doubtful that he ever knew what had delivered the blow, so intent was he upon receiving a miracle. The people on their knees certainly saw it, though, as did Salvo and Miksa. From where they were up the road they saw the priest crumple to the ground like an empty sack; they saw the crowd of people leap to their feet and rush to him. They were too far away to hear either the dull thud of the cross's impact or the sharp crack that followed as the priest's skull split in two. Likewise they could not see his blood and brains spill out over the ground, where they softly imbued the parched earth.

Miksa seized his son by the arm and pulled him along. He knew that when the initial shock wore off, the *gadje* of the church would seek retribution. He knew this as sure as he knew the sun would set that evening, as sure as he knew it would rise the next morning. They would have to leave this town, and fast.

Salvo wrenched his arm free and ran beside his father. He was ashamed to be treated like an errant urchin.

"Why do we always run away when there is trouble?" his brother András had once asked.

"We do not run away," his father had said. "We leave when it is time, and we go to a better place." It seemed to Salvo that once again they were on their way to a better place, at a much accelerated rate. Still, he knew better than to argue with his father. He ran as fast as he could, his throat closing from thirst and his chest burning.

"The priest," Salvo panted, "he is dead?"

His father didn't look at him. "Yes."

The road began to slope upwards before it passed a cluster of tinder-dry brush and turned sharply to the right.

The town where the Ursari family lived was a modest place, home to seven hundred people, mostly Hungarians mixed in with some Romanians and some Slovaks. There were very few Roma. Nearly all were either Christian or Muslim, and there were some Jews as well. The only things that almost everyone had in common were a lack of food and a hatred of gypsies.

A main road ran through the town, which comprised a market-place, some shops and a tavern. There was a stable on the south side of the street, next to a blacksmith's. From the main road ran several smaller side streets that were closely crowded with houses, some better kept than others. At the very end of the worst of these side streets stood the two-room house where the Ursari family lived.

It was not much of a house. There was one low, narrow wooden door in the front of the building and one tiny window on the side. The walls were made of rough stones covered with a crude plaster that was chipped and cracked and stained. The roof, constructed of sticks thatched together in a haphazard fashion, gave the house the appearance of sporting a shaggy head of hair.

The inside of the house was nearly always dark. They owned a small kerosene lamp, but there had been no fuel now for nearly five years. Salvo slept in the front room with his brother, András, and his father's tools, and his parents and the baby slept in the back room. They had lived in this house since just before the war had started; this was by far the longest they had ever stayed in one place.

Directly to the right of the house, a ring of blackened stones enclosed a circle of lightly smoking ash, marking the fire that the family meals were cooked over. The residence had no fireplace, and before the drought, when it had rained, Salvo and his brother had held a sheet rubbed with grease over the fire to keep off the rain while their mother cooked.

Azira Ursari was at this fire, preparing a painfully sparse meal, when she saw her husband and youngest son come running up the street. She instantly knew something was wrong from the way they ran; Miksa would never run like that for any reason other than danger.

At twenty-six, Azira had been married to Miksa nearly half her life. She had bore six children, buried three, and if there was one thing she could recognize with absolute clarity, it was imminent disaster. Remaining calm, so calm that a casual observer might not have noticed this shift in her perception, she straightened the scarf that corralled her inky hair and wiped her hands on a threadbare skirt. She picked up the baby that sat naked at her feet and went into the house to gather up the family's belongings.

As they reached the house, Salvo caught a glimpse of his mother, disappearing into the darkened doorway. He took in large gasps of air, bent at the waist with his hands on his knees, trying to catch his breath. His father didn't even seem winded; save for the sweat on his brow there was little that would indicate how far he had just run. Seeing him, Salvo stood up and ignored his screaming lungs.

Miksa scanned the area, shading his eyes with a hand. "Where's András?" he asked.

Salvo shrugged. He didn't know any more than his father.

"Go and find your brother. We have to leave this place." He headed towards the house.

"Where should I look?"

His father turned, anger in his face. "How do I know? Just go and find him, Salvo, and do it quickly."

Salvo nodded and jogged down the street. On the next street over lived a girl that András was fond of. Maybe he was there, Salvo thought. Of course, he could be almost anywhere. András was a fantastic wanderer, a true Rom. You never knew where he would go, and neither did he. He could be ten miles from here or he could be right behind you. There was no way to tell.

There were, however, places that he most definitely would not be. That was how it was in this town when you were a Rom. Some places you went and many you simply did not. The Roma lived on one of two streets, an unstated rule that was known by all, whether Roma or *gadje*. Similarly, there were stores and market stalls that Roma went to and those that they did not. No one seemed to know who had instituted these rules, and no one much cared. Most Roma didn't want to associate with *gadje* any more than most *gadje* wanted to associate with Roma. It was very much a mutual feeling.

There were exceptions. Salvo himself had no particular misgivings towards *gadje*, other than a healthy measure of wariness when dealing with them. His mother's sister had even married a *gadjo*, a Hungarian, and they now lived quite happily in Budapest. Salvo had visited them before the war, and he remembered his aunt and uncle as kind people. He also remembered the old priest, who was a good man, but he was a priest and thus subject to different conditions than an ordinary *gadjo*.

He continued his jog down the road and turned onto the street of the girl who András liked to visit, but when he got there all he saw was an old woman attempting to milk a goat that was little more than skin over bones. Salvo went further down the street, hoping to stumble upon him, until he reached the end of the road, at the foot of mountains, where there was a withered bit of forest few ventured very far into. He backtracked up the street and onto the main road. He ran for a short distance and turned onto a street where no Roma lived, but where there was a man who often bought goods of dubious origin, a man that the Ursari family and András in particular often had dealings with. The man's shop was closed up, however, and there was no sign of his brother.

There was a place back on the main road where Roma went to drink gritty coffee and smoke acrid cigarettes, and it occurred to Salvo that his brother might very well be there. He was beginning to worry that he had been gone from the house for too long. He wondered how long it had been since he had started his search. Perhaps half an hour? Maybe longer? He had no way to tell. Salvo was still contemplating how much time had elapsed when he stopped dead in his tracks. Coming down the main road like a legion of ants was a mob of *gadje*, brandishing clubs and sticks and various other weapons. Some, the ones who had been soldiers, even had rifles. They were shouting, swearing, and they were moving fast.

Salvo ducked into the stable beside the blacksmith's, moving rapidly towards the rear of one of the horse stalls. He didn't see the smith and didn't know if the smith had seen him. He edged in beside a sable mare, putting his head up against the horse's flank, smelling the horse smell and speaking softly to the animal. As the throng grew closer the horse became agitated, shaking its head and snorting and stamping a poorly shod hoof against hard-packed earth. Salvo was afraid that the horse would crush him against the side of the stall, or catch him with one of those steel-clad hooves, and he realized that if he were to be discovered hiding here, it would be assumed that he was attempting to steal the horse. He cursed himself for not having taken the time to find a better hiding spot.

As the mob passed the stables he knew that he had made the right decision. He heard the words *gypsy* and *revenge* stand out among the furious drone, and he knew that if he had seen the mob, it was at least possible that someone in the mob had seen him. He was only one pair of eyes and there were many contained within the crowd.

Just when he thought that the raven horse was about to squeeze out what little breath was left in him, and just when he was sure that someone would discover him, the mob had passed. He could hear it moving down the street in the direction he had come.

Salvo waited until he was sure the mob was well away before emerging from the horse stall. He thanked the horse for not crushing him, the sound of his voice soothing the frightened animal. The street outside was quiet and deserted. It was hard to tell if the people who were supposed to be there were hiding from the mob or if they had left to join it. Either way, there was no one on the street but himself. He stayed to the side of it, ready to conceal himself if he encountered anyone he shouldn't, but he went all the way to the last place he thought his brother might be without seeing a single person.

The café was empty but it was not locked up, and there were tin cups of coffee sitting on some of the tables. The coffee was still warm. In the corner, a lit cigarette lay on the floor, its wispy smoke wafting upwards. The people who had been there had clearly left very recently, and they had left in a hurry. It suddenly dawned on Salvo where the mob had been heading. His chest clenched, and he turned and ran as fast as he could in the direction of his house.

Miksa Ursari had gone into the house as soon as Salvo left. Azira was in the back room assembling clothing and other necessities, and Miksa began to collect his tools. He put them into a brightly coloured trunk, its corners battered and caved in by rough travel. Azira came into the front room and looked at him questioningly. As quickly as he could, he explained to her the church and the steeple and the cross falling on the priest. She did not interrupt him even once, and when he was finished she placed one hand lightly on her stomach and pointed at the door with the other.

"Go warn the others," she said.

"There is no time."

"Yes. These *gadje* will go for any Roma who are left."

Miksa swallowed. She was right. Their anger was about more than a dead priest.

"Go. You must. I will do what must be done here."

Miksa nodded in agreement. "Salvo has gone to find András. He should be back soon." He stood and ducked through the narrow doorway into the blinding light.

The first place Miksa ran to was the Romany café. There were about ten men there, and he told them what had happened and advised them to leave this town until things settled down. No one needed to be told twice; this was not the first time such a thing had happened.

Avoiding the main street, Miksa ran to the road where Salvo had first gone. There was no time to go to each house, so he went up and down the road yelling as loud as he could, "The *gadje* are out for blood. Everyone should go away from here." There was no way to tell how many people heard him, but some did. They came into the street and saw that it was him, and they went back inside their houses to gather their things.

He did this again on his own street, where there were fewer people. He was at the point where the side road met the main road when he heard the approaching mob. They were moving fast, and Miksa was tired from his recent exertions in the heat. He forced his legs into a run and sprinted for the house.

Salvo reached the top of the road just as the mob spotted Miksa darting into the house. Such was Salvo's haste that he nearly caught up with the crowd and stumbled into them; only their preoccupation with his father saved him from detection. As the mob rushed his house, Salvo slipped behind a cart that lay abandoned in the tall grass outside a house belonging to a Rom who was imprisoned in a Romanian army camp up the road. No one knew quite why the man was being held, but his house had gone untouched since his incarceration four months ago.

Salvo peered over the top of the cart and watched as the mob swarmed around his home. Someone tried to open the door, but it had been barred from the inside, and the window was too small to crawl into. Besides, someone else speculated, this Rom was dangerous and could not be trusted to submit to punishment without violence.

That Miksa Ursari had no intention of surrendering himself was true, but he also had no intention of fighting the mob. He looked at Azira and the baby crouched in the corner of the front room, and he knew that the situation was dire. He began to assess his options. If he were to go outside, the crowd would, at the very least, throw him into some jail for a deathly long time, but he thought it more likely that they would kill him. He remembered being somewhere in Germany and seeing a crowd rip apart a man accused of raping a girl. They had torn his limbs right off and flayed the skin from his bones and ripped out his eyes in a matter of minutes. He shuddered to remember the sight. No, he thought, it's no good to go out there.

So he would stay in the house. The door was strong, and unless someone in the crowd got overly ambitious, they should be safe. It would not take long for the mob outside to grow restless, and he hoped that when they did they would move on, looking for an easier target.

It is likely that Miksa would not have come to this conclusion if he had been able to see what Salvo did. Once the crowd realized that they couldn't get into the house and the people inside were not going to come out, someone called for a torch. Salvo's mind seized; surely they would not light the house on fire with his father and mother and sister inside it. But with every subsequent action taken by various people in the crowd, it became more and more apparent that that was exactly what they planned to do.

There was one man in particular who seemed to be spearheading the burning of Salvo's house. Salvo recognized him from the church. He had never seen him before that, and he thought that he must be one of the ex-soldiers who had moved into the village immediately following the Romanian annexation of Transylvania. He was a large man, nearly six feet tall, with a neatly trimmed beard that grew into a point at the chin. His hair was brown and his forehead was creased with wrinkles. When he called for a torch Salvo heard his voice, rough and deep, his tongue thick with an accent the boy could not quite place.

The man was handed a torch, and he lit the oily rags with an expensive silver lighter. Salvo had never seen such a lighter. A long, thin flame rose out of it, spreading onto the torch and into the sky. Even though it would still be several hours before the sun went down, the light from the torch was clearly visible to Salvo, and he could see wavy lines of heat radiate from it. A sticky line of tar-black smoke followed the heat skyward. The man returned the beautiful lighter to his pocket and moved to the edge of the house.

Other people had been reluctant to go right up to the structure, perhaps afraid that the inhabitants would be armed, but this man was not, or if he was he hid it well. He casually walked around the perimeter of the dwelling, as though on a lazy Sunday stroll, stopping occasionally to hold the torch to the desiccated limbs that formed the roof. He lit the house in five places, showing no emotion as orange streaks of flame shot up the roof. He stepped back to evaluate his work. Seemingly satisfied, he tossed the torch through the tiny window and returned to the crowd.

The fire seemed to have a hypnotic effect on the mob. Where before there had been much shouting and pushing and jostling, now the crowd stood relatively still and quiet, as though transfixed by the flames.

Salvo watched from his hiding place as the fire engulfed the roof. He desperately wanted to rush forward, to individually smash apart every member of the mob and cut a path to the house, but he knew he could not, and he forced himself to stay where he was. He knew his father, and thought it was only a matter of time before his family would emerge from the burning building. As the flames grew brighter and the smoke thicker, he began to worry, his fear reaching a crescendo when a part of the blazing roof collapsed.

When Miksa Ursari first realized that the mob had set his house on fire, he yelled to Azira to lie down on the floor and cover herself and the baby with blankets. He hurriedly emptied the trunk he kept his tools in. When the torch was thrown into the front room, he stamped it out as best he could and hurled it into the back room. With a medium-sized pickaxe he put two holes in the bottom of each side of the chest and dragged it to the centre of the room. Ignoring Azira's protests he took his daughter, Etel, from her arms and placed her in the chest. Over her he draped the tanned hide of Good Bear the Bear. The girl did not cry as he closed the lid, but after it was closed he heard her shrieking. He went to where Azira lay just as a shower of fire fell from the roof. Its debris landed beside him, continuing to burn on the dirt floor. He never had any intention of leaving the house. He did not think that the walls would burn, being made of stone and plaster. As he pressed his face to the earth, trying to escape the smoke that was rapidly filling the air around him, he knew that while he would probably not burn to death, there was a good chance that he and Azira would be suffocated.

He remembered something he had heard about poison gas, and he thought that it was possible that it would help here too. He removed his shirt and tore it in half. Then he rolled onto his back and pulled open his pants and urinated on the two strips of cloth as best he could. He gave one to Azira but she would not put it to her mouth. He held his soaked rag to his own mouth with one hand, and with the other he forced the second rag over his wife's face. After several seconds she stopped resisting him, surrendering to the necessity of the situation.

The rags dried quickly with the intense heat and did not seem to help. Miksa did not know how long they had been lying on the floor of the burning house when Azira stopped gasping and lost consciousness, but the fire was still going strong as he felt himself slipping away. He felt as though he was inside hell's own furnace, and he could not control his coughing. He briefly thought about trying to make it to the door and out of the house, but found he could not move. It was then that Miksa Ursari knew he was going to die. He found he did not want to die, which surprised him. He'd always liked to think he was ready to accept whatever came. That he wasn't ready for death somehow gave him some small consolation. If he were to have no sorrow over losing his life, then it wouldn't have been much of one. This fleeting notion was soon overwhelmed by despair, though, and the tears that ran down his face were not entirely the result of smoke.

As the room rapidly faded, Miksa thought of his children. They are Ursari, he told himself. We are a Lazarus stock.

Although it did not take long for the house to burn, it seemed to Salvo that his whole life passed in the time it took the flames to die. When the roof fully collapsed, he slumped down to the ground at the base of the wagon and hid his face in his hands, no longer able to watch. It would be dark very soon and a cool wind had picked up, pushing scattered blackened clouds across the sky. He thought of his father and mother and how they were almost certainly dead, and the baby, Etel, too, and he tried to remember better times, when his brothers and sisters were all still alive with Good Bear the Bear, but he could not. He could hear the fire and the mob, and he could taste the smoke in the air, and he could smell the house he had lived in for most of his life becoming a pile of ash. The memory of good things was lost to him at that moment.

Then he grew angry. Where was his brother, András? They shouldn't have waited for him. And why hadn't his parents come out of the burning house? Why had they just stayed inside and died like sheep? This mob, though, he thought, they are the worst of it. They should feel their own rage. They should burn like my parents. They should burn now like they someday will when they must answer for what they have done here today. But as soon as he had thought it he knew that no one would be held accountable for his own actions. Not by the authorities, and not by God. Well then, he told himself, I will hold them accountable. They will answer to me.

As the fire began to burn itself out, so did the mob's vehemence. There were some who were as keen as ever but most were satisfied, and a few even looked as though they felt things had gone too far. As the sky darkened the mob dispersed, some crossing themselves with fallacious piety as they left the Romany street. When they were all gone, Salvo emerged from his hiding place and cautiously crept towards what remained of the house. The roof was completely gone, save for a piece that lay smouldering beside the building. The walls had not burned, but they were charred black from the smoke. Salvo did not enter the house. He peered through the tiny window and saw the bodies of his mother and father lying under some sooty blankets. He was surprised to see that they did not appear to be burned; they looked so much like they were sleeping that he almost called out to them. He did not see the body of his baby sister, and he assumed that she was somewhere in the back room, or under the blankets. He did not think to look in his father's tool chest, which lay undisturbed in the centre of the room.

Salvo walked back up the street to the house of the man who was in prison. In it he found some rags and some thick oil. He took these to his own house, and with a piece of wood from the ground, he made a torch. He lit the torch on the smoking ashes that lay beside the walls of the house, and after a final wordless goodbye to his parents and sister, he turned and left that place.

Avoiding the main road, he skirted around the edge of the town, keeping a wary eye out for anyone who might be watching him. The wind was blowing hard now, and he had to walk backwards in places to keep his torch from being extinguished. When he was clear of the town he walked on the road, ready to jump into the brush at the first sign he was not alone. There was no moon, and the clouds that were coming made it unusually dark. Salvo was glad for the light of the torch.

He passed through the front courtyard of the church and past the dead tree where he had spent much of the afternoon. In the dark he could not see whether there was a stain on the ground where the priest's head had split open, but he imagined there was and took great care not to tread on that spot. He looked up at the church for a very long time, admiring the building. There was nothing magnificent about the church. It was a plain building, but it had a sort of quiet sadness about it, as though it had witnessed a great deal in its time and the things it had seen left its heart on the verge of breaking. Salvo felt sorry for this old church, sorry that such wicked people worshipped within its walls, sorry that tonight it would burn to the ground.

He pushed his regret out of his mind. Fate did not rest in the hands of those it governed, and surely this church knew that as well as he did. Neither of them was above the whim of man or God, and if it was to be that Salvo would burn down this sad, old church as revenge for his parents, then that was how it was to be.

But revenge was something his father would never have considered, Salvo knew. Maybe revenge was only a way of fighting with fate. And certainly God would not want him to burn down a church, no matter how evil its inhabitants were. Or would He? Salvo did not know.

He caught a whiff of the torch, and the greasy smell reminded him of why he had come. His resolve strengthened. The church would burn regardless of his own damnation. Salvo lowered the torch and held it to the door. His hands did not shake.

The moment the door began to singe, he felt a drop of rain splash down on his cheek. He looked up just in time to see a streak of lightning skid across the sky, followed seconds later by an explosion of rolling thunder. The promise of rain diluted his resolve. His desire to see the church in flames was replaced with something bigger. He knew his quarrel did not lie with this old church. He jerked the torch back from the door and kicked out the small flame that crept up the wooden slat. He stepped away from the church and dropped the torch to the bare ground at his feet. The raindrops were few and scattered, and he stood and waited for them to hit him. His eyes focused on the dying torch. With his foot he rolled it back and forth on the hard-packed dirt, until it was extinguished. Lightning shattered the sky again, the thunder coming sooner than before, and Salvo knew that soon it would pour and the drought would be broken. He looked up at the steeple to where the cross had been, and he knew what he must do.

He leapt into the tree by the side of the church and went up it like a cat on a pole. From the tree onto the roof and up he climbed, as quick as if he were walking down the side of the road. He danced along the crest of the roof, his feet light and his legs strong. As he reached the steeple and stepped onto the first of the nails, he remembered a story his father had told him when he was very small and repeated many times as he grew older, a story he would never hear again except in his mind.

"Once, in a village like this one, at the foot of mountains like the ones near here, there was a Rom who was not a good man but a truly wicked man who stole the souls of other Roma. Some said he had magic, which may be true or may not. Then it came that a man who was a good man and a great thief, who never stole from those who could not afford it and certainly never from another Roma—and most certainly he never stole any man's soul—this man came to the village at the foot of the mountains."

Salvo climbed fast, and he climbed the spire very efficiently, much better than his father had done. His balance was perfect, and he had no fear of heights. He went from one nail to another to another so lightly that he barely even stepped on them. When he reached the end of the square section of the steeple it began to rain a little harder.

"When the Rom who was not wicked found out what was going on, that men's souls were being stolen, he made a pledge to the people there that he would find their souls and return them. The people were grateful to hear the man's offer, but they told him that it would not be possible, for the evil Rom had taken their souls to the top of the mountains, and there was no way to climb there. The Rom assured the people that he would do exactly that, and he set off early the next morning.

"When he reached the mountains he began to climb, but before long he got to a place that he did not think he could climb, and he stopped. He thought for a very long time about what to do, and then he spoke aloud to God. 'God,' he said, 'here is a place that I do not know if I can go, but there are men's souls beyond, and so I will try. I will do this knowing that whether I fall or not will be up to you. You are the master of my fate. So if

I must fall then that is fine, but remember that there are souls that depend upon my success.'"

Salvo wrapped his arms around the rapidly narrowing steeple and shimmied his way upwards. The rain had made the wood a little slippery, but it did not slow him down. That he was nearly eighty feet off the ground did not bother him at all. He was in a place that was not Transylvania, not Romania, not Europe. He was in a place where only his father had been before, where no one else alive could go. Here, there was only him, and maybe God. He gained the top of the steeple and the rain poured down over him.

"The man climbed to the top of the mountains without falling, and there he found the wicked Rom guarding over the souls he had stolen. There was a great fight, in which both men were mortally wounded. When the wicked Rom died, the ground opened up and swallowed him. The Rom who was not wicked was frightened, and wished not to die. He did die, very soon after, but the ground did not open up. Instead, the man began to rise up towards heaven. As he ascended, though, he looked back to Earth and saw that the stolen Romany souls still lay on the mountains. He struggled to return to retrieve the souls and managed to do so.

"When he arrived in heaven he was not allowed to enter with all these extra souls. 'You did not fall,' he was told. 'That is enough. These souls are no longer your concern.' But the Rom remembered his promise to the people of the village, and so he struck a deal that he himself would not go into heaven if the stolen souls were admitted. As a result, he was destined to stay in limbo for all eternity.

"When other Roma found out how this great hero had been treated, many cast their own souls out of their bodies in protest. The Rom who was not in heaven was moved by this action, and he gathered their cast-out souls and returned them again to their owners. There is a consequence to casting out one's soul, however, and the descendants of these loyal Roma have loose souls that sometimes escape from their bodies. Without their souls, they sometimes do things they otherwise would not do. The Rom who was not wicked knows about it, and he collects each soul for safekeeping until such time as that person is ready to take it back."

Salvo stood atop the cusp of the steeple and stretched his arms out wide, palms skyward. The rain was warm and soon he was soaked to the skin. Tears ran down his cheeks and were diluted by sweat and rain, but he did not sob or shake or move a single muscle. He closed his eyes and willed his soul to leave his body. When it would not leave voluntarily he ripped it out, and he could feel it fall to the earth, where it lay in the mud. His tears stopped. He felt his soul rise up, only slightly at first and then with preternatural speed. It shot straight up the height of the church, hung even with him for a moment and was gone.

Back on the ground he could not remember having descended. The rain had eased up a bit, and Salvo realized he was hungry. He looked back in the direction of the town, pulled his sodden shirt tightly around him and set off in the opposite direction, northwest, towards the Transylvanian mountains and, far beyond, Budapest.

THREE

───────

It was a cool October day, and Esa Nagy sat rigidly in the front room of the apartment she lived in with her husband, László, and her son, Leo. Cradled in her hands was a steaming teacup. At a casual glance it might have appeared that Esa had company over; she seemed to be holding a polite and restrained conversation. But the fact was that she was completely alone. Esa Nagy, who had recently turned thirty-two, was having an imaginary tea party.

She knew that it was an odd thing for a grown woman to do, and every time she engaged in the fantasy, she told herself afterwards that she would do it no more, but her resolve never held and she was beginning to wonder what the point of fighting it was. She had never actually been to a tea party, or anything that even remotely resembled one, and she was therefore unsure precisely what went on at these gatherings. They belonged to a whole world outside of hers, but she didn't think her one indulgence could be harmful to herself or others in any way. Still, she knew it was definitely not normal.

Normal, what is normal? she asked herself. She thought she heard a knock at the building's main door and turned her ear to the street, which was one floor down. Maybe this craziness is what keeps me sane, she ventured. Maybe everyone should do this. Maybe then things in Hungary would go back to normal. Whatever that is.

But now her brief respite was ruined. She couldn't tell whether there was someone down at the building's front door, but like a person prematurely awakened from a dream, she knew there was no going back.

She rose and moved herself into the room that faced the street. This room served as both a kitchen and an eating area, and was the warmest room in the house on cold winter days, thanks to the coal stove that stood in the corner. A large arched window allowed her a view of the street. Esa leaned out the window and searched the area surrounding the door. She saw no one at first and then, just as she was sure it was all in her head, she saw, protruding from the edge of the entrance alcove, an arm. It was a small arm, and no sooner had she seen it than the arm disappeared from view.

Esa stood in the kitchen and listened, like a mouse who suspects that an owl is near by. For a long while she heard nothing, and then—faintly, tentatively—came the sound of knuckles on wood, emanating from downstairs. Esa's brow furrowed. From about eight o'clock in the morning until nine o'clock at night, the main door to the apartment house was left unlocked. So why was someone knocking?

Esa considered going down to see who it was. Three years ago she would not have hesitated, but now things were in a state of upheaval, governments falling like raindrops, some new revolution always threatening the last, and in this time of instability it was hard to know the right thing to do. But surely there could be no harm in answering a knock at the door, could there? she asked herself. Maybe if her husband László were here he would know what to do. But he was one of the lucky ones who still had a job. Most of the others who hadn't fought in the war were not so fortunate. No, it was a good thing that László Nagy was not at home in the middle of the day.

Well, she decided, we are still living in a civilized country, and in civilized places when a door is knocked upon you answer it. She smoothed her skirts and walked out of the kitchen, into the front room and through the main door. The door opened onto a catwalk that ran along the front and sides of the apartment house, and was exposed to the middle of the building, where there was an open courtyard. Esa walked the length of the catwalk, past two other apartments, to a large curving staircase that led down to the ground floor. She kept a firm hand on the banister as she descended, wary of a fall. The treads of the staircase had been worn dangerously smooth by generations of feet, and it was easy to slip. There had once been an ornate newel post at the foot of the stairs, but in the years following the apartment house's prime, some irreverent children had sawed it level to the banister so that they could slide down the rail unobstructed.

The apartment house at 7 Viola Street was in one of Budapest's rougher neighbourhoods, and it stood out like a pine tree in a desert. A three-storey building made of blocked stone, it was built in the early nineteenth century, intended as apartments for the city's wealthier citizens. Now, a century later, the area was not one that anyone with a lot of money would want to live in, and the larger apartments had been subdivided into smaller ones. Despite the gradual disappearance of many of the building's more ornate touches, it was still an undeniably fine residence, especially when the unusually reasonable rents were considered.

Esa reached the bottom of the staircase and entered the hallway that led to the front door. There was a row of mail boxes which, before the end of war, had contained letters on a frequent basis. With the chaos that followed the loss of not only the war but much of Hungary's territory, and the subsequent governmental uncertainty, the mail had slowed to a mere trickle. It made little difference to Esa, who could neither read nor write, save to sign her own name, which her husband László had taught her to do.

There had once been a thick green carpet covering the floor of the hallway, but it had been removed in the latter stages of the war, exposing a wooden floor, its varnish unmarked. Signs of wear were now beginning to show, a trail of scuffs and water damage leading through the hall from the door to the staircase. Esa, who had never lived in such fine places before she had married László, was shocked to see that people would treat such a beautiful old building so poorly.

Esa braced herself and swung the heavy wooden door open. It gave way noiselessly, its hinges having been recently oiled by the building's caretaker; this was one of the few jobs he did with any sort of regularity. A rush of cool air chased the opening door, sending a chill down Esa's spine.

In the doorway leaned a thin, sick, exhausted Salvo Ursari. At first he was not sure whether this woman who stood before him was his aunt Esa or not. She looked like he remembered her, sort of, but it had been five years since he had last seen her, and even then he had only been four years old so he was not completely confident in his memory. There was no way to know if his aunt and uncle even lived in the same place. Salvo had, like any good Rom, correctly remembered the address on account of the street bearing the name of a musical instrument. The house number he had not been so sure about, but as soon as he saw the apartment building at 7 Viola Street, he knew he was where he was supposed to be.

His aunt Esa had been a very beautiful woman when she had defied Romany law and custom by marrying a *gadjo*, his uncle László. Her mother and father disowned her, as they were obliged by rule to do, and Esa moved to Budapest with her husband. When her parents died shortly before the war, she did not go back for their funerals. Her younger sister, Azira, Salvo's mother, had ignored her banishment and visited her sister twice in Budapest, once before Salvo was born and the other time when he was four years old. Salvo's father had accompanied them to Budapest, but he had refused to shake László Nagy's hand and would not sleep under his roof. Salvo did not know whether his father's hostility stemmed from personal reasons or if it was an attempt to avoid any possibility of the shame of László and Esa's relationship attaching itself to the Ursari family.

That mattered little now, though. It had taken Salvo two months to get to his aunt Esa's house, and he didn't care if she was an outcast or not. He remembered almost nothing of the journey; he had been in a haze of hunger and grief and fatigue. But he had made it. There had been times when he had thought he would not, but he was here and what would happen now did not matter because, finally, he had reached the end of his travels. Salvo fell to the ground.

His aunt Esa stepped back, startled, one hand on the door. "What do you want?"

Salvo was unable to speak. His mouth moved like that of a fish removed from water, gulping at the air.

"What do you want?" his aunt repeated.

Salvo closed his mouth and, with every ounce of strength he could muster, called up his voice. He received one word for his efforts. "Ursari," he croaked.

His aunt's face remained blank for a moment, and then her eyes flashed recognition as she realized who he was. With a strength far beyond the usual capability of a woman of her size, she scooped Salvo into her arms and carried him upstairs.

~~~~~~~~~~

Esa Nagy tossed three large sausages into a pot of boiling water. She found sausages to be strangely ironic things. Take the intestine of an animal and stuff it with its own flesh or that of another animal. It was like you were eating a creature that had eaten itself. Still, sausages were cheap, easy to cook, and László couldn't get enough of them. As hard as he was to please in nearly every other area, if she put a sausage on his plate he was happy.

The winter of 1921 had been an unusually cold one, she reflected, glancing out the window of the kitchen. Or maybe it just seemed that way. After all, didn't every winter seem colder than the last? That was, Esa decided, the very nature of winter. It had a way of making you think your suffering was new. A good trick, she thought. A very good trick.

The children, Salvo and Leo, were in the front room playing. When Salvo had first arrived, Esa worried that they would not get along. More specifically, she worried that Salvo would treat Leo harshly because of his clubbed foot. She knew how the Roma treated those who were disfigured. She herself remembered how, when she had been a Romany child, she and her playmates had thrown rocks at a man with one eye. She did not wish for Leo to face that from Salvo.

This had not proven to be the case, however. From the very beginning, Salvo had taken to protecting Leo from any special attention that might be accorded him due to his being a cripple. Three years his senior, Salvo acted the part of older brother far better than any real older brother would have been likely to do. He was, as far as Esa was concerned, a blessing upon the Nagy family.

Salvo, for his part, felt that the Nagy family had done him a small miracle by letting him stay for these past two years. He missed his family, sometimes so much he could hardly imagine what it had been like not to miss them, but without Esa and Leo he knew it would be worse. He also enjoyed the *gadje* lifestyle far more than he ever would have imagined. The Nagy apartment was, by Salvo's standards, a palace, and they ate far better than Salvo had ever eaten in his life. As for Leo, Salvo liked the sickly boy, and seeing as how the child didn't seem to care who Salvo was or where he had come from, Salvo decided that he didn't care about Leo's physical shortcomings. Besides, it wasn't as if there were a lot of other kids for him to play with. Most *gadje* children wouldn't play with a Rom, and László had strictly forbidden both Salvo and Leo from consorting with gypsies. So Salvo really had no choice.

Salvo and Leo sat on the floor. Today they were bandits on the run, huddled around a makeshift fire, their voices low, eyes nervously scanning the night for signs of their pursuers. The head bandit, Salvo, told stories to pass the time.

"Sometime in the past, in a place that is not this place, there was a village of *gadje* who could not talk to God. They had lost His voice, and wanted badly to get it back. But it would not come, no matter how they asked for it.

"Then one day they asked, even begged, a Rom who lived on the edge of the village to help them hear Him again. The Rom was suspicious, but he felt badly for them, so he agreed to help. The Rom went and climbed the steeple of their church and asked God to speak to these people again. But there were things this Rom did not know.

"He did not know that God had stopped speaking to these people for a reason. He went silent because the people were wicked. He went silent because the people were greedy. He went silent because these people were no longer His people. None of God's opinions were known by the Rom, but maybe the Rom would have agreed with God. After all, it is not often that God is mistaken.

"So the Rom, in his ignorance, asked God to speak again to the *gadje*. Because God loved the Rom, He granted this request. But He refused to lie to the *gadje* and tell them good things about themselves, which is what they wanted to hear. He told them the truth, which is never what anyone wants to hear. The pain of hearing it caused the village priest to fall down dead where he stood.

"The *gadje* did what *gadje* have always done, which is blame the Rom. They found him in his home and they killed him. But killing a Rom is nothing; it will not stop him. The ghost of the Rom returned to the *gadje* church and went to the top of the steeple and called again to God. God told him that from that day forth, He would no longer speak to the people, not one word. And He spoke no more."

Esa stood in the doorway. "I have never heard of this story."

Salvo blushed. He hadn't known she was listening.

"Is it true?" Leo asked, eyes wide.

Salvo nodded. "It is, or may I be dead."

"You will not die of this, but that story is not true, and you would be wise to watch where you repeat it." Esa returned to her kitchen of sausages.

"Maybe now," Leo said, "God isn't mad. Maybe you could talk to him."

Salvo shrugged. "Maybe you could too."

"Nagys aren't Roma," Leo said. "Mother used to be, but she stopped."

Salvo nodded. She had stopped. And his uncle László was no Rom, that much was obvious. Salvo knew his aunt was right; he should watch what he said. He shouldn't make up stories that served no purpose except to aggravate his well-being in this house. Being a Rom had caused him trouble enough already.

The knob on the front door turned and the door swung open. László Nagy drooped into the apartment, shedding his heavy coat and scarf and hat and gloves into a frozen lump on the floor. It was only a ten-minute walk to the glass factory where he worked, but that was long enough for his moustache to have frozen stiff, with two icy rivers extending from his nostrils.

He nodded to Salvo and Leo and crossed through the front room into the kitchen, where he stood by the stove and let its warmth seep into him. Esa kissed him on the cheek and brought him a cup of hot tea. It was too hot to drink, so he set it on the sill of the window to cool. "I'll burn my mouth if I drink that," he said.

"Sorry." Esa took the cup from the window and poured it out. She set another one to steep, wary of its temperature.

László Nagy watched his wife as she tended to whatever was on the stove. When he had first met her, he had thought her the most beautiful thing he had ever seen. It had not mattered to him that she was Roma; after all, no one can help what they are born into. He had offered her a better life, and she had accepted with little hesitation. She had known as well as he had that if she married him she would be disowned by her family, something he had thought to be a not altogether bad thing.

Since then, though, for some reason he found Esa less compelling than when he had first laid eyes on her. She certainly had not changed that much. No more than he had. To be sure, she was still beautiful. But there was something about her now, something he thought she saw in him that he did not like and for which he felt great guilt. He often wondered what it was she saw. A part of him knew that there were things inside him that were worth being ashamed of.

Like his feelings towards Leo. He knew that it was foolish of him, almost stupid, but for some reason he could not look at his son without seeing his deformed foot. And because of this failing, he knew that some of him did not love his own son. Not as much as Esa did, anyway.

Then there was his job. Although by most standards it was good work, and many men would love to have a job such as his, László felt deep inside that he was capable of better, that he held the promise of something more. And he hated himself for ignoring this potential. But there were mouths to feed, so he had no choice. And because it was easier, he blamed the source of these necessities instead of himself. He resented Esa. He resented Leo. Lately, though, he mainly resented Salvo.

That his wife had taken in an orphan of the relatives who had shunned her was admirable. True. But he always remembered that it was easy for her to do so because she was not the one who had to go to a glass factory every day to support him. Not to mention the fact that the boy, Salvo, made the hair on his spine stand on end any time they were alone in a room. There was something about him that made László very, very nervous.

Esa saw that he was staring at her. "Sausages," she said.

"What?"

"For supper. Sausages."

"Oh." She handed him the new cup of tea, temperature just right, and László resolved to find a way to love his wife again. He could do such a thing, he told himself. It would be no trouble at all.

In the front room, Salvo and Leo had abandoned the game of bandits. Now Leo sat on the floor, and Salvo entertained him with acrobatics. Quiet ones, as they had to be careful not to raise the ire of László. Salvo took a wooden chair with a high back and placed it in the centre of the room. He stood on the seat of the chair, put his hands on the back, and as smoothly as if he were rolling over in his bed, he did a handstand on the back of the chair. Leo beamed. If it were not for the noise it made, he would have clapped his hands together and cried out. Salvo decided to take the trick a little further. Still holding his handstand, he leaned the chair back until the front two legs came off the ground. He remained upside down for ten seconds, and despite his best efforts, Leo could not stop a tiny squeal of delight from escaping his lips. Salvo let the chair rest on all four of its legs, then reverted his body to an upright position and dismounted.

Salvo had never been taught how to do this manoeuvre. He had always had good natural balance; when he was only nine years old, he had, after all, climbed the very steeple that many grown men had failed to conquer. One day he had looked at the chair, and it occurred to him that if he wanted to, he could probably do a handstand on the back of it. It was relatively difficult at first, but after a few dozen times it became quite easy. Tipping the legs off the ground was trickier, but he'd mastered that as well.

László entered the front room just as Salvo returned the chair to its proper place. László had not seen any of the balancing. He set about picking up his winter clothing from the floor, setting his coat on the hook by the door. He looked at Leo, who was rubbing his lame foot. "Cold today," he said.

"Too cold," Leo replied.

"Maybe hell's frozen over," László said. It was supposed to be a joke, but his tone of voice hadn't given any cue. Both boys' faces paled and their mouths dropped.

Leo looked to Salvo. "Did that happen?"

Salvo shrugged. Anything was possible.

"No, don't worry. This isn't hell. It's only Hungary," László said. Once again, it was a joke that was above the heads of children. Cynicism is always lost on the young ones, he thought. "Winter will be over soon."

Again Leo looked to Salvo. "Ask God for us if this is hell."

Salvo's breath caught in his throat. László looked at him, puzzled. "You're talking to God now?"

"No," Salvo said. His hands began to shake.

"God used to talk to the Roma. Maybe he will again," Leo said.

László seized Salvo by the shoulder and pulled him into the kitchen. With a look, Esa knew this was trouble.

"Who has been telling Romany stories to my son?"

"I'm sorry." Salvo said. László's fingers were digging into his shoulder, which was rapidly going numb. Tears began to well up in Salvo's eyes.

"Your stories are not to be in this house. Filth. My son will not be a thief. He will not be a liar. He will not be dirty and he will not be poor."

"Yes, Uncle."

Esa remained quiet, but she was becoming angry inside. She had been Roma once, and she was neither dirty nor a thief nor a liar. László had no right to say such things.

"You want a story? I've got a story for you, then. There were these three travellers: a Hungarian, a Jew and a Rom. They went to a farm one night, looking for a place to sleep. The farmer told them that he only had two beds; one of the travellers would have to sleep in the barn. The Hungarian wasn't selfish, so he said he'd sleep in the barn. When he got there it was full of animals, and it was too foul to sleep in. He returned to the farmhouse and told the Jew to sleep there. The Jew went to the barn, but there were pigs there and it was not kosher for him, so he came back to the farmhouse and paid the Rom to take his place.

"So the Rom went to the barn to sleep. After a while there was a knock at the door of the farmhouse. It was the cows and the pigs and the chickens. 'Look,' they said, 'let us sleep here with you. We can't sleep in that barn with a dirty Rom.'"

Esa watched László's mouth form a sneer, and she struggled to keep silent. This was not her battle. She had decided she would lose this fight a long time ago. Her choice had been made, and she had chosen László over her people. She didn't know if she had done the right thing, but it no longer mattered. She loved her husband. This meant she must continue to love him, even during times like these. That was how things worked, whether she was Roma or *gadje*.

Satisfied he had made his point, László released his grip on Salvo's shoulder.

"You understand what I've said?"

Salvo felt his arm prickle as circulation was restored, and he rubbed the sore spot with his good hand. "Yes, Uncle."

László nodded and strode out of the room. Salvo choked back tears. Maybe his uncle was right about the Roma. No good had ever come from his being one. Only trouble, only misery. His aunt had stopped being a Rom, maybe he could too. But he did not want to. His father was Roma, as were his mother and brothers and sisters. They had died because they were Roma, and he would not be made ashamed of what he was. Instead he would become more Romany than ever. Someday, he would become like one of the Roma his father had told stories about.

Esa watched Salvo's face and felt a twinge of sorrow for what she knew the boy was enduring. She said a silent prayer that he would come through this torment with his spirit intact. "Come and sit," she said, placing a hand on his shoulder. "Have some sausage."

———

Etel Ursari would never remember being locked inside the burning house. She had no memory of András opening the trunk, lifting her out and carrying her from the house, keeping his body between her and the still figures that had been their parents. Her earliest memories were of a winter spent in a hunter's shelter deep in the forest, of being hungry and cold. She could not recall the faces of her parents, or of Salvo. Only András.

For nearly two years they had stayed hidden, András fearing for their lives if they should be found. They ate what András was able to forage, risking a fire only when absolutely necessary. He dared not even trust other Roma. Eventually they ran out of options. The woods were becoming increasingly dangerous as more and more people fled the turmoil of the war's aftermath. András decided that they would be safest in a large city, far away from the provincial town that had destroyed their family. It was a hard thing; at twelve years old he was an orphan, penniless and in charge of a baby girl.

Hardship was something Etel knew from her first memory, a fact that stood in front of her since thought began. It was not worn as a burden, and there was no regret attached to it. It simply was, and things went forward from there, it naturally being assumed that life was a wrenching endeavour that lent no favours to unfortunate Roma.

András, though, had known other things, and he was unable to put his sorrow aside. Though he had long considered making the trip to Budapest to seek out his aunt, he did not go. Either this place was not done with him or he was not done with this place.

He vowed revenge; he savoured the prospect. His days were spent waiting, full of patient anger, his chest heavy with a dull ache he was sure would never go away.

In the spring of 1921, shortly before Etel's third birthday, they made their move. It was their intention to make their way to Budapest, where there might be work for András, and even the possibility of family. First, though, there was something András wanted to do. Young as she was, Etel knew immediately that it was something serious, something that was beyond her reckoning. She could tell that her brother would rather not have brought her along, but there was nowhere else for her to go. They waited until well after the sun went down. There was no moon, and as they moved quickly through the streets of the town that had once been their home, Etel grasped tightly to András's back. In his arms he carried a large, sloshing, metal can. She did not have to be told to make no sound.

As their destination approached, András remembered running down a muddy road in the middle of a thunderstorm, seeing the charred house, seeing his mother's eyes wide open, his father's mouth agape. He had heard Etel's cries from inside the trunk, felt a wave of relief when he opened the lid and saw her, frightened but unharmed. He was seized by panic, fearing that his parents' killers would return to finish the job. He wondered where Salvo was, scooped Etel into his arms and fled to the forest.

These memories were placed aside when they reached the church. András put Etel on the ground beside a thick tree at the edge of the clearing, telling her to stay out of sight. András moved quickly around the back edge of the church, dousing the siding with kerosene. He stood still for a long minute, staring up at the steeple with no cross at the top. Etel heard nothing until the sharp snap of a match igniting, and a *whoosh* as the hungry wood consumed its flames. Before she even realized what he'd done, András was scooping her up and carrying her into the woods.

Peering over his shoulder she could see the church burn; she could smell the smoke of the fire and feel its heat. When they were a distance away, cries of alarm rose from the church, but by then it was too late to stop the fire. It never occurred to Etel to wonder whether anyone had been inside. It had occurred to András, but he didn't care. They moved slowly through the woods, choosing stealth over speed, going all night without stopping. András had no idea if there were pursuers behind him, but he felt it best to assume that there were. Etel watched over his shoulder for signs that they were being followed. All she could see was fire, long after it had disappeared from view.

They worked their way towards Budapest, staying clear of towns and main roads wherever possible. They slept in farmers' fields and spent a comparably luxurious night in an empty barn. Etel wondered where the animals were. András knew they had all been slaughtered.

About a week later, they were trudging along a desolate side road when the sound of wagons came up from behind them. András ushered Etel into the underbrush, where they crouched amongst the brambles, waiting for the wagons to pass.

After a while a pair of horses came into view, good strong horses. They pulled a brightly painted wagon driven by a man wearing a gaudy hat. Several more wagons followed. A man rode a white horse beside the third wagon. He was dressed in new clothes, and he looked like he ate regularly. Behind him were four or five more wagons, and voices could be heard from all around. It took András a second to realize that the voices were speaking Romany. Etel did not know the difference between Romany and

Hungarian, her language being a mishmash of the eastern dialects that András knew bits and pieces of.

When the man's horse cáme astride the spot where András and Etel were concealed, his rider bade him stop. The man remained frozen as the wagons continued, and then, as if smelling the children, he turned and looked straight at the bushes that hid them. He whistled sharply between his gleaming teeth and the wagons stopped smartly, like soldiers on parade. He slid off his horse, his hand moving to his side, where the hilt of a knife thrust upwards from his belt.

"Who is there?" he said in Hungarian, his voice solid and commanding.

András froze, wondering how the man had known they were there. Etel, however, let out a frightened squeak, and immediately the man was joined by three other men whose clothes were not as good as his. "Robbers," one of them hissed in Romany. He had a rifle, and he raised it at the children's hiding place.

"No," the man answered, "I do not think so." He placed a hand on the rifle, gently pushing its barrel downwards. "Come out," he called again.

Etel made as if to move forward, but András grabbed her arm and held her still. The rifle again rose, and this time the well-dressed man made no move to stop it. A shot exploded from the rifle and the ground sprayed dirt in their faces.

"Stop," András called in Romany, instantly wishing he hadn't. Now they were revealed. Rough hands pulled them from the brambles and stood them in front of the well-dressed man. He looked at András first—a long, hard, assessing look that made András sure the man could see into his bones. Less attention was paid to Etel, but enough that she felt close to tears, though she never cried. "Roma," her brother had often told her, "do not weep for fear."

The man nodded and his cohorts released them. "You are Roma?" he asked.

András nodded.

"Funny thing. A few days ago, we went through a village that was looking to harm Roma. One in particular, a boy about your age. Seems he had burned down a church. You know about this?"

András said nothing, but his hands began to shake.

"We were lucky to get away. They knew we had nothing to do with it but did not care. To most *gadje*, we Roma are all the same." The man grabbed András's hand, and before the boy could pull it back, the man held it to his nose and inhaled deeply. "Kerosene," he said, a slow chuckle rolling from the back of his throat.

András smelled his hand, detecting no scent of kerosene. "I smell nothing," he said.

"Neither did I," the man answered, "but your actions tell me everything."

András looked down at his feet, ashamed to have been tricked so easily. The man squatted down and brushed Etel's hair out of her face. "What is your name, little one?"

Etel stood up as tall as she would go. "Etel Ursari," she said.

The man smiled. "Ursari. You are a bear, then?"

Etel growled her meanest bear growl, intending to intimidate, and the man laughed. He stood up. "I am Anosh Mór. I lead these Roma. If you like, you may travel with us."

"We're fine," András said.

"I don't think so. People are looking for you."

András looked at Etel, and felt his stomach tighten from emptiness. He knew that he had little choice but to trust this man.

"We have food," Anosh Mór said, and András's mind was decided.

Anosh Mór was called simply "Nosh" by everyone else. The twenty or so who followed him were mostly related in one way or another. The family had come from Russia to Hungary in the early part of the century, and since the war they had travelled throughout the continent, sometimes away from this army or that, but mostly to wherever a fast profit could be made. The war had been good to them on this account.

When there was a scam to be had, everyone worked, even Nosh. He was an expert horse trader and had a million tricks for making a poor horse look well. Grey on a horse's muzzle was dyed black again. One horse that was lame in his left foot had a tiny nail driven into its right foot, so that it was unable to favour either. The best trick of all was the trained mare who, at the first possible opportunity, would bolt from her new owner, only to be brought back in short order by an honest stranger, who usually received a small reward for his trouble. After this happened three or four times, the new owner usually came to the easily found caravan of the Mór Roma and demanded a refund, which was grudgingly given. The honest strangers were of course Mór Roma themselves, but hardly anyone ever noticed, most considering themselves lucky to receive a refund on the bad horse. If the new owners did not return the horse for a refund, then the mare would be stolen in the night, and the Mór Roma would not be so easily located. Even if they were, the mare would be nowhere to be found, though a similar horse of another colour would be in plain view.

András got a rush from these schemes, not in their success but in their execution. He enjoyed duping the *gadje* immensely, regardless of the prize. The Mór Roma had treated the Usari children well, almost as though he and Etel were two of their own. There was a distance that András sometimes noticed, though, a look that held a quiet malice, as if the Roma knew some larger truth that he did not. It concerned him but these times were rare, and without anything more substantial he was of the opinion that a good thing need not be tampered with.

When they were in larger cities, the youngest of the Mór Roma were given crutches, slings and eye patches and sent out to the streets to beg. András was surprised how much could be earned once he learned how to play the game. Etel always earned the most, though. People would push past the throng of them only to stop at Etel, who stood silently with a bandage over both her eyes, a bowl at her feet. They nearly always put a coin in her bowl without her moving a muscle.

At first Etel didn't mind the begging. She didn't give it a second thought, because as far as she was concerned she wasn't even there. With her eyes covered over she lived in her dreams, imagining for herself a life that did not involve being at the mercy of others. She imagined that she lived the life of a *gadji*, or at least what she thought the life of a *gadji* must be like. But as she got older it became harder and harder to keep back the world around her, and after three years with the Mór Roma she could do little else but stand still and sing herself songs in her head.

It was in the fall of 1925 that László Nagy's hard work came to fruition. For the previous four years he had spent as much time as he possibly could perfecting his craft, staying late after his shift at Sándor Glassworks, often working through the night. The foreman was a kind man, and he did not object to László using company equipment for his own purposes, as long as it didn't affect his work. After all, the more László learned about glass, the better an employee he would be. He even watched with interest as László perfected various techniques for colouring and shaping his hand-blown glass, and every once in a while, when a setback was suffered, the foreman felt nearly as badly as László, though he never let on.

Since the preceding spring, however, László had been keeping the subject of his work a secret, and although the foreman occasionally caught a glimpse of a piece of something here and there, he had never seen exactly what László was making until that day after work when László took him aside and showed him his magnificent creation.

Similarly, neither Salvo nor Leo knew what László was up to. All they knew was that he seemed to be in a much better than usual mood lately, and that he was hardly ever home. As both these things were sources of comfort for the two boys, they did not put much effort into questioning László's whereabouts. Esa, however, was fully aware of her husband's work, but even she had no idea what to expect the day that László finished.

The door to the apartment opened quickly and unexpectedly, which startled Esa. She had been in the kitchen preparing a midday meal, fully expecting László not to arrive home until late at night, so she had not made a portion for him. Leo's foot was aching, so she had made him soak it in warm water and salts. Salvo had helped her lift a basin into the front room, and the two boys were there now, Leo trying to teach Salvo to read, Salvo paying half-hearted attention. Esa was wondering if maybe she should ask Leo or László to teach her how to read when the door had burst open. She immediately thought that the police were there to take her away. When she saw that it was László she was relieved, and thought herself rather silly. Why would the police take her away? she chided herself. She had done nothing wrong. After completing this mental reprimand, she noticed that László was carrying a wooden box about two feet wide and tall, and she wondered what was in it. "You're home early."

László nodded, appearing to Esa to be out of breath. There was a strange look on his face, an expression she could not recall ever seeing before. She wasn't sure what sort of mood the look was indicative of; there was a smile on his face, or at least the hint of a smile, which for László qualified as a beaming grin, but his forehead was scrunched down so that his eyebrows protruded awkwardly from his head, much like the way the snow on a roof can bulge over the eaves, seeming to defy gravity for a time before collapsing under its own weight. Esa decided that whatever László was feeling, it was new and extreme, and for a fleeting moment she envied him the scope of his emotions.

She watched as László gingerly set the box down on the floor. He removed the lid and reached inside. His hands emerged with rags and crumpled papers, which he carefully placed in a neat pile on top of the box's lid. He looked up towards Esa, and then to where Salvo and Leo were and, appearing satisfied that he had their full attention, his hands delved back into the box.

"Maybe you have thought that I am a stupid man," he said, looking mainly at Salvo. "Maybe you have thought this because I make windows all day, and I do not tell fine stories or play music or know a hundred ways to cheat a man out of his property." Here his gaze shifted towards Esa, but she pretended not to notice. "Think what you like," he continued, "but never say that I can't take care of my family, or that I can't do a great thing that few others can do."

Tenderly and far more delicately than Esa had ever seen him handle Leo, even when he had been a baby, László gripped whatever was in the box and lifted it out. Esa gasped and brought a hand to her mouth, another to her breast. László held a figurine, over a foot tall, of a Hungarian soldier in full ornamental dress. Every detail down to the brass buttons on his coat was fashioned from glass, and the soldier shone, almost glowed, from the light it absorbed and reflected. What struck her most were the soldier's eyes; they were a deep green, with coal-black pupils. But it wasn't just that they looked like real eyes—in itself reason enough to marvel. It was that they were the same as hers. For that matter, those eyes were the eyes of her ancestors and family, the eyes of her sister, Azira, Salvo's mother, and even the eyes of Salvo. That László would re-create these eyes, eyes that were Romany eyes, shocked Esa to her bones.

Salvo saw the eyes too, but he did not recognize them at first. All he could tell was that the glass soldier seemed to be looking straight into him. What the soldier could see was unclear, but it was definitely something. Salvo did not know whether he loved or feared the soldier, or both. All he knew was that those eyes sent a shiver down his spine.

László couldn't tell what others saw in his soldier, but he knew what he saw when he looked at it. He saw hours and hours of work; he saw all the pieces that he had built twenty times before he got them right. He saw his entire body of glass-making knowledge embodied in a single piece of work, and he saw perfection. As far as he was concerned, the soldier came as near to complete beauty as any man, and more specifically himself, was ever likely to get. He also saw inside the soldier the promise of a better life for himself and his family. To him, the eyes were only eyes.

There would be no more Sándor Glassworks for him. He would open his own shop, where he would make more figurines to sell to the wealthy citizens of Budapest. His skill as a craftsman would erase the shame of having a Romany wife and a crippled son, and maybe he could convince Esa to let him find somewhere else for Salvo to live. He did not like the way the boy was always looking out the window, towards the tops of buildings, as if there were somewhere he would rather be, as if László's house was not good enough for him. When the boy had come here he had nothing; for the past six years László had put a roof over his head and kept him fed and clothed far better than any Romany family would have been able to do. The boy should be grateful, but instead he stubbornly insisted on appearing as though he wished he were elsewhere.

Never mind the boy, László thought. His hand moved to the inside pocket of his threadbare coat, where there was an envelope that only this morning had contained more money than László had ever seen in his life. It was a down payment for the soldier, which had already been purchased by the agent of a local collector, a rich man whose name was known not only in Budapest and Hungary but throughout Europe. László had already gone to his landlord and paid two years' rent in advance for the apartment, as well as paying off his and Esa's debts. Most of the down payment was gone now, but there was a little left, enough for a good celebration, and then tomorrow when the agent came to collect the soldier he would receive even more money, the equivalent of nearly three years' salary at Sándor Glassworks.

He returned the soldier to its box, replacing the rags and paper that protected it. He carried the box to the far corner of the front room and laid it down in the corner. Then, as clearly as he ever had before, László smiled. He had a treat in store for the family, his way of showing them that he was not always a hard man. He told everyone to change into their best clothes as quickly as possible. Leo and Salvo rushed to obey, and he refused to answer even Esa's questions as they changed, telling her that she would see when they got there. When everyone was ready, László led them out of the apartment, down to the street. They rode the electric streetcar into the inner city of Pest. At the terminal for the subway that ran underneath Andrássy Avenue was Gerbeaud's, the famous pastry shop, but László wouldn't allow them to stop. There was no time, he told them. Perhaps on the way back.

Salvo's regard for the subway was the same as it was for the rest of his life in Budapest. He enjoyed it because it was unlike anything he'd ever encountered elsewhere, but he could never quite shake the feeling that there was something wrong with it, that even though it took him to places he'd never been, it somehow also confined him. On the subway you were forced to go where it took you. A part of Salvo knew that his father would have hated this underground train, and Salvo did not like that he didn't entirely agree.

The subway took them under the city, northeast, away from the Danube, towards City Park. As they walked past Heroes' Square, the sound of a crowd became more and more concentrated, until they reached the bank of the lake and there it was.

By most standards it was a small circus, an outdoor troupe of no more than ten people, who made their living by performing in various public areas throughout Europe. People stood and watched the show, as there were no seats save for a few scattered park benches, and a small boy, who was at the very most six years old, circulated through the crowd with a hat that people put change into.

Salvo stood beside his aunt and watched as two clowns performed a series of slapstick follies with a ladder, one climbing up the ladder while another briefly held it and then pretended to get distracted, letting go of the ladder and sending the other clown flying. The audience gasped, and then, realizing the performer was unharmed by his fall, laughed as the aggrieved clown chased his unreliable assistant, swinging wildly at him with the ladder. Even Salvo was forced to laugh.

Next came a man and a woman who juggled flaming torches between them, first two, then three, then four, until they had eight flying through the air separating them. Then they switched to knives, demonstrating the instruments' sharpness by slicing through a paprika tossed into the air. As the knives reached their maximum speed, a third woman came and stood directly in the path of the darting blades, calmly eating the two halves of the bisected paprika. The crowd cheered when they stopped and the woman emerged unscathed. People tossed coins into the child's hat freely and without hesitation.

Strung between two tall poles, twenty feet above the ground, was a wire. The audience's attention was directed upwards, and a man wearing tight pants and a sleeveless shirt stepped onto the wire. As the man moved slowly and tentatively across it, Salvo felt his chest tighten. The man moved with a grace and ease Salvo had never before witnessed. He knew immediately that this man was engaged in something of value, something few could do and something that was worth doing. This man was in a different world. And he seemed to Salvo to be at complete peace with his surroundings. He might as well have been walking along the sidewalk, or so it appeared.

The man walked the length of the rope, about forty feet, three times, until the crowd's contributions to the hat began to wane. He descended to applause and in a loud voice he announced that the troupe would be performing there for the rest of the week. After imploring people to be generous with their donations, the circus began to pack up their belongings.

Salvo was awestruck. He wanted to approach the man but found himself unable to move. What would he say to such a person? He had a brief moment where the thought of running away and joining the performers made his palms slick with sweat, but he put it out of his head. He was lucky to have found his home among the Nagys; it would be stupid to leave them for what cold logic told him must be the foolish dreams of a fifteen-year-old boy. If his time among *gadje* had taught him anything, it was that he had a tendency to dream outside the scope of reason. Salvo forced himself to stand still as the wire walker moved through the crowd and out of his view.

As they made their way through the park, back to the subway station, Salvo tried to think of a way to thank his uncle. Though still wary of him, he had seen a side of László Nagy today that he had never seen before, or even suspected existed. He wondered if it was possible that he had misjudged the man. They rode the subway in silence, Leo leaning heavily on Salvo, his foot raw and sore from the afternoon's exertions. When they got off the subway, Salvo decided that the best way to thank his uncle was just to come right out and say it. László was a straightforward man; that was how you did things with him, Salvo supposed.

László spoke first. "Here," he said, reaching into his pocket and picking a bill out of an envelope, handing it to Leo. "This is for the streetcar. And you can buy your cousin and yourself something from Gerbeaud's."

Esa looked startled. "Why should they need their own money?"

"Because," László said, "you and I are going to the opera house, and boys their age would not appreciate such a thing."

Esa's eyes lit up. All her life she had wanted to go to the Budapest Opera House. Even Salvo knew that. But it was expensive.

"Go on, now, you two. We have to hurry," László said. Esa kissed Leo and Salvo on the cheek, and then she headed off down Andrássy Avenue, linking arms with László.

"Thank you, Uncle," Salvo called after them. Whether he was heard or not he could not tell. László never turned around.

As they walked up the street, Esa tried to imagine what the opera house would be like, what the people would be wearing, what they would talk about at the intermission, how the music would sound. She could not stop herself from smiling, and after a while she gave up trying. It was better than any daydream; this tea party was going to happen.

Salvo and Leo went into Gerbeaud's and bought four large pastries. They sat on the sidewalk, leaning up against the wall of the pastry shop. Salvo was sure that the pastries were the most delicious thing he had ever tasted. By the time the streetcar returned them to their neighbourhood and they opened the door to the apartment, Leo was nearly weeping from the pain in his foot, so Salvo gave him some of the laudanum Esa kept for such occasions, which put Leo almost immediately to sleep.

Salvo sat in László's chair in the front room. He did not normally sit here. It was not forbidden, but neither was it encouraged. Salvo had never particularly wanted to sit in his uncle's chair; why would you sit in the chair of a man you knew disliked you? A rabbit would not sleep in a fox's den. But tonight was different. Salvo didn't know if it would last or if it was an eclipse of normal circumstances, but on this night Salvo did not fear or hate his uncle. Nearly the opposite, Salvo sat in the chair and held a measure of admiration in his heart for László Nagy, forgiving him his harsh manner and his attitudes towards Roma and the way he scorned his crippled son.

His eyes settled on the crate in the far corner of the room. He knew that he should leave it be, that no good could come from tampering with it, that it was not his business, and he continued to tell himself as much even as he rose from the chair and walked across the dimly lit room and opened the lid. The rags and paper inside parted readily before his eager fingers, and as he lifted the soldier out of the box, he was surprised by how heavy it was. He set it down on the floor in front of him and stepped back.

In the flickering light the soldier almost looked alive. It seemed to smile at him, a sly, knowing smile, as if it knew what he was thinking, what he had ever thought and what he had ever seen. Salvo's breath quickened, and he looked deeply into the soldier. He looked into the soldier like a man who sees a miracle and isn't sure why he has been chosen to bear witness but nonetheless has, in spite of himself, found religion.

Even as a part of him continued to scream against it, Salvo pulled the cuffs of his shirt over his hands and picked the soldier up. He did not want to leave finger smudges on the glass. He raised the soldier high above his head, remembering both his father and himself on the steeple of the church, remembering how they stood high above the ground and did not fall. Below them, that was where the trouble had happened. That was where things had gone bad. With the soldier above him, it was as if he was back up on that steeple, with his father this time, and they rose higher and higher, far away from the *gadje* and Transylvania and Budapest.

Then Salvo felt the soldier slip from his hands. He didn't know for certain whether it was an accident or not, but he did know that he could catch the soldier as it fell, or at least he could try, but he didn't. Instead he watched as the soldier fell to the ground, spinning head over heels over head, hitting the hard wood of the floor and shattering into oblivion. Even as he heard the broken glass skitter across the room he remained calm and still. Although he knew that a terrible thing had just happened, a truly horrible thing, he was peaceful, at complete ease, like in that perfect, abeyant moment before falling asleep.

Salvo got a broom from the kitchen and swept the scattered remnants of the soldier into a pile in the centre of the room, lay down on the floor, and waited.

○ see page 262

The Mór Roma spent the majority of their days on the road. They were true Roma and their feet got itchy quickly. These travels were long and hard, everyone happiest after they had made camp for the night, eager for a warm fire and a good meal. After they had eaten, the music began and, with it, the stories.

There was an old man named Vedel Mór who told the best stories of the group. He chose his moments, however, and would not tell a story every night, or even every second night. When he did, it was a special occasion, and everyone listened that much harder. People knew that Vedel would not live forever, that there would come a time when his untold stories would disappear with him. When he told a story he would often choose one person and speak as if only to them, or at least they would feel it was so. He began his stories the same way always.

"If it is not true, then it is a lie. Little Etel, and larger András, we have taken you in, and we would do so again, because we Roma are scattered throughout the earth, and we have been for a long time. But it was not always so.

"Once a Rom and his family were all together in their wagon. Their horse was a nag, not worth his weight in flesh, and he lurched forward under the wagon's weight. It was not all this horse's fault, for the wagon was filled to the top with Romany children. There were so many that the Rom could not count them all, and as the wagon lurched forward on the rutted road, the children fell out behind it. Because of the number of children, the lost ones were not missed, but the wagon travelled far across many lands, and everywhere there were young Roma left behind. This is how we came to be scattered about, all of us the children of that Rom."

All the Mór Roma nodded their heads approvingly. They had heard this story many times since they themselves were children, and it had become a welcome and familiar beginning to an evening. These stories were for the young ones, so that they would know where they came from, what it was to be Roma.

Not everything was like this. There were other stories that the children were not supposed to hear, but as Etel had no parent besides András, who did not know better, she was able to hear several of them before Vedel realized she was there.

"If this is not true, then it is a lie. Once there was a Rom, a wealthy Rom, who did not steal but traded horses and lived in a large house and had many friends. He wanted for nothing save a woman to share his happiness with. It came that he was riding through the forest at night when he happened upon a band of Roma, all of them feasting and dancing and playing music. For a reason he could not tell, he was afraid of them, so he hid in the trees and watched them from a distance. They were gathered in a circle, and in the middle danced the most beautiful woman he had ever seen. The Rom was captivated, and he watched her for hours. The revellers sang and danced into the night, and just as dawn approached, the woman looked out into the trees, and the Rom was sure she saw him, and he was sure she smiled at him. His heart leapt, but he was still afraid to approach.

As the sun broke they disappeared into their tents, and the Rom overcame his fear. He ventured forth, hoping to speak to this beautiful woman. When he looked inside the tents, however, he found they were full of dismembered bodies, limbs hacked from torsos, heads severed from necks. He instantly realized that these Roma were a caravan of the dead, but he was by then so in love with the woman he had seen dancing that he had become irrational, and so he found her corpse and stole it away.

"When night fell the woman rose up, startled to find herself separated from her family. The Rom introduced himself and professed his love for her, but she bade him to return her at once. The Rom refused, but she implored him. 'You do not understand,' she said. 'My brothers will find me, and they will do you harm.'

"The Rom did not care, even though at that very moment he could hear the hooves of her brothers' horses approaching. He grabbed the woman and they mounted his fastest horse, galloping through the night with the dead Roma close behind. Just as the sun was about to rise they caught him, and they ripped her from his arms. They would have killed him, but the minute they raised their swords, the sun came up, and they fell to the ground, lifeless. He retrieved his love's body and fled, resting little before the day was done.

"Night fell and again she rose to life, and again she begged him to return her. He heard her brothers' horses, and he fled with his beloved. Just as dawn broke the brothers caught them, but again he was saved by the rising sun. So this went on for weeks.

"Gradually, though, the woman began to fall in love with this Rom who would give up so much to be with her. Finally, she could deny him no longer, and she told him how to stop her brothers. 'You must wait until the day breaks, and then you must bury their bodies properly in the ground under a cross. You must bury me likewise, else a curse will befall us.'

"The Rom did not like the sound of this. 'What will happen to you? When will I see you again?' The woman hid her face in her hands. 'One night a year, I will come to you. Beyond that, I will be with you in the next life.'

"The Rom did not like these terms, but seeing no other way, he agreed. When the day came, he took the bodies of the dead Roma and he buried them in consecrated earth and marked their graves with a cross. He put the woman in her grave, but he saw her lovely face before he covered her over, and he could not bring himself to do it. He removed her from her tomb and waited for night to fall.

"Darkness came and the woman rose to life. 'What have you done?' she cried. The Rom told her he was sorry, that he couldn't bury her, that he loved her too much. 'We can be together now,' he said. He moved to touch her—such was his folly—but the moment his skin met hers he turned to dust, and the woman was forced to wander the earth, untouchable, to pay for his sin. So may she still wander."

All was quiet around the fire as the sombre story was reflected upon. Vedel slowly stuffed his pipe with cheap tobacco. After a short time someone took out a fiddle and the mood lightened, and soon people were dancing and singing. No one saw Etel shrink under her blanket. She lay as still as she could, trying not to shiver. She did not want to dance. I am dead, she thought. I have been dead for my whole life and no one knows. And though she did not entirely formulate the thought, she began to understand that the dead must not be loved.

It was dark in the beer hall. Salvo had to squint his burning eyes through smoke and flickering light to see his way across the room. It smelled of beer, sweat, meat and the pungent decay of every other tavern in the wide world.

Salvo had been making his living amidst smells like these for the three years since Esa Nagy had ordered him to leave the apartment on Viola Street and never return. She had told him this calmly and without malice, but there was no hesitation in her voice or manner.

When László Nagy had seen his soldier shattered on the floor, he had died a succession of tiny deaths. He died to think that his beautiful, wondrous creation was destroyed; he died to think of the money he would not be paid for the obliterated soldier; he died to think of the money he would have to return to the collector to repay his deposit, money he no longer possessed; and he died to think of the likelihood of debtor's prison, or worse. He crashed to the floor, where he lay with his mouth and eyes wide, making no sound, refusing to be roused, refusing to respond to Esa or Leo or Salvo. After Salvo left, Esa picked him up, moving his limp form to a chair. He didn't speak a word.

A part of Salvo wished László had reacted differently. He was ashamed of what he had done, how he had brought this ruin upon them, his family. They had taken him in, and he in turn had destroyed their lives. He would have accepted any punishment to undo the damage. He did not think he would ever forget the way Leo had looked at him as he backed out the door of the apartment. It was as pure a look of hatred as he had ever seen.

Although Salvo was now eighteen, more than old enough to be on his own, he had no trade, no skills, no friends and was barely literate. Salvo Ursari was still a Rom, and no one wanted to hire a Rom. So he made a living in the taverns, performing handstands on the backs of chairs for whatever money the drunk and delirious saw fit to give him.

His situation was, Salvo believed, exactly what he deserved. Though he spent many hours trying to figure out why he had destroyed the soldier, and with it his aunt's family, he was unable to arrive at any firm conclusion. Not for the first time in his life, Salvo wished he were someone else.

It was a poor way to live. He was perpetually hungry and in constant danger of being robbed, beaten up or otherwise injured. At least once a week some souse would attempt to replicate his feats of balancing, and—upon failing, which they always did—turn violent. Or even worse, not turn violent. Instead, they would hold their grudges tightly to their chests like a child's toy, and then the next week or month Salvo would feel a kick at the leg of his chair, which he sometimes recovered from and sometimes didn't.

There was also the police. It wasn't illegal for Salvo to balance for tips, but it was required that he purchase a licence, which cost far more than Salvo could ever hope to pay. Therefore, he had to be forever on the lookout for police, from whom he faced a combination of jail, beating, fines and robbery if caught.

This night in this tavern started out the same as any other. He moved from place to place, and this was his fourth stop that night. It was a place he usually skipped; it was favoured by a clientele that had little money to spare and plenty of ill will. On this occasion it seemed marginally cheerier than usual, and it had been a slow night for Salvo, so he went in.

He worked his way to the back, where the bar was, and after receiving a permissive nod from the man in charge, selected an empty chair in what was roughly the centre of the room. Round tables were scattered randomly throughout the bar, and while some people sat at these, others preferred to sit with their chairs against the wall or huddled in tight groups.

Salvo wiped the sweat from his hands and brow, adding to a darkened smear on the front of his shirt. After scanning the faces of those in his immediate vicinity and recognizing no one whom he knew to be a threat, he gripped the back of the chair and, with a grace that was startling to see in such a gaunt, dirty young man, neatly inverted himself. A few people directed their attention towards him, half-heartedly observing his efforts. Salvo shifted his hands towards each other until they were touching squarely underneath his head, then removed one of them from the chair. He released his grip and balanced with only one palm on the chair. A few more people took notice of Salvo, turning to watch. Salvo extended his free arm until it was perpendicular to his body and then jerked it towards his torso. His body spun a full 360 degrees around, so quickly that some of the drunker members of his growing audience missed it. He switched hands on the chair and spun in the other direction, and no one missed it this time. Nearly everyone in the room was watching him now, even those who had seen his act before. Salvo felt the blood pound in his head, felt his muscles strain. But he was only getting started.

He crept his hand to the edge of the chair's back and, with a deft shift of his weight, its front two legs lifted off the ground. He spun around to the left and to the right, and was rewarded with a few scattered cheers and approving laughs. He wrapped his fingers around the back and again shifted his weight. Salvo balanced upside down, with only one of the chair's legs touching the ground. There were more cheers and laughs, and some patrons clinked their glasses in appreciation.

Abruptly, as if from nowhere, a face appeared in front of his. It appeared upside down to Salvo, the sly smile a pouting frown, the wide nostrils tunnelling deep towards brain. A slight kick rattled his chair, but Salvo recovered. Then came a harder kick and a more tenuous recovery. Deciding that the person was not going to go away, Salvo flipped off the chair, landing on his feet. Before him stood a fair-headed man with twinkling eyes and what appeared to be a trustworthy smile.

"That was some good balancing," the man said, tossing him a coin. Salvo caught it without averting his eyes from the man's gaze.

"I don't like people kicking my chair," he said, trying to sound threatening.

The man laughed. "You should probably get out of here quickly, boy."

Salvo was about to argue with the man when he saw the policeman advancing towards him. He had not seen what the man had seen: two uniformed policemen entering the tavern, one pointing Salvo out to the other, then moving to the rear of the room, where they exchanged words with the owner. One of them stood behind Salvo now, the other between him and the door.

Salvo turned away from the policeman advancing towards him, only to see the other coming up behind him. He turned back towards the door. He was trapped.

The policeman between Salvo and the door moved in, a step ahead of his companion. The man who had kicked Salvo's chair stumbled, sending a chair into the legs of the policeman. Salvo leapt over him as he fell and bolted for the door. He felt a hand grasp his arm but pulled free, and seconds later he emerged from the dankness of the beer hall into the sharp chill of the night air, followed closely by the two officers. One of them gave up the chase almost immediately, but the other persisted until it became obvious that Salvo could easily outrun him. Salvo left him wheezing in the street, his breath billowing out like smoke from a fat, angry dragon.

There would be no more work for Salvo that night. With the money the man had given him, he rented a piece of floor in a dingy room and slept a fitful sleep, waking up every half-hour, terrified that the police were at the door, even though he knew they weren't. He awoke in the early morning tired, hungry and broke.

ALTHOUGH HE DID NOT DARE RETURN to the scene of his near capture, it was not very long until Salvo walked into another tavern and saw the man who had kicked his chair. He hesitated, not knowing what the man's intentions had been or what would have happened if the police hadn't interrupted. He remembered the man's gold coin, though, and with this in mind he approached him.

The man saw him coming. "Well," he said, his face flashing what could have been either a smile or a sneer, "if it isn't the balancing boy."

Salvo's eyes were drawn to the table, where a plate of the kind of sausages Salvo had grown especially fond of while living with his aunt and uncle lay half eaten.

"You hungry, balancing boy?"

Salvo nodded, not yet able to bring himself to speak. The bravado he had possessed on their last meeting had abandoned him.

The man picked up a sausage and held it out to Salvo. When Salvo reached for it, however, the sausage was pulled out of his reach.

"How about a handstand?" The man smiled, which did little to reassure him.

Warily, Salvo placed his hands on the filthy floor and swung his feet into the air. The man remained motionless for several seconds, observing him, then placed a hand on Salvo's foot and, very lightly, began to push him to one side. At first it didn't noticeably affect his balance; it was more of an annoyance than anything else. But as the steady sideways pressure persisted and Salvo's legs grew more and more skewed, it became harder and harder to maintain the handstand. When his legs were very nearly at a right angle to his body, Salvo could no longer hold the floor and was forced to put his feet down and abandon the handstand.

"Very impressive," the man said. "Very impressive, balancing boy."

He thrust the sausage in Salvo's direction and this time did not pull it back. Salvo greedily engulfed the sausage and ate it so fast he could hardly be seen to have chewed.

"Slow down, slow down. You'll hurt yourself, eating like that," the man said, handing Salvo another sausage that he tried to eat more slowly, with limited success.

"Thank you."

"Let me ask you a question, balancing boy. Are you afraid of heights?"

"No," Salvo said.

The man paused, thinking, before reaching into his pocket for a piece of paper. "Can you read?"

Salvo nodded. "A bit."

"Can you read this?" He handed the paper to Salvo. It was an address, the street in a rough part of Pest that Salvo knew well.

"Yes."

"Good. Come by tomorrow around noon, and we'll see if you can do more than handstands."

Salvo's heart skipped. "A job?"

"Maybe. We'll see."

"I work hard," Salvo said.

"You will indeed. What's your name, then, balancing boy?"

"Salvo."

"Salvo," the man repeated. "My name is Tomas Skosa. Tomorrow, then."

SOMEONE WAS KNOCKING AT THE DOOR. Tomas Skosa rolled over in bed, head pounding, and tried to shake out his cobwebs. He was momentarily startled when something shifted beside him, then he remembered the girl. Her breathing suggested she was sleeping. He was surprised she was still there. She probably had pegged him as a meal ticket. He'd have to see about that. It had taken him a pretty penny to get her stumbling the night before, and when they got back to his room she'd protested nicely at first, all whimper and howl, but she'd settled down relatively quickly. Too quickly for Tomas's liking, in fact, and if things hadn't been so far gone, he likely would have lost interest. He'd have to see how things went. Tomas was easily bored, and a girl like this often brought risks that gave him pause.

Though not at all handsome, Tomas Skosa was not without charm. He was quick to discern between a woman who saw him as a provider and someone who saw him for what he was but, being self-destructive, wanted him anyway. Few saw him as he really was. Not in the beginning, at least. Most saw a man who loved to dance, a man who could be funny one moment and serious the next, a man who spent his money freely, who appeared to listen when others spoke. They believed in all these things because they were true. But there were other things about Tomas Skosa that they didn't know and would like to find out.

He pulled on his pants and stood, his shift in weight waking the sleeping girl. She looked at him, bleary-eyed and disoriented. Then, seeming to remember where she was, she pulled up the bedclothes to cover her nakedness, shame in her face.

Tomas smiled; this girl had plenty of latitude left in her.

Salvo waited at the door. He double-checked the address, confirming he was at the correct place. A rustling came from the door, which opened tentatively.

"Balancing boy. Are you early?" Tomas ushered him inside.

The rooming house was reflective of a poor quality of tenant. Someone had kicked a hole in the plaster at the base of the stairs, from the looks of it quite a while ago, and the walls were streaked with stains and handprints. He followed Tomas up the stairs to the second floor and into a room at the back of the building. The room was cluttered with bottles and clothes and smelled of stale cigarettes and dirt. There was a chair and a small table in one corner, a bed in another. A coal burner stood beneath the window that overlooked an alley. Salvo was startled to see a girl, two or three years younger than him, sitting on the bed, her legs drawn up and arms laced tightly around them, her whole body wrapped in a blanket.

Tomas sat in the chair, motioning for him to sit on the bed. Salvo declined, remaining standing. "You have a job for me?" he asked.

"That depends. What was your name?"

"Salvo Ursari."

"Yes. I am Tomas Skosa. You have heard of me?"

Tomas seemed irked when Salvo replied that he had not. He shook his head and went to the window. It opened with ease. Tomas turned his back, unbuttoned his pants and pissed out the window. "Introduce yourself to the girl," he said.

Salvo turned to the girl, who was visibly shocked by Tomas's actions. "I'm Salvo," he said.

She looked at him but did not respond.

"Tell him your name, girl," Tomas said without moving.

The girl swallowed. "Margit." She flinched at the sound of her own name.

Tomas buttoned up his pants and motioned Salvo to the window. It faced a narrow alley, affording a view of the windowless back of another building, twenty-five feet away. A thin wire stretched from directly below Tomas's second-storey window to the other building, anchored by a hook at each end. Below, the alley was mud and trash.

"Can you walk it?" Tomas asked.

"Walk what?"

"The wire. If you can walk the wire, I may have a job for you. If not, you can go."

Salvo hesitated. "I don't know. I can learn."

Tomas sighed. "Anyone can learn. I will give you one afternoon. If at the end I think you could be of use to me, you will have yourself a job. Otherwise . . ." His voice trailed off.

Salvo considered this proposition for a moment. "I can do it." An ongoing association with this man did not appeal to him, but the wire did. Since the steeple, since he had seen the wire walkers in the park, he had felt a nagging inside him that now declared itself again. "I will do it."

Tomas looked at him, assessing him, and nodded. "Take off your shoes." He turned his attention to the girl. He reached into his pocket and threw a coin onto the bed. "We will need food. And a bottle of wine. Be quick about it."

Margit hesitated, looking at her clothes, which lay in a heap at the opposite end of the room. "My clothes," she said, her voice almost a whisper.

"What about them? I've seen what you have already, girl." Tomas's eyes darted sideways to Salvo, who looked down at his feet. He heard Margit gasp as Tomas yanked the blanket from her grasp. Salvo kept staring at his feet as the girl sat stunned, then bolted across the room, dressing as hastily as possible. When the door shut behind her, he bent down and removed his shoes. Salvo hoped she would not return.

Tomas turned his attention to Salvo. "Your balance is good. That will help you. But the wire is not about balance." He put a hand on Salvo's shoulder. "There are two things out there: there's you, and there's the wire. If you let anything else exist, it's over. Out you go." His hand thrust Salvo roughly towards the open window.

Gingerly, Salvo stepped out the window and placed one foot on the wire. It was cold and felt as though it was cutting into his skin. "Position the wire between your biggest and second toe. Let it run down the centre of your foot. Now the other foot. Knees bent. Upper body straight. Now stand. Still."

Salvo stood as still as possible on the wire. The ground was fifteen feet below. If he fell it would hurt, but he would probably not be seriously injured.

"Immobility," Tomas continued, "is what you strive for, but immobility is impossible. You could not move your arms. You could not move your legs. Even if you could fix your eyes on one point and not blink, you would still see. And your blood would still flow, and your heart would still pound in your ears. Yet you must always *try* for immobility. The wire must have a time of its own, so that each movement of your body is as natural and unconscious as breathing, so that there is as little difference between mobility and immobility as possible. First you will learn this lesson. Then you will walk."

Tomas slammed the window shut, leaving Salvo standing alone on the wire. How long he stood he had no idea. It could have been minutes, it could have been hours. Eventually, though, he felt he could stand no longer. His legs ached and his feet felt as though they were being sliced in half. His knees buckled and he fell to the ground. He was shaken but unhurt. The window above hadn't opened, and there was no way to get back up on the wire.

He walked around to the front of the rooming house, opened the unlocked door, went up the stairs and down the hall. He knocked on Tomas's door. There was no answer. He opened the door and peered in.

Tomas leapt forward and slammed his fist into the side of Salvo's head. Salvo dropped to the floor, where he was met by a kick to the stomach. At first all he felt was blinding pain. Gradually the pain began to recede to a dull throb, and he once again became aware of his surroundings. Tomas pulled him to his feet.

"If you ever let yourself fall again, I will make that seem like a handshake," he said. "You stay on the wire no matter how tired you get. If you fall, you grab the wire. You crawl to the window, and you get back on the wire. But you never give up and seek ground. Understand?"

Salvo nodded, but his jaw was set and his face was hot.

Tomas pushed him to the window and opened it. "Out you go."

As he stepped out the window he saw Margit sitting in the corner of the room. She watched him with wide eyes, her hands clutching a piece of bread. He wished she hadn't come back. He couldn't know that she had not gone straight to the store, that upon leaving the rooming house she'd run fast in no particular direction, desiring only to be away from there. He couldn't know that she had stopped, heaving for breath, and turned back in the direction she had come, stopping to buy food and wine for Tomas. He didn't understand the way Tomas did that she had nowhere else to go, and that the streets were for her a very different place than they were for Salvo.

As it had before, the wire stung his feet. Before sliding the window shut, Tomas offered one last piece of advice. "Make the wire yours."

Salvo again stood until he thought he could stand no more. He wanted to give up, to drop to the ground, but he wouldn't allow himself. He would neither fail nor give Tomas the satisfaction of seeing him fail. He forced himself to stay still.

Time stopped. His body ached, muscles strained past caring. He concentrated on immobility, on remaining motionless, on the stillness of his movements. Slowly, the wire began to reach into him. It snaked its way up his shins, through his calves, up his spine. It pierced his brain and was gone.

Salvo was warm. He saw the faces of his father and mother, his brother, András, and his dead sisters. He saw his Uncle László and Aunt Esa, his crippled cousin, the girl Margit and the new priest and the villagers. He saw everyone he had ever known and everything he had ever seen. Then, it all vanished. It was night, he was in a freezing alley on a wire, standing above mud and garbage and the piss of a man he knew he hated but needed, and he was untroubled. None of it mattered.

The window opened.

"Come inside," Tomas said. "I have a job for you."

※※※※※※

Despite the welcoming nature of the Mór Roma, after five years András still didn't feel as though he was one of them. There was something about them that he didn't share, and he could tell that they knew it as acutely as he did, even if no one could quite put their finger on what it was.

András remembered his father's stories well, and he often thought that they were far better than Vedel's, but he never said as much. His father would tell his stories no more, so there was no point in wishing to hear them, and anyway, one does not frown in the face of hospitality.

There was one story Vedel told that András initially liked. It was a favourite with many, and often it was told by others when Vedel wasn't in the mood. They never got it right, András thought, and he hardly ever listened unless Vedel was the one telling it.

"If this is not true, then it is a lie. Troka, you pay attention to this," he would say, and everyone would laugh at Troka Mór, a boy a little older than Salvo whose pathetic attempt at a beard was much maligned.

"There were two men, one a Rom and the other a *gadjo*. They were friends, not the sort who would die to protect each other, but the sort who would compete over anything, like jealous brothers. But they did like each other, that much for sure.

"The *gadjo* had a beard, a very fine beard, thick and long, and the Rom grew no beard at all." At this point Vedel would usually look pointedly at Troka, and many would laugh.

"The Rom became jealous of his friend's beard. 'Friend,' he said, 'that is a very beautiful beard you have. How would you like to sell it to me?'

"The bearded man gave this some thought, and he decided it was not a bad idea. They agreed upon a price, but the Rom had a condition. 'I will buy your beard, but it has to stay on your face.'

"The price was good, so the *gadjo* accepted this condition, and a sale was made. Every day the clean-shaven Rom would come and see his friend, and he would take care of his beard. He trimmed it well and washed it in expensive lotions. Often he would bring people by to admire the beard, not caring if the man whose face the beard was on was busy or not.

"He would cut it into a point, or put a hole into the middle of it, or pour scented oils on it. If his friend protested, he'd say, 'What's mine is mine, friend. You sold me this beard. The law is on my side.' And he was none too gentle, either, when tending the beard, often pulling it and tugging it, sending his friend to tears.

"Eventually, the man whose face the beard was attached to had had enough. 'Please, friend, sell me back my beard. I'll pay whatever you ask.' The Rom refused. 'No,' he said, 'I'm very happy with this beard. It's very soft and thick, and it's strong.' He yanked on the beard to show his point, and the poor man yelped. 'I'll give you any price you ask. Just let my beard alone.' 'Sorry, friend,' the Rom replied, 'but it's not your beard.'

"Finally, after many weeks, the Rom agreed to sell back the beard, and he made a good profit on the sale. The *gadjo* went straight to the barber and had his beard shaved off, and he never grew it back as long as he lived."

András liked this story for the same reason the others did; he enjoyed hearing of a *gadjo* being tricked. What he did not understand, however, was why the *gadjo* didn't beat the living blood out of the Rom for abusing his beard so. The more András thought about it, the more he was convinced that this was in fact what the *gadjo*, or for that matter, any reasonable man, would do. That was the problem with so many of Vedel's stories: in many of them the *gadje* were stupid and easily tricked, the reality of the likelihood of violence ignored. He'd seen for himself that it took quite a bit of work to trick the *gadje*, and that they were more than willing to inflict physical harm on the Roma who had duped them.

Most Roma probably already knew that. But what András also realized—after wondering why the bearded man had tolerated such behaviour—was that every time they pulled one over on the *gadje*, the *gadje* hated them even more. As long as they kept it up, *gadje* would always hate Roma. He had little remorse for this fact, and didn't wish to change it, but he saw it nonetheless.

ANDRÁS KEPT TO HIMSELF as much as he could, avoiding conflict except when necessary. He was, at seventeen, stronger than most adult men, which brought a fair amount of trouble to him. There was always one boy or another seeking to prove his manhood by challenging him in some way.

There was one Mór Rom who paid special attention to András, a striking young girl, fifteen years old, named Jeta. She had large eyes and an entrancing smile, and was easily the most beautiful of Nosh Mór's daughters. She took quite a liking to András, despite his seeming ambivalence towards her. This infatuation did not go unnoticed by others, and it inspired a great deal of jealousy. András was unfazed by any of it, though, intent only upon the raising of his eight-year-old sister.

As time went on, Jeta began to take András's perceived snubbing of her advances to heart. She stayed in her tent, refusing to eat, until finally Nosh came to speak to András.

"What have you done to my daughter?" he said, his voice low so that others would not hear.

"I have done nothing."

"She is in love with you. She wishes to marry you."

"Yes. But I have no intentions towards her."

At this Nosh Mór became angry. "You think I would allow you to marry my daughter, orphan? I have overlooked many things. You burn a church, a bad omen. You do not become one of us. You do not sing with us. You do not share the stories I know you have. All these things I overlook." He took a deep breath, collecting himself. "You would not be fit to marry Jeta. But for you to think yourself above her is another matter."

"I do not think myself above her. I simply do not love her." András did not say that neither did he love any of the Mór Roma. If pressed for an explanation he would have been unable to supply one; he could not pinpoint why he was unable to fit in with this group.

"Love?" Nosh spat. "Ursari, that is the least of your worries."

Etel burst into the tent. Tears ran down her face. András forgot Nosh Mór and focused on his sister. Never in her life since she had been a baby had he seen her cry, let alone with such ferocity. He knew at once that something terrible must have happened.

"*Vyusher*," she said. "*Vyusher*." She was too upset to say more. András understood what she was talking about, and he went where Etel led him, Nosh following right behind.

One of his favourite stories that their father Miksa had told—and one that András had repeated to Etel since she was old enough to listen—was the story of the Rom and the wolf.

"Not so long ago," he would begin, trying his best to sound like his father, "an old Rom who was once a great leader of his people but was now sick and weak sensed that his tribe was about to turn on him. So late one night he crept from their caravan and slipped into the deep of the forest, where, with his remaining strength, he set to building himself a shack. One day, when he sat down to rest, he was cornered by a pack of hungry wolves. He was unarmed, having left his axe at the edge of his clearing, and had no way to defend himself. The wolves were just about to devour him when their leader, a strong silver giant of a wolf, leapt between the Rom and the wolves and bade them leave him alone. The wolves grumbled at this, but they respected their leader's authority and retreated into the brush.

"A few years went by, and soon the silver wolf was not so strong, not such a giant. He was old, and though he still had cunning, he could feel his control over the pack waning. So one quiet night he fled into the forest. The other wolves heard him leave, however, and they took after him. They were nearly upon him when he reached the Rom's shack. The Rom, remembering the favour this silver wolf had once done him, took him into his house and saved him.

"From that time on, the Rom and the wolf lived together until their days were done, dying only moments apart, and they were as happy as they had ever been."

The Móra Rom camp was full of dogs. They were never consciously collected; they just arrived one day and travelled with the wagons, content to live off discarded scraps and whatever was seen fit to give them. Many of them were affectionate towards their human providers, and many were indifferent, but none was vicious. They were smart dogs, and they had quickly learned that any aggression towards humans led to an abrupt end. The dogs were, however, quite violent amongst themselves, fighting often and without mercy. There was one dog, a small brownish cur, that Etel found one day dragging part of its stomach behind it, having had its gut torn open in a fight. Etel picked the creature up and brought it to András, who was inclined to put the poor thing out of its misery, but Etel begged him to try and save it. They washed the distended pieces, pushed them back into the dog and wrapped a bandage around it. András doubted the dog would last the night, but there it was the next day, still alive, and the day after that, and so on, with Etel looking after it, washing its wound and feeding it, as well as keeping the other dogs at bay. Until one day the dog was well enough to get up, and eventually it appeared to be fine. Etel remembered the story of the Rom and the wolf, naming the dog *Vyusher*, the Romany word for wolf.

They became inseparable. Vyusher was always beside her, licking her swollen feet after a hard day of walking, guarding over her while she slept. Etel, for her part, fed the dog half of all her food, brushed its fur with her own hairbrush and kept other dogs from injuring Vyusher further.

That had been over a year ago. As András arrived at the bare spot of earth where Vyusher now lay motionless, he knew that this time the dog would not recover. Its head was caved in on the side, unrecognizable as the former face of a dog, an iron pipe on the ground beside it.

"Who has done this?" he asked Etel.

"Nicolae and Dilaver," she replied. "But all of them were there."

András looked at Nosh. Nicolae and Dilaver were two of his sons, one a year older than András and one a year younger. They did not like András, nor the idea of their sister being in love with him, and they liked it even less that he did not care for her. They were too afraid to come after him, having felt his fist at their heads more than once, but there were other ways, they knew.

"It's just a dog," Nosh said.

"It was my sister's dog. You do not kill a child's dog."

"They love their sister."

"And I mine." András stared Nosh Mór hard in the face, and his glare was returned with a smirk. András, infuriated, lunged towards Nosh, his hands at the man's throat.

Etel opened her mouth but no sound came out. She had never seen András lose his temper before. In all his fights he was never the one to make the first move, and even afterward he did not appear angry. That was usually his advantage.

As András lunged, Nosh dissipated before him, there and not there. András felt a breeze at his side, and from behind him a cool, hard pressure at his throat and solid flesh constricting his wrist. He grasped with his free hand to keep Nosh's knife from going into his neck, but Nosh's arm was strong and he had no effect on its position. For a moment András thought he was dead, but death did not come, and he knew that if Nosh had wanted him dead, he would already be so.

"You have made a bad mistake," Nosh whispered into his ear. "I should kill you where you stand."

András said nothing. He couldn't think of anything that was certain to make things better, and he didn't want to risk making the situation worse.

"I took you in five years ago, when others would not have. I protected you from those who thought you should pay for burning down their church. I fed you and your sister. You shared our fire. And for this you first bring shame upon my daughter, then you come at me with fists. Tell me one reason why I should let you live."

András thought for a moment. "Because you would do the same thing for your family. You would kill to protect them."

Nosh released András, shoving him to the ground. András was unprepared and lost his wind as he connected with the hard earth, and he lay on his back, gasping.

"You look like a dying fish," Nosh said. His dagger was already back in its sheath at his waist. Neither András nor Etel had seen it come out or go back. Nosh turned to Etel, who knelt beside her dead dog.

"I am sorry for your friend," he said. "All over the world other dogs will be sick of broken hearts for his absence." Nosh looked at András. "Be gone before sunset. Your sister may stay, but if you are here in the morning, you will not see noon." Just then others began to arrive, drawn more out of intuition, a feeling that trouble was near, than by the commotion that had been raised. Nosh pushed his way past a group of onlookers and disappeared into his wagon.

No one spoke to András. He was, from the moment of Nosh's pronouncement, outcast from the entire group. Whatever personal feelings any of them held, and a few did think that Nosh was overreacting, they did not go against his word, nor hold out a hand to András as he got up off the ground. They looked at their feet as he moved past them, and they walked away silently once he was inside his tent.

Etel took one last look at her friend Vyusher and followed her brother.

András gathered together what few belongings he had. He watched Etel in the doorway, wondering what to do. A part of him believed that she would be better off staying with the Mór Roma, that without him they would accept her as one of their own, and that in time she would come to understand why he had left her. Another part of him, a larger part, needed her to come with him, could not fathom the thought of leaving without her. Do not be selfish, he told himself. She has a right to a better life than you can provide.

"It is a bad thing about Vyusher," he said.

Etel nodded. "Hearts are broken, dogs' and mine."

András did not like her rephrasing Nosh, but said nothing. "I must go."

Etel stepped back. "And me?"

"I think you should stay."

"I will not." She held her hands tight at her sides.

"It's best. The future will be difficult."

"I will go with you." Etel made herself as big as she could go. "Ursaris hold together. You will not leave me."

András agreed, not letting on how relieved he was. Her loyalty made him proud, made him happy to leave the Mór Roma. The prospect of a life on the streets of a large city was less daunting, almost appealing. She's right, he thought. Ursaris hold together.

FOUR

On the wire, thought of any sort was the first step towards a fall. Salvo learned as much as soon as Tomas bade him walk. What was on the wire was unlike what was on the ground; walking on the earth was a one-sided proposition. The wire was animate, the wire breathed, and the wire was always stronger than anyone who walked it. The only way to live was to work with the wire, to breathe in such a way that would not disturb its breathing, to walk softly at times and on places that the wire didn't mind.

Tomas had been right; Salvo learned quickly, far more quickly than the others Tomas had tried to teach. In less than two months he was proficient enough that Tomas felt sufficiently confident in him to book some performances, to trust Salvo with his own life.

Training the girl, Margit, had been a more difficult proposition. Tomas wanted her to be part of the act, but while she was satisfactory in other areas, she did not take naturally to the wire. Tomas did not require her to walk, only to be carried or to balance, but it was clear that the girl didn't trust him, which made her a difficult student. He resolved to use her in the act as sparingly as possible, limiting her to one or two tricks. She would still be useful on the road.

The act was a simple one. Tomas was not a fan of skywalks, preferring instead the confines of a hall or a tent. Tomas would start the show with the dance of the drunk, in which he would lurch across the wire as though intoxicated. It was a good opener and always got a cheer. Next he would do some somersaults, which were more difficult. Then he would send Salvo out to do some handstands. On Salvo's last handstand, Tomas would carry Margit out on his back, place a chair on the soles of Salvo's feet and lift the girl onto the chair. He would then sit on the wire and eat an apple while Margit howled, only half pretending to be terrified. When he finished his apple, he would retrieve Margit from the chair, where she would first slap and then kiss him, much to the delight of the audience. Salvo would return to the platform for a short rest as Tomas prepared the finale. Both Tomas and Margit wore a belt with a brass ring at the front. Tomas would lead Margit to the middle of the wire and secure a rope between their two rings. As he lowered Margit from the wire, Salvo rejoined him. With Margit dangling in the air below them, suspended horizontally, Salvo would climb up Tomas's back and do a handstand from his shoulders. It was a very difficult trick, and it always brought the audience to their feet.

Whenever Salvo did this trick, he had to work very hard not to look at Margit's face. He knew she was there, staring up at the wire, and he knew that if he looked her in the eye, he would lose his focus and fall. In general, he tried to have as little to do with her as possible. She was not Roma, that was certain, and the way she sometimes looked at him made him feel as though she might not like him. That they had much in common mattered little; the circumstance of each being a needy beneficiary of both kindness and cruelty from Tomas Skosa had not made them allies.

Salvo's training had been harsh. Tomas's violence had ensured that lessons learned were not soon forgotten, but it had not been without cost. Since Salvo had arrived in Budapest he had been plagued by irrational fears, and though he was nearly twenty now, he experienced the sorts of dread commonly reserved for children. Chief among these was a fear of the dark. He knew this was irrational, but this did nothing to allay his fear and much to make him feel like a fool.

Sleep was his only recourse, but the road to sleep made it worthless. In the moments before slipping away, surrounded by darkness, he was visited by memories of his parents' burning house, of the cross falling on the new priest, of the glass soldier shattering on the floor. Other times, he had memories of things that had never happened: he was drowning, he was cut, he was crushed, lost, imprisoned. A thousand catastrophes heralded slumber. On the verge of sleeping, he'd be startled awake by his terror. After hours of this torture he would finally be so exhausted that even his fear could not rouse him, and he would sleep for a few hours.

It was a little better once Tomas took their act on the road. As they criss-crossed Europe, Salvo felt his fatigue so acutely that his fears had less energy with which to manifest themselves. He slept on trains when he could, otherwise attempting to sleep during the day. When they weren't travelling, Tomas usually rented a cheap room for the three of them, where Salvo was intended to sleep on the floor, but after several nights of listening to Tomas and Margit, he more often than not slept in the hall.

Salvo knew that Tomas Skosa was a very good wire walker, if also a brutal teacher. Salvo knew he must do exactly as he was told, and once he mastered the basics he found that there was much more that he could learn from Tomas—not only the mechanics of walking the wire but the psychology as well. Despite his many faults, Tomas Skosa knew the wire inside and out. He was known by other wire walkers wherever they went. Some hated him, others admired him, but none disputed his excellence.

His past was a mystery. Everywhere they went Tomas seemed to know people, but no one appeared to know where he came from, how he learned to speak so many languages: Hungarian, French, English, German, Italian and, Salvo suspected, Romany. Whenever they arrived in a new town, Tomas would disappear for several hours, not saying where he was going, and was equally tight-lipped upon his return.

It was during one of these vanishings, this time in Munich, that Salvo and Margit had what Salvo later realized was their first real conversation. They had checked into what was, for them, an unusually nice hotel, and Salvo was resting for that night's performance, grateful for the peace that Tomas's absence had afforded. Margit sat in a chair by the window, mending a tear in one of Tomas's shirts.

"I do not like the hanging trick," she said, startling Salvo. She rarely spoke.

"Why?" Salvo asked. It was by far their most popular trick.

"I just don't."

"Oh." Salvo closed his eyes, assuming the conversation was over.

"He is an awful man," she said.

Salvo did not answer, his eyes darting towards the door, expecting it to burst open.

"To both of us, he is awful."

"He taught us the wire," Salvo offered.

"He taught you the wire. Me, he carries. He will teach me nothing. Besides, he only teaches you so that he has someone else to perform with. He is doing you no favours."

Salvo shrugged. "What can we do? It's not so bad."

Margit's eyes returned to her sewing. "Someday . . . ," she ventured, but she did not finish.

That night, as Salvo did his handstand on Tomas's shoulders, he was for a brief moment unable to keep himself from looking at Margit's face. She met his gaze and held it, her face expressionless. Salvo looked away.

He felt something brush his cheek, light and soft. Close as it was to his face, he could not see what it was, and he started to panic. An orange-and-yellow blur fluttered into view: a butterfly, Salvo realized. It bumped into him again, harder this time, and then disappeared from sight. Salvo froze. He couldn't see the butterfly, and he was paralyzed by fear. When Tomas gave him the signal to end his handstand, he couldn't move.

"Come down, boy," Tomas growled.

Unable to speak, Salvo remained upside down, his mind stuck in a loop: *I don't want to die.*

"I said come down. I can't stand like this forever."

Tomas's legs began to tremble. His strength was fading. Still Salvo couldn't move. Finally he caught a glimpse of the butterfly, several metres to his left, drifting away from them. His fear subsided enough to allow him movement, and he dismounted Tomas's shoulders and helped him pull Margit to the wire. The crowd extolled the trick, unaware of how close the troupe had come to falling.

Afterward, Salvo was sure that Tomas would beat him. He was determined to take it standing up, not to let Tomas see his pain. He did not flinch when Tomas's arm cocked backward; he stared Tomas straight in the eyes. To Salvo's surprise the blow never landed. Tomas's arm hung back, stuck in mid-air. There was something new in Tomas's eyes. He knows, Salvo thought, that violence no longer affects me. He may as well punch a piece of meat.

"If you ever freeze on me again, I will kill you." His voice lacked conviction, but still Salvo knew he meant it.

"I'm sorry," he said, but Tomas had already walked away.

From the corner, Margit smiled out at him.

The next night they did not perform. They would leave Munich the following day, bound for Stuttgart, Nuremberg, Frankfurt, Bonn, Cologne, Dortmund, Hannover, Bremen, Hamburg, Berlin. They went to a beer hall in a working-class part of the city. Salvo and Margit sat at a table in the back, while at the other end of the room Tomas met with a strange man. The man, though he wore clothes of the same manner as everyone else in the tavern, looked out of place. There was something about him that did not fit in. He was trying too hard to look like a man without secrets to hide.

The man listened intently to Tomas, his eyes scanning the room, assessing each new person who came through the door. After five minutes of what was essentially a one-way conversation, Tomas placed a piece of paper on the table. The man pocketed the paper and pushed an envelope towards Tomas. He stood and without shaking Tomas's hand exited the tavern.

Salvo didn't pay as much attention to Tomas's conversation as he might have if he wasn't half drunk. Not usually much of a drinker, Salvo had consumed three mugs of strong German ale already and was halfway through his fourth. He hadn't been drunk more than three or four times in his life, and his head was swimming. A polka band had set up on a makeshift stage, and as they launched into a song a few scattered patrons got up to dance. Salvo stood, surprised at his own unsteadiness. He extended a hand to Margit.

"Dance?"

Surprised, Margit stood and followed him tentatively towards the space of floor that had been cleared for dancing. She started a polka, then stopped and stood still, eyes darting from side to side nervously.

The dance Salvo danced was not a polka. In his mind, the music he heard was different. His eyes were closed, and his feet were moving to a tune he hadn't heard since he was a small boy. He had been drinking to chase away the panic that had been battering his eyelids since the night before, leaving him sweaty and shaking. But the drink had only amplified his fears. Then he had remembered a story told to him by his dead father, and he had had a sudden urge to dance. He heard his father's voice as he moved, an overscore to the music in his head.

"Once, long before you were ever born, in another place that is not here, there was a Rom who could hear the voices of dead men, angels, God and the devil. He heard voices so loudly that he thought he would die, and so many that he could make no sense of anything they said.

"All the other Roma thought he was crazy. Some wanted to kill him because they suspected he was possessed. Others thought he might be some sort of angel, so he was not killed. But both those who thought him devil or angel feared him, because he spoke of things they did not understand and did not want to understand.

"As always there came a time when there were people that wanted to do harm to the Roma. It was obvious they must go to a different place, and with much haste, but it was not known where they should go. On all sides there could be danger, a peasant army approaching from any direction.

"A child was playing a fiddle by the fire. The Rom who heard voices noticed that when the boy played his fiddle the voices were not as loud, nor were there as many. He told the boy to play faster and louder, and when the boy did, one voice began to come to him more clearly than the rest.

"But the voice was still not loud enough, so the Rom who heard voices called for the great musicians of the tribe to bring their instruments and play the best and most beautiful music they knew. They hesitated to do this, not sure whether this Rom was leading them to death or wasting their time, but they were makers of music above all else, so their desire to play won out over their suspicions.

"As they played their best and most beautiful music, the Rom who heard voices began to dance. As he danced, the voices subsided one by one by one until there was only a single voice in his head, one clear, loud voice that spoke with such authority that the Rom who heard voices knew it immediately as the voice of God.

"God told the Rom who heard voices where the peasant army coming to kill them was, and where they would find safe haven. When the Rom stopped dancing and told the others what he knew, many did not believe him. He told them he was going where he had been directed, and it was up to them whether they came.

"The other Roma were moved by the strength of his pronouncements, and the clear, not-at-all-crazy look in his eyes— a look that had never been there before—and they decided to go with him. When they were safely delivered, the Rom who heard voices was no longer considered crazy, and many times in the future he danced before the fire, always able to hear the voice of God over the voices of lesser demons. And if he is not dead, he may still live."

Salvo had heard no voices, but he was plagued all the same. Since the appearance of the butterfly his fears had grown. They were irrational. They were constant. As he danced, he willed them away. But they did not listen. They were ever-present.

The music had stopped, the song Salvo wasn't dancing to having ended. Many people, including Margit, were staring at him. He stood, wondering what to do.

A voice from the crowd called to him harshly. "We don't do those dances here, Rom." Salvo was too drunk to completely understand their German, but he caught their tone and the word *Rom*. He saw Tomas moving towards him but was unsure of his intentions; Tomas had never expressed any opinion one way or another about the Roma. Salvo felt rough hands on his shoulders and was pushed to the floor. He barely pulled his face out of the way of a worn leather boot, then felt another sink into his ribs. He yelped with pain, then heard the sharp crack of fist impacting jaw. From the ground he watched as Tomas slowly and calmly beat back his attackers, mashing one man's nose, tearing at another's ear.

Margit pulled at his arm, and with her help, he staggered to his feet. If he were not so drunk, his ribs would have hurt more, a consolation that mattered little to him then. Tomas's ferocity had not gone unnoticed, and those who before had seemed likely to join in the trouble had apparently thought better of it. When the three moved towards the door of the tavern, leaving four men on the floor with varied injuries, no one made a move to stop them.

With Salvo leaning heavily on Margit, they walked back to their hotel. No one spoke. Every breath sent a spark of fire through Salvo's broken ribs, and the cold, fresh air had sobered him enough that he was able to think a little more clearly. "Thank you," he said to Tomas, who was walking in front of them.

Tomas said nothing and kept walking.

"I'm sorry. I shouldn't have drank so much."

Tomas stopped abruptly, turning around. "That dance you did—"

"I won't do it again."

Tomas paused, appearing hesitant. "It was a good dance."

Salvo was taken aback. "Thank you."

Tomas nodded and continued towards the hotel. Salvo looked at Margit, who appeared equally shocked, and then they, too, resumed their walk.

That night Salvo slept soundly. He was too tired to be afraid of anything, even himself.

✺✺✺✺✺

After leaving the Mór Roma, András felt more acutely that he hadn't been one of them. They were not his family. In light of the circumstances of their parting, he was glad.

He realized, however, that this feeling of dislocation might be lessened if he were again surrounded by kin. And then there was Etel. She would need family, something outside of him, to keep her from withdrawing from the world. Though he had long ago decided that he would give his life for his sister, he knew chances were that that would not be enough; it would be an empty and useless gesture. Partly because nothing he could do alone would be sufficient, and partly because they had nowhere else to go, András and Etel made the journey to Budapest.

Like his brother before him, András remembered Viola Street. He could not, however, remember exactly where on this street his aunt and uncle lived. After asking people in the neighbourhood, he finally found someone who recognized their name. The woman did not know Esa or László Nagy well, but she remembered where they lived.

Etel stood behind András as he knocked on the door of 7 Viola Street. When no one answered, she followed András as he entered the foyer and made his way up the stairs. The building was musty, but Etel didn't mind; she almost enjoyed the smell. At the top of the staircase András stopped, and Etel bumped into him.

"Sorry," she said.

András smiled, his eyes moving from doorway to doorway, looking for something familiar.

"Is this the right place?" Etel asked.

"Yes. I think it's this one," András answered. He motioned to the door of an apartment facing the street. Slowly, they approached it. András knocked.

Immediately the door opened. András barely recognized the thin, greying woman who answered the door. He remembered his aunt Esa as a beautiful, proud woman. She could not have turned into this tiny, sad figure who stood before him.

"Aunt Esa?" he said slowly.

"My name is Esa, but I am not your aunt."

"It is me, András Ursari. Your sister's son. And this is Etel, your niece."

"I know your face. Salvo thought you were dead."

Andreas stepped back, shocked. "Salvo is alive?"

Esa Nagy nodded and spat on the floor. "He was here, and he has ruined us."

Peering into the apartment, András saw that it was empty. There was no furniture and the walls were bare. "Salvo isn't here now?"

"No. He will darken our door no more."

"Where is he?" András stepped forward, insistent.

Esa backed up, her hand ready to slam the door shut. "I don't know. He is a wire walker, I heard."

"What has he done?" András could not believe that Salvo could have done something that would make his aunt hate him so much.

"He has destroyed our lives. Because of him my husband must work two jobs, is working himself into a grave, and my son must live in agony because we cannot afford his medicine. Everything we had is gone." Esa's voice rose in volume and timbre, and she stood up straighter.

"Maybe," András said, surprising himself, "we can help."

"How could you help? Do you have money?" Esa took another step back.

"No. But maybe I could find work. We're family."

Esa's eyes narrowed, her lips pursed. "I already told you. You are not my family." And she shut the door.

As the lock clicked, Etel stood, transfixed. She hadn't heard a word Esa Nagy had said. All she could do was stare. That, she thought, is my mother's sister. That is what my mother looked like. Hair, eyes, hands—these fragments were as much as she would ever see.

She took András's hand and followed him down the stairs and out onto the road. She did not see Esa watching them from the window as they retreated up Viola Street.

"András," she said, her voice a whisper, "is that what our mother looked like?"

András paused. He looked down at her, tears in his eyes. "No. Our mother was a million times more beautiful. She was nothing like that woman."

Etel nodded, but she did not believe him. From then on, whenever she would think of her mother, she would see the face of Esa Nagy.

***

Months and then a year passed. Tomas Skosa and Salvo and Margit travelled Europe, walking for the poor and the wealthy and criminals and royalty. Salvo saw no more butterflies. On the wire his mind was clear; he was peaceful and unafraid. He was at least as good a wire walker as Tomas Skosa, if not better. He was twenty-one years old, as tall as he would ever be, but not as filled out as he might have been if he'd been able to eat properly and regularly.

They had been in Warsaw for a week, and would be moving on to Budapest the next day. Salvo had spent the morning exploring the city, returning to their hotel in the afternoon to rest before their evening performance.

Entering their room, Salvo saw the floor was covered in blood. Tomas Skosa lay face down, arms splayed, naked below the waist. At first Salvo thought he was dead, until his leg moved slightly and a low moan gurgled from his lips. In the far corner of the room Margit crouched, her eyes fixed on Tomas, her hair a tangled mess. Beside her lay an iron kettle with a dent in one side.

"What happened?" Salvo asked, rushing to kneel beside Tomas. Margit stayed where she was. "He will use me no more."

Tomas stirred slightly. He grunted, and his arms and legs retracted, coiling underneath him as he tried to stand. Salvo attempted to aid him, but Tomas brushed him aside. He managed after much effort to stagger to a chair and collapse onto it with his full weight. His hand gingerly touched his head, fingers locating a four-inch gash that was steadily leaking crimson down his cheek and onto his shirt. Salvo handed him a cloth, which he pressed to his wound.

Slowly, Margit walked to where Tomas sat. She drew herself to her full height and stared down at him. "You will use me no more."

Tomas smirked. He pulled his hand back as if to strike her. Margit flinched, and Tomas lowered his hand. "I will do what I like," he said, his voice a growl.

"No," Salvo said. "You won't."

Tomas turned to Salvo. "What?"

"You won't touch her again, Tomas. Not a finger." Salvo's voice wavered, but he held his ground.

Tomas tried to stand, but he was unable. He hit the floor hard, then vomited. He looked up at Salvo, blood running into his eyes, sweat on his brow. "Help me."

116

Salvo pulled him to his feet and shuffled him to the bed, where he gently lay him down. "I will get a doctor," he said.

"No. No doctor." Tomas's speech was slurred.

"You are not in charge any more." Salvo's eyes were hard. He was not going to lose this battle.

"Fine. It's your act now. I don't care. But no doctor. No doctor." Tomas seized Salvo's arm. His grip was strong.

"All right," Salvo said, and Tomas's hand slackened as he lost consciousness.

Margit moved to the edge of the bed. "Will he die?"

"I don't know. Maybe."

Margit bit her lip. "I hope he dies."

Salvo stepped back. "I do not think you do."

"Yes I do," she said, nodding her head. "And you shouldn't think you know what other people wish for."

<hr />

Not long after he took Etel to see their Aunt Esa, András got a job in a stable. He did not mind the work as much as he would have thought; the horses were easy to get along with, and some of the people who worked there were tolerable enough. András also discovered that he took to a set routine quickly; for a Rom, he knew, this was unusual. He had fought against such a notion from the time he was born until he left the Mór Roma. After that, necessity won out over any ideas of how things ought to be. Besides, the job paid enough to rent himself and Etel a warm room and put food in their stomachs.

It was, however, physically demanding work, a seemingly never-ending amount of shovelling. As time went on, András grew to loathe the act of shovelling, and his job became harder. He could feel his mind growing numb. He began to long for a change.

After one particularly tedious day, András waited to cross Andrássy Avenue, when his gaze drifted to a sign that was taped to a lamp-post. He could not read well, but he recognized his brother's name, or at least he thought he did, and it was possible that the person who walked the wire in the poorly lithographed poster was Salvo. András seized the arm of the first person who passed.

"Excuse me," he said, seeing the man had taken his gesture as hostile. "Can you tell me what this says?"

The man examined the poster. "There's a wire act in Serpent Square tonight. Seven o'clock."

"And the name there?" András pointed at what he thought was Salvo's name.

"Salvo Ursari."

András was unable to speak. The man pulled his arm from András's grasp and continued down the street, looking back and shaking his head. András stared at the poster. His brother was in Budapest. This could not be true. He must not allow himself to believe it.

Realizing that it was already past six, András turned and sprinted the five blocks that separated him from Etel. He found her sitting on the front step of their building, smoking. He did not think she should be smoking. It was not a habit for women, let alone twelve-year-old girls. Normally he would have told her as much, but he decided not to say anything this time.

"Come with me," he said.

Etel stood up, flicking her cigarette into the gutter. "Where are we going?"

András paused, wondering if he should tell her. "There's a show in Serpent Square." It was better that she not know until András saw for certain whether the performer was Salvo or not. There was no point in building her up for a disappointment.

They reached the square just as the walk was about to begin. A wire had been strung across the square, attached to a building at each end, about forty feet above the ground. A sizeable crowd had gathered, and Etel had to hold on tight to András's shirt to keep from being separated from him as they pushed their way to a better vantage point.

When the walk began, Etel did not look up right away. Instead, she studied the faces of the people who stood eyes skyward, the way their faces gained intensity and relaxed their hardness as they lost themselves in the event. When she finally did look up at the wire, Etel was unable to stop a rush of air from escaping her, as though she had been hit in the stomach. On the wire she saw a ghost. A thinner, younger version of András, with the same unruly shock of coarse, uncombed hair. Etel remembered the story of the Rom who loved a ghost, and she was afraid, thinking that perhaps this spectre had come to claim her, that her time among the living, which she already considered to be illegitimate and stolen, was at an end. She wanted to run away, but found she couldn't move.

If Salvo was a ghost, he did not feel like one at that moment. He felt the opposite, utterly alive and mortal. He had done few outdoor walks of this type before, and Margit had done even fewer. In addition, this was the first large outdoor walk he had done since Margit had ended Tomas's wire-walking days, and even though Salvo had never particularly relied on Tomas for support during a walk, he would have been glad on this day to have him on the wire instead of down below, where he was no doubt frowning with disapproval.

Salvo tried to stop thinking as he made his way across the wire. Margit was a few paces behind him, and he knew that she looked to him for guidance. He must not show his reluctance, for her sake. The thought of others counting on him helped collect him. There was a power in responsibility that was new and exciting to Salvo. By the time he reached the middle of the wire he was in full control of himself, and he knew there would be no mistakes today.

He turned to face Margit, and when she reached him he bent his knees, squatting on the wire, the palms of his hands level with his chest, facing the sky. Margit put her hands on his, and with a spryness she had never attained under Tomas's tutelage, she sprang into the air, her feet arcing above her head. When she had her balance, Salvo raised himself from his crouch. He brought his hands together as Margit shifted her weight. Then she removed her left hand from his and held it at a right angle to her body. Below they heard the people in the crowd applaud. Salvo was happy to hear them; a two-high one-handed stand was one of the most difficult tricks he and Margit could do.

To Etel, the impressiveness of the handstand served only to solidify her belief that Salvo was something other than human. But for András it had the opposite effect. Seeing his brother execute such a risky feat made him real. It took Salvo out of memory and placed him squarely back in the world. Slowly, as he watched Salvo lower his partner to the wire, András began to understand that Salvo, his brother, was indeed very much alive.

András suddenly felt a wave of apprehension pass over him. He did not know what sort of man Salvo had become, and he didn't know if he wanted to bring him out of the past. In memory, his brother was a slightly irritating but likable, almost noble, boy. András knew that he would not be able to bear having that image destroyed. He had lost too much of his family already.

He remembered Etel and turned to her. He could tell that she knew who Salvo was, that he was their missing brother, and he lost his nerve. He did not catch any inkling of Etel's true feelings, that she was afraid and would gladly have fled. If he had they would have been miles away by the time Salvo came down. Instead, they stood at the door of the building that had supported one end of the wire, waiting for Salvo to exit.

As Salvo stepped through the door and onto the street, it took his eyes a moment to adjust to the light. He heard cheers as people recognized him, and he linked his hand in Margit's and raised their arms in salute. For several minutes he shook hands with admirers and well-wishers, saying little but smiling and nodding graciously as warranted. Slowly he became aware that someone behind him was watching him; he could almost feel eyes boring into his back. He turned to see who was there.

Salvo would later describe the sensation as similar to being suddenly immersed in ice water. He instantly recognized András. His mouth went dry, and his throat constricted.

András forgot all his hesitations and fears, and stepped forward, embracing his brother. He wept freely and did not let go of Salvo until his tears began to abate. "I'm sorry," he said. "I'm sorry."

"For what?" Salvo asked, finally able to speak.

András half laughed, half began to cry again. "I don't know."

Then Salvo saw Etel. He did not know who she was, but he knew somehow she was related. She could not have looked more like an Ursari.

"This is our sister, Etel," András said, seeing Salvo's confusion.

"But she is—"

"No. Our father placed her in his tool trunk during the fire. She survived."

Salvo felt weak in the knees. "I didn't know. I watched the house burn. I didn't know you were in the trunk."

Etel said nothing. She was still not sure what to make of Salvo, though he seemed less and less like a ghost. She moved towards him ever so slightly. "I don't remember it," she said, her voice a whisper.

András stepped between them. "Why did you leave so quickly?"

"I was afraid. I went to burn the church. I found I couldn't." Salvo hung his head, ashamed.

András locked his eyes on Salvo, waiting until he raised his head. "I could," he said, his voice serious.

Salvo nodded, understanding. "They would have been looking for you."

"They were. I think they have stopped now."

Etel listened as her brothers exchanged small details of their recent lives. Salvo seemed real enough. Maybe he actually was her brother. She smiled slightly at the thought that it could be true. But a voice inside her told her to be careful.

"Where did you learn to do that?" she asked, pointing at the wire.

Salvo put his hands in his pockets. "A man taught me."

Etel thought about this. If Salvo was not a ghost, if a person could actually do what she had seen him do, then she would like to do that. "Can you teach me to do that?"

Salvo looked at András. "Yes, I can."

András shook his head. "We could not learn that."

"Of course you can. You are Ursari."

Etel smiled a wide smile. She had two brothers now.

⁂

The two couples danced on the wire, the men with their backs to each other, the women opposite their partners, moving in perfect time. Below, the Viennese gentility marvelled at their grace. The music stopped, and the women retreated from the wire, as did the older-looking of the two men. The remaining wire walker—almost handsome, with green eyes that shone all the way to the ground— paused, patiently waiting for the audience's full attention.

He faced the end of the wire and from a standing position fell backwards, sending the crowd into a collective gasp. Before the gasp died he was on his feet again, having executed a seamless backwards somersault. A young woman with the same eyes walked out, handing him a chair. He placed the chair on the wire, the length of the wire running down the middle of the seat, the four legs dangling. As though gravity did not exist, the man's own legs rose into the air, and his hands came to rest atop the back of the chair. His handstand was flawless, which impressed the crowd, but not as much as when he wobbled slightly, placing one hand perpendicular to his body for balance, deftly recovering. They did not know that he was never in danger of losing his balance, that this was done simply for effect.

He returned his feet to the wire and, lifting the chair to his waist, was rejoined by the man and the other woman, by far the smaller of the two, blonde hair instead of black. She stood between the men. The chair was placed behind her, and as she sat it was hoisted to the men's shoulders. The Viennese clapped, astounded. This stunt they hadn't seen before. The woman was returned to the wire, and the wire walkers returned to the platform, where they bowed graciously. The next day the newspapers would run a story recounting this evening's feats, and many would wish they had not missed the show.

Tomas Skosa was at the performance, but he did not perform. He hadn't in the two years since Salvo had effectively taken control of the troupe. His connections with booking agents and intimate knowledge of the cities of Europe were valuable, though, maybe more valuable than his skills on the wire. He was not a young man any more; he doubted whether he could have walked the wire, even if he wanted to. As he watched the others perform, he was coming off a very bad day—not the worst he had gone through since Margit had attacked him with the kettle, but definitely on the negative side of things. That morning he had been unable to pull back the blankets on his bed or tie his own shoes, even the simplest tasks of coordination presenting difficulty. He felt better as the day went on, but not so much that he wasn't presently having trouble lighting his cigarette. He dropped his lighter and smiled as the woman sitting next to him retrieved it and ignited his cigarette for him. He leaned the tip of his cigarette in and inhaled, relieved. "Thanks," he mumbled self-consciously, awkwardly taking back his lighter and fumbling it into his pocket.

The woman was pretty, and there was a time when he would have asked her out to dance. Tomas thought of the good time they would have had, how their bodies would have soared with music and movement. No more, he knew. On a day like this one his feet would be frozen, his arms jerking as if in a hanged man's death spasms. When such days came along, he was forced to consider whether life was still worthwhile.

He turned his attention to the wire. The boy Salvo, who was no longer a boy, had treated him far better than he would have expected, and, Tomas realized, far better than he had ever treated Salvo. A part of him hated Salvo for his kindness. If he were not obliged by circumstance he might have left. But what kept him there more than anything was the simple fact that this Rom was without a doubt the best wire walker Tomas had ever seen. His brother and sister weren't bad either, and even the girl Margit, once properly taught, had shown more skill than Tomas had thought her capable. But none of them was in the same class as Salvo.

Whether Salvo had any idea of his talent, he never indicated. When he was on the wire he appeared as though he was oblivious to everything else, which, Tomas reflected, was exactly what he had taught him. His pride in the boy, a pride he kept secret, kept him with the troupe as much as the people he needed to contact in various cities or the many duties he had.

Margit, when she spoke, which was rarely, did not speak to Tomas. For two years she had managed to avoid saying more than a few scattered words to him. The thing was, she didn't seem to be afraid of him. She wasn't. Margit had discovered that Tomas had no more power over her, that his days of doing as he liked were over, and she need no longer fear him. To Margit, Tomas Skosa was already a memory.

András and Etel, who were never seen apart, had adjusted quickly to their new lives as wire walkers. It was not, András knew, so different from the life of a Rom. The main difference was that wire walkers could, if they were good, enjoy the respect and admiration of *gadje*, if only for the moments when they were performing. András took a strange pleasure in knowing that they were cheering for him. The wire was not the only trick that was going on.

Where Tomas had been harsh with Salvo's training, Salvo was patient. The concepts were the same, and failure was no less an option, but Salvo preferred to coerce rather than threaten. Besides, Salvo would never have struck a woman—either Margit or his sister especially—and he would likewise not strike András, who could easily thrash him.

When they had begun to train, Salvo was stunned when it was András who took to the wire least. Margit had some training already and had a definite head start, so he wasn't surprised there. Etel, in spite of her enthusiasm, had worried him most.

"If you fall, you die," he told Etel sternly. The look she gave him made him feel as if he had just insulted not only her but himself somehow as well, so he gave up such admonishments. He had commenced training the next day.

First they learned immobility. Margit had no trouble, as she had already learned it, and Etel caught on almost immediately. It took András a week. After that they took their first steps. If they lost their balance, which they often did, they were not allowed to fall. Always they were made to grasp for the wire, hold onto it, then drop to the ground. If they missed the wire, or did not attempt to catch it, Salvo would have to fight hard to control his rage. "You just killed yourself," he told them, "and probably one of us, too." His voice made them ashamed, and after a month they could cross back and forth and no one ever fell.

Balancing and tricks came later. These took time, repetition and a sense of balance that was only perfected after hours and hours on the wire. Negotiating the wire had to become second nature before any tricks were possible. In time, though, they were ready, and even now Salvo continued to teach them any trick he knew, had seen or was able to envision. After two years, he was able to confidently trust each of them with his life, but he still preferred to be alone on the wire.

In the last six months Etel had grown four inches. Soon she would be as tall as Salvo. If her hair was cut and her nose was larger, she could have passed for a younger version of either of her brothers. In temperament, though, she resembled neither. Where András was slow, Etel moved with a quickness reminiscent of a hummingbird. Where Salvo was secretly fearful of very nearly everything, Etel was secretly afraid of nothing. She hid her courage, not wanting to appear brazen. She spoke in a voice softer than her own and often slouched, embarrassed by her height. She made no effort to keep herself clean, constantly having to be reminded by András or Margit to wash her clothes and face. And she smoked incessantly; she loved the smell of it.

IN 1937 THEY SECURED A BOOKING in one of Europe's most prestigious venues, Berlin's Wintergarten. It was a lavish setting, its curved stage and superior acoustics the envy of theatres across the continent. Its patrons, dressed in their finest tuxedos and gowns, ate meals worthy of royalty as they were entertained by the best acts Europe and the world had to offer. As each guest entered the Wintergarten a star on the ceiling was lit, and when the house reached full capacity the ceiling was ablaze with a splendour that rivalled nature.

The wire was strung between two velvet-ensconced private boxes, sixty feet above the stage. Below, a twenty-piece orchestra scored the act, strategically scattered in case one of the wire walkers fell. The house was sold out, as usual.

There was a rumour circulating that Cole Fisher-Fielding was expected to be in attendance, which sent Salvo into a panic that left him aching, his hands sore and stiff from the frightened fists they were permanently contracted into.

Nearly fifty years earlier Cole Fisher-Fielding had, along with four of his brothers and two of his sisters, started the Fisher-Fielding Extravaganza, a meagre spectacle consisting of seven or eight acts, most of them involving at least one family member. In less than twenty years the Fisher-Fielding Circus Company had come to employ over fifteen hundred people and was the undisputed giant of the North American circus world.

Cole Fisher-Fielding was the second youngest of his siblings, and the youngest to enter the circus business. Of his thirteen brothers and sisters, only half had taken an interest in the circus, although sooner or later they had all taken an interest in its financial prosperity. Cole Fisher-Fielding was the sole surviving member of F-F's original founders, sixty-six years old, twice married and twice divorced. He would almost certainly die without an heir. Such was the fate of the majority of the Fisher-Fieldings; of the seven who had started the business, only three had produced children. It baffled many, for the sexual proclivity of the Fisher-Fieldings had never gone unnoticed. It was widely speculated that there was many a Fisher-Fielding who bore a bastard name wandering the streets of America.

That Cole Fisher-Fielding outlived his brothers and sisters was no accident; more than one associate of the F-F Circus Company had remarked that Cole would bury the entire family, some with malice and some without. He was the sort of man it was impossible not to have a strong opinion about. But whatever could be said of him, none could argue that he hadn't earned the title of King of the Circus. During the early 1930s, when the Depression had broken most, if not all, of their competition, the F-F under Cole's direction had not only survived but turned a profit. In fact, in the fifty years that the Fisher-Fielding Circus Company had operated, it had never once missed a pay call. There was no other circus on earth that could make that claim.

Their formula for success was simple. Intimates of Cole had heard his mantra a thousand times if once, and could repeat it asleep. Number one: Never try to cheat the customer. The circus runs on repeat business. The best advertisement was a happy customer. Number two: Hire the best acts and keep them. Number three: Take care of your own. F-F workers were the best fed, best paid, best treated in the business. Simple as that.

It was his second tenet that had brought him to Europe. He had a nose for talent. Most of the top acts of the American circus had been discovered by Cole Fisher-Fielding and everyone knew it. Including Salvo Ursari.

It was no real surprise that he would show his face at the Wintergarten. After all, he was after the best acts in Europe, and the Wintergarten was the best venue. One naturally followed the other. What made Salvo nervous, besides the prospect of performing in front of this famous man, was what might happen if the troupe were offered a spot in the F-F Extravaganza. It had been much discussed among them, and sentiments were split down the middle, with Salvo undecided. András and Etel were keen to move to America, lured by the promise of a new land and the security of belonging to a large circus. Margit was reluctant to leave, wary of America, uninterested in stardom. Tomas Skosa was adamant that he would not go; he refused to even consider the possibility.

"Why not?" András had asked him. It was a rare occasion for András to speak to Tomas. Hardly anyone except Salvo spoke to him.

"Because this is where I am," Tomas said. "There is work to do here."

"But—"

"No but. You go if you like. I must remain."

"No offers have been made," Salvo said. "There is no point to this discussion."

"If there is an offer, I will go," András said. "I owe this place nothing."

"Go, then, Rom. No one will complain."

András, angry, set his jaw, but he did not move.

"No offers have been made," Salvo repeated.

Etel looked at him. "Do you think there will be one?"

Salvo shrugged.

"What would Fisher-Fielding want with us?" Margit said. "There are plenty of wire walkers around."

"We are good," Etel said.

"Yes, but to be in the Fisher-Fielding Company you must be great," Margit said.

"You are not great," Tomas said. Everyone looked at him. Inside, they all suspected he was right, and they despised him for it. He could feel it. He curled his lip to them, rose from his chair and left.

András's eyes stayed on the door long after it had closed, then he turned to Margit. "You should have killed him when you had the chance."

"Enough," Salvo said. "We should rest. Tonight is a big one."

Later, as he lay down, Salvo shook on the bed, his clothes soaked in sweat, his stomach lurching. He didn't know what made him so afraid. It wasn't the walk; he had no fear for that night's performance. Yet Salvo was afraid. He closed his eyes, waiting for the fear to subside. It took a very long time.

ONE BY ONE, THE STARS ON THE CEILING of the Wintergarten were lit. After the final star glowed, the band began to play. When they finished their song the evening's performance would begin. The audience, which consisted heavily of uniformed government officials, waited with palpable anticipation.

The high wire would be the final act. In a cramped dressing room Salvo waited with András, Etel and Margit for a stagehand to tell them it was time to go on. No one talked. Salvo could not wait to be on the wire. The others were nervous. They would be trying a new trick this evening, one that was guaranteed to be a showstopper, one way or another.

For the previous two months they had practised the act daily, repeating it long after their arms and legs were sore and their will to continue had faded. Salvo demanded and received such attention. In the past two weeks they had done the new trick over a hundred times without incident, but everyone knew that doing a trick in practice and doing it in a show were very different prospects. And this was not just a show, this was a show at the Wintergarten, with Cole Fisher-Fielding of the great Fisher-Fielding Circus Company in attendance. It was also, as far as they knew, the first time anyone had attempted a trick like this one.

So they waited in silence as the jugglers juggled and the dancers danced, did not sneak a look at the trained seals or the boneless woman. They didn't care that the other performers thought them elitist. They did, in a way, consider themselves different than the other performers, for they were risking their lives. If a juggler dropped a ball, no one died. It was rare for a trained seal to go berserk and cause injury. But one slip on the wire and that was it for them. That fact set them apart from the others, whether the others were willing to acknowledge it or not.

They had been asked to use a net for this performance out of concern not only for their safety but the safety of the audience and band members. Salvo had refused. It was his feeling that a net made things more dangerous, gave them a false sense of security. And a net did not prevent injury or even death. Salvo knew of a wire walker who had fallen into one from a relatively modest height, only to be bounced off and impaled by his own balancing pole. He would entertain no talk of nets. None of the others questioned him in this conviction, although secretly they wondered whether Salvo wasn't motivated more by the excitement that working netless added to the act than by concerns about safety.

Salvo was surprised that Tomas hadn't showed up for this performance. He often didn't, but this show was different, and every time he heard a noise in the hall outside, Salvo glanced at the door, expecting it to open and Tomas to enter. When it finally did open, it was not Tomas but a stagehand, telling them that they were the next act.

As they walked to the stage, Salvo leading, followed by Margit, then Etel, then András, the other performers averted their eyes. Behind them someone whistled. Salvo's hair bristled; it was bad luck to whistle before a walk, something everyone in the Wintergarten knew. He wasn't worried about the whistle itself. There was no room for superstition on the wire, he believed. It was the ill intent of the person who had whistled that caused him worry. Sabotage was not unheard of.

Still, Salvo did not offer up a prayer as he climbed the ladder that led to the wire. He would fall when and if his time came. Nothing could change that. Margit prayed, though, as did Etel and even András, although it was not normally his custom. This show was different, and whatever else András thought about God, he believed that He was a part of the wire, and for this show it seemed right to ask for special consideration. He felt a little cheap as he did it but shook his head clear. The wire called.

Salvo stood on the platform. When he had silence, he stepped onto the wire. There was a method to the act: Salvo believed that contrast was the key. As loud enhances quiet, dark begets light, Salvo maintained that danger implied safety. So he always started the act with the safest of wire walks; he crossed from one platform to the other, and then back again. Next, they did the wire dance, followed by another solo, Salvo performing a backwards somersault. With András and Margit they did a three-high with a chair, then it was time for the new trick.

A quick pause on the platform, everyone ready, then they took to the wire in a line: Salvo, Margit, Etel, András. When they reached the middle of the wire, Salvo and Etel reversed direction, so that András and Etel were facing each other, as were

Salvo and Margit. Salvo dropped to a knee, and Margit placed her hands on his shoulders. As he stood, she leapt off the wire and towards him, perfectly upside down as he reached the full height of his stance. András and Etel repeated this procedure, and Salvo and András each took a step towards the other, with the women holding handstands on their shoulders. Salvo and András stayed steady, as Etel and Margit each arched their backs, leaning as far back as they could, until their feet touched. From the ground, the four of them looked like the beams of an A-frame house.

They held the position for ten seconds, no one faltering, and then Etel and Margit straightened, and Salvo and András stepped away from each other. Etel and Margit swung down so that they were sitting on the men's shoulders. Salvo and András turned 180 degrees and walked off the wire to opposite platforms.

The Wintergarten's audience had enjoyed the new trick very much, and indeed the entire performance. As the troupe returned to the ground, many left their seats to congratulate them, and the theatre manager shook Salvo's hand so hard and happily that Salvo thought it might fall off. Cole Fisher-Fielding was nowhere to be seen. Nor was Tomas.

Afterward András took Etel and Margit back to their hotel while Salvo waited for their pay. Salvo wasn't quite sure how to go about it since Tomas usually collected their fee, so he waited nervously outside the manager's office. He could hear that there were people inside, and he didn't want to disturb them. It sounded as though a heated conversation was in progress.

Finally the door opened, and a handsome, older man in an immaculate black suit emerged. The man was taken aback, appearing to recognize Salvo. He spun around, re-entering the manager's office.

"Filth!" he swore, his German betraying some sort of accent. "He's been right outside your office the whole time. Who is it you think you're dealing with? I suppose he's waiting to be paid. Honestly, Franz. Why I do business with you, I'll never understand."

The man came outside again and extended a hand to Salvo.

"Cole Fisher-Fielding. You've heard of me?" He spoke in Hungarian now.

Salvo nodded. He was afraid to speak, in case he said something stupid.

"Great act. Absolutely first class. How'd you like to work for the F-F?"

Salvo's mouth opened, but no sound emerged.

"Look, you think about it. You want to work for me, you come to America, all expenses paid. You work steady, forty weeks a year, for top pay. Hell," he paused, "you can even have your own railcar." He thrust a card into Salvo's hand. "I have a train to catch. You decide you want to work for the biggest show in the world, you contact me."

Cole Fisher-Fielding flashed Salvo a million-dollar smile, winked and strode down the hall. Salvo was paralyzed. He was unable to believe what had happened.

The theatre manager approached. "Arrogant prick," he said. "Where's Skosa?"

"I don't know," Salvo said.

"No matter. Here's your pay. Nice show." The theatre manager looked at Salvo for a moment, then returned to his office. As Salvo walked towards the exit, he called to him. "If I were you, I'd think twice about going to America. Lots of people have found it a disappointment."

Salvo considered the manager's words for a moment, before pushing open the door and heading for the hotel.

He ran most of the way and was fairly winded by the time he reached the room. At first, as he tried to catch his breath, he didn't notice that things were not as they should have been. But he soon saw that the room was a mess. Their suitcases had been opened, everything emptied and strewn across the floor. Tomas's had been cut open, the lining exposed. There was a smear of blood on the wall and a hole in the plaster. Before he had any more time to examine the room, he sensed a presence behind him and felt two sets of hands seize his arms. He did not have to look long to realize that these hands belonged to Gestapo officers, seven of them in all. He had seen these uniforms before, both on the street and in the Wintergarten, and of course he knew them by reputation. He had no doubt that his life was in danger.

He was taken by car to a castle on the edge of the city, where he was locked in a room that admitted neither light nor sound. He was in this room for what seemed like hours, all the while trying to guess why he was there. He had heard rumours of Roma being rounded up by these people, and he believed them, but he had considered himself exempt because he wasn't German and because he was a performer. He now wondered whether he hadn't been incredibly naive in his assumptions.

He was worried for András and Etel and Margit as well. He did not know if they had been caught too; for all he knew, they could be in the room next to him. He tapped on the wall, hoping that someone might tap back, but no one did. Without warning, the door opened. Even though the light in the hallway was anything but bright, Salvo squinted his eyes at its intrusion. He got to his feet, and when a rough voice commanded him to step out of the cell he did. A pair of guards escorted him up a narrow staircase and into a large open room. He was thrust roughly into a chair in the centre of the room, and his guards retreated to the doorway. Salvo scanned his environs, looking for a way to escape, seeing none.

A man in a black uniform strode into the room, his boots echoing sharply on the stone floor. He sat at a desk opposite Salvo and for a long time he said nothing, shifting papers on his desk in what Salvo assumed was an attempt to make him nervous. It was successful.

"I assume you know why you are here," the man said.

"No," Salvo said.

"You are an intimate of Tomas Skosa?"

"Yes."

The man nodded. "How long have you been an associate of Mr. Skosa?"

"Since 1928. He taught me to walk the wire."

The man looked at Salvo for a long minute, a frightening, assessing look. "I have seen your act. It is very good."

"Thank you," Salvo said, taken aback.

"Tell me, are you afraid when you are up on that wire?"

"No," Salvo said. "Only when I am on the ground."

The man gave him another long look, then wrote something on the papers on his desk. "You should be more careful about who you choose to associate with, Mr. Ursari. Tomas Skosa was not a man to be trusted."

Salvo nodded. He knew this as well as anyone, but he was unsure why the Gestapo would have any feelings either way about Tomas. The man's use of the past tense when referring to Tomas made his mouth go dry.

"You may go," the man said. "I do not believe you are involved in this matter. Be aware that you are being watched. I have made an exception in your case. I would not like to regret it." The man raised an eyebrow, watching to gauge Salvo's response.

"Thank you, sir. I am involved in nothing."

The man motioned for the guards, who came and removed Salvo from the room. He was taken back to his hotel in a similar car. When he got to the room the blood was gone from the wall, and there were three dollops of fresh plaster at chest height. Their belongings were still scattered across the floor, and he cleaned these up, wondering what had become of the rest of the troupe.

Soon the door opened and András entered hesitantly, Etel and Margit behind him. "They let you go?" he asked.

Salvo nodded. "Yes. You were taken too?" He looked past them into the hallway, afraid they were not alone.

"No," said András. "Margit saw the black cars parked outside the hotel and we kept walking. We watched them take you from across the street."

"Tomas is dead," Salvo said. He was surprised to hear his voice crack with sorrow.

Margit stood, looking Salvo straight in the face. "He was a spy, Salvo." Her voice betrayed no sadness.

Salvo knew then how fortunate he was to be alive.

"Did you get our pay?" Etel asked. Without it they would be stuck in Berlin.

Salvo checked his pockets, fearing the money had been taken when he was searched. It was still there. He exhaled, relieved.

Etel took the money from him and began to fill their suitcases. "Then we should probably get away from here."

"Who was he spying for?" Salvo asked, looking at Margit.

She shrugged. "I think he was working for a lot of different people."

"We should go," Etel said again. "They may be coming back."

"You knew about this?" Salvo asked Margit.

"No. But I can see it now." She looked Salvo straight in the face. Her look did not convince him she was telling the truth.

"We should go," Etel said once again.

"Quiet!" yelled Salvo. "We will go soon enough." He lowered his voice. "We are going to America."

András stood. "Fisher-Fielding?"

"Yes."

"I will not go," András said. He crossed his arms in front of him and paced between the window and the bed.

"Yes you will. You said you would go before."

"I will not run away."

"We are not running away," Salvo said. "It is time to go, and we are leaving for a better place."

András stopped, remembering where he had heard those words before. He did not like that Salvo had invoked the memory of their father at a time like this, but he was forced to concede to the necessity of the situation. "All right."

Etel said nothing, but Salvo knew she would go where András went.

Salvo turned to Margit. She was the only one remaining who had not wanted to go. She sat on the edge of the bed.

"I will go." She looked cold.

They left Germany the next night. Though Salvo feared they were being followed, they crossed the border into France without incident, and four days later they boarded a freighter bound for New York, their passage having been arranged by Cole Fisher-Fielding. As they left port, Salvo was finally able to relax for an instant, before he began to think about the possibilities that the Fisher-Fielding Extravaganza held, and his moment ended.

———

FIVE

Somewhere in the middle of the Atlantic Ocean, Salvo lay on the metal decking of what he had come to consider hell. He'd just completed retching his insides into the sea and knew he'd probably have to do so again any moment. Etel sat beside him, quietly smoking, reasonably sure that no one had ever died of sea-sickness. The motion of the ship didn't bother her, nor did it seem to bother András or Margit, who were asleep in their bunks. Salvo seemed to be the sickest person on the boat, so sick that most of the other passengers had trouble believing that he was the same Salvo Ursari that walked on a wire high above the ground.

Etel knew who he was, though, because she recognized herself in him. She knew that Salvo did not know this, that he even thought she did not like him, which was not true. She held Salvo in awe, his ability on the wire worthy in her eyes of such reverence.

Pushing her thick black hair out of her eyes with long, tobacco-stained fingers, she tossed the butt of her cigarette into the ocean and lit another. She inhaled, savouring the smoke as it entered her. Margit often complained that Etel reeked of smoke, even after she bathed, and she knew it was true, but she didn't care. Etel loved smoke far more than she loved Margit.

She exhaled sharply. Salvo seemed a little better. "What will the Fisher-Fielding Extravaganza be like?" she asked him.

"I don't know," he mumbled weakly.

"Will there be animals? And many other people?"

"Probably."

Etel frowned. She did not think she would like such sur-roundings, and she knew that Salvo wouldn't. "How do you feel?"

Salvo didn't answer her. She pushed a cup of water towards him, but he made no move to drink it. She picked it up and drank some herself, then pushed it back to him. He managed a feeble sip.

It felt strange to Etel to be going to America. Though she had moved from place to place her whole life, somehow having something as large as the ocean between where she was and where she was going made this different. And though no one had ever said as much, Etel knew they would not be returning.

"Do you know what today is?" Etel asked.

"No."

"It is my nineteenth birthday."

"Congratulations," Salvo said. Then his stomach contracted and he spilled a little more of himself into the ocean. Etel shook her head, silently willing the five days that must pass before they would reach land to go quickly.

TRAVELLING ON A MUCH FASTER SHIP and without particular misery, Cole Fisher-Fielding reached New York a full week ahead of the Ursaris. He used this time to prepare for the upcoming tour.

It was a circus born of the imagination of Cole Fisher-Fielding, and to a lesser extent, his brothers and sisters. They were not a circus family; their parents had looked down on such pageantry, even after the achievements of their children. The sib-lings who had chosen to make their living in other professions were shown an obvious favouritism; even those who managed to fail spectacularly at mundane aspirations were preferred over the circus children. Though far less successful than their siblings, they were in respectable professions, which mattered greatly to their parents, who held aristocratic ambitions. Following the deaths of the Fisher-Fielding parents, the families of the original seven founders rarely spoke to the families of the seven who spurned the big top. Instead of healing, the rifts grew wider.

The Fisher-Fielding big top was the largest there was. It could seat ten thousand people in relative comfort, along with animals and performers, rising sixty feet in the air at its apex. The outer circumference was supported by numerous minor poles, each twenty feet high. Oval in shape, the big top was ringed by bleachers on the shorter sides and seat wagons on the longer lengths. These wagons consisted of twenty rows of seats ascending from the ground, higher at each consecutive row. The seats folded out from the wagons, requiring minimal set-up. Inside the wagons performers waited for their cues, and attendants kept a watchful eye out for people, mainly children, trying to sneak under the side walls of the tent. Down the centre of the big top ran a line of sixty-foot poles, each topped with a flag, forming the high point of the tent. Guy wires, ropes and sub-structures made up the rest of the skeleton of the big top. Over all this stretched the canvas, made by sail makers specifically for the F-F for a sum that few circuses could afford. It fit together in sections laced and unlaced at each venue by expert hands.

Once the big top was up, the animal menagerie was erected and the seat wagons and bleachers were unfolded. The rigging for the various aerial acts was checked and rechecked. Outside, the midway began to be assembled, and preparations commenced for the "spec," a free parade designed to entice people into the big top.

By the time the Ursaris arrived in New York everything was set to go. The F-F was opening the season with an indoor show at Madison Square Garden, as it always did. Salvo couldn't believe the scale of the F-F. It made the Wintergarten look like a tavern. There had to be at least a hundred clowns. Two trapeze acts. Wild lions, tigers, panthers. Elephants. Sword swallowers. Equestrian acts. Anything and everything the circus could dream up, the Fisher-Fielding Extravaganza had. It frightened Salvo beyond belief.

Salvo had revamped the entire act for the North American audience. In the big top they were much higher than they had been before. They would use balancing poles whenever possible. Also, the tricks had to be more complex; it was harder to sell a wobble, because it was harder for people to see one. The biggest change was the use of bicycles. None of them liked using bicycles, but other high-wire walkers used them and audiences liked them, so they didn't have much choice. Salvo resolved that if they were going to use bicycles, they would use them spectacularly. And they wouldn't use a net.

András was furious when Salvo told the rest of them that there would be no net. "Who are you to decide this for us?" he said, slamming his hand on the pole that supported their rigging.

"It is better this way." Salvo did not allow András to scare him. He knew he must win this argument.

Etel looked at András, then at Salvo. She said nothing, knowing there would be no changing either of their minds. Both ways were the same to her.

"Better for who?"

"For all of us. If you have a net, your mind will know that you can fall. But you can still get killed if you fall. You bounce out, maybe a bicycle falls on you—anything can happen."

András shook his head. "A net can save you."

"No." Salvo put his hand on András's shoulder. "The only way is never to fall. A net makes falling more likely. So we will use no net."

Salvo turned and walked away. He didn't look back. He wanted to, but even more he wanted to appear strong. He and András had had this discussion before, and Salvo wanted the issue settled once and for all.

When his brother was gone András swore in Romany, uttering a phrase that Etel understood but Margit did not, though she could tell as well as Etel that he was upset.

"He is wrong," András said.

Etel shrugged. "Maybe he is. Or maybe he isn't. If we ever find out, it will be too late to do anything. He knows more about the wire than any of us, though."

"So you're taking his side?"

"No, I'm taking no side." She pushed a coil of hair out of her face.

"You can't do that."

Etel looked András square in the eye. "Yes, I can." She held his stare for several more seconds, then left. There was no talking to him when he was agitated.

András watched her leave. There had been a time when she would have sided with him. He did not want to feel betrayed, but he did.

Margit had moved and was standing next to him. "You are with Salvo on this?" he asked her.

Margit smiled at him. "Take me for a walk," she said.

"But what do you think about the net?" András knew what she thought, but he wanted to hear her say it.

"I think it is a nice night and I would like to see the stars." She took his hand. "I think we spend far too much time talking about what we do on the wire."

143

András sighed. Maybe she was right. He was beginning to wonder if he cared that much about whether they used a net or not, or if he wasn't more concerned with not losing an argument. "All right," he said.

As soon as they stepped outside they realized no stars would be visible from the depths of the city. Margit was disappointed.

"This has happened before," András said.

"No stars?" She leaned closer to him.

"Yes. There was a time once when a giant fish leapt out of the sea, high into the air, and this fish swallowed up all the stars. People everywhere were very unhappy, as they had grown to love the stars, and without them the sky seemed empty. They searched the world for someone who could catch the fish and put the stars back in the sky, until finally they found a Rom who was said to be the most clever man ever to live. This Rom missed the stars as much as anyone, so he agreed to help.

"He went to a great king and begged him to loan him a diamond. This king was not a fool—one does not just give every Rom who comes to their door a diamond—but when he found out what it was for, he agreed.

"So the Rom took the diamond and tied it to a line, and one night when the moon was right he cast it into the sky above the sea. Sure enough, the fish leapt up and swallowed the diamond. When the fish realized it was snared, it put up a fight that lasted the whole night and the next day and the next night. After three days the fish had no more fight left in him and he gave up the ghost.

"The Rom sliced open his belly and the stars floated out, back to their proper places in the sky. The Rom told the king that his diamond had been lost in the struggle, but the king was so happy to have the stars back that he did not mind. The Rom gave the diamond to a beautiful girl, and she fell madly in love with him. From then on things have been as they are."

Margit laughed. "That's a good story. Where did you hear it?"

András's shoulders lowered. "My father told it to me."

Margit stopped laughing. "Do you miss him?"

"Yes." András did not tell her that there were times when he had trouble seeing the faces of his parents in his mind.

"And Salvo. Does he miss your father?"

András nodded. "He does."

"He never speaks of him. He never speaks of anything that has happened to him."

András thought about this. "He was on his own. Etel and I were together, but he had no one. That's why he's different."

"I'm glad you're not like that." Margit smiled again.

I could get used to that smile, András thought. He took her hand and they continued walking. They had no destination in mind.

WHEN SALVO INFORMED COLE FISHER-FIELDING of his decision not to use a net, his reaction was mixed. The pure circus enthusiast in him loved the idea. And he knew audiences would go for it. But the F-F was known as a safe circus; no one had ever died while performing in the Extravaganza. He expressed his safety concerns to deaf ears. In the end Cole relented.

Their first night was a sell out, as most of the dates were that year. They would be in Madison Square Garden for another week, and then they would take the big top on the road, playing dates across the continent for the summer and early fall. The Ursaris followed the cat act, waiting nervously on the platform as the crowd marvelled at the animals' surly obedience. Finally the cats were directed back to their cages, and the band played the Ursaris onto the wire.

For the first trick, Salvo and András each rode a bicycle across the wire. Salvo handed off his bicycle and they crossed back on András's bike, Salvo doing a handstand on the handlebars. Next, Etel and Margit made a crossing on foot, stopping in perfect synchronicity to lean forward and place their poles on the wire, simultaneously executing handstands. As they did this trick, Salvo and András each strapped on a harness that secured a six-foot pole between them. When Etel and Margit arrived at the platform, Etel boosted Margit onto the pole, where she balanced as Salvo and András crossed. Etel rode the bicycle back across the tightrope then, so that both bicycles were on the same platform. Next came their final trick, by far the best one.

Without removing the harnesses, Salvo and András took to the bicycles, András in front, Salvo behind. Etel, an eight-foot balancing pole in her hands, stood on the pole between the bicycles. Margit stood behind her, without a balancing implement, holding on to Etel's shoulders. On Salvo's cue, the bicycles started forward. After they were in motion, Margit leapt up onto Etel's back, her feet resting first on her hips, then under her arms, then on her shoulders. With what looked like minimal effort, she paused in a squat. Then, with no more hesitation than if her feet were firmly planted on the ground, she stood.

The effect took the audience aback. Fifty feet above them, a woman stood on the shoulders of another woman who stood on a pole supported by two men riding bicycles on a wire. And there was no net. As they reached the middle of the wire, more than one gasp involuntarily escaped from the audience. The woman on top had placed her hands on the shoulders of the woman below her and inverted her body in a handstand. She wobbled slightly as the performers moved to the end of the wire, and a woman in the audience screamed. The crowd was otherwise so quiet that people on the opposite side of the ring heard her husband's admonishments. They reached the far platform, finally, after what seemed to those watching like hours.

At first people were too shocked to know what to do. After several seconds, they stood, almost in unison, clapping, yelling and cheering wildly.

Up on the platform, Salvo completely misread the audience. To him they sounded angry, and many were whistling loud, shrill whistles, which in Europe was dangerously unlucky and a sign of extreme disapproval.

"Come quickly," he said to the others, and he slid down the rope ladder as fast as he could and retreated to their corner of the performers' area. There they huddled, András and Etel and Margit all agreeing with Salvo's impression, believing that the crowd had hated their act and was calling for their heads.

A stagehand ran towards them, looking confused. "What are you doing? Get back out there," he said, pulling on Salvo's arm.

Salvo refused to budge. "Are you crazy? They'll lynch us."

"You've got it wrong, Ursari," the man said. "They loved you. They want a bow. This is an ovation."

It began to sink in. As they climbed the ladder to the wire and looked at the faces of individuals in the stands, they saw that indeed they were not angry, that they had thoroughly enjoyed the act. From the platform they gave a bow, waving, the enthusiastic crowd responding with a crescendo of applause.

Later, as they sat in their railcar, the others chided Salvo.

"They'll lynch us," Margit laughed, mimicking Salvo.

András said nothing, but smiled.

"Can you believe them?" Etel said. "They were crazy for us."

"We're a good act," Margit said. "Maybe the best in the circus."

"Be careful where you say that," András said. He had already seen firsthand how jealous some performers could be.

Salvo sat off to the side, not joining the conversation. He was exhausted and worried. The act had not been as tight as he felt it should be. He could feel during the last trick that their timing had been off. They would have to practise harder. "We get up early tomorrow," he said. "We have much to work on."

Margit, her back to Salvo, made a face, which made András laugh, but no one said anything. There was a knock at the door, and before anyone could answer it, the door swung open.

Cole Fisher-Fielding, immaculately groomed and tuxedoed, strode into the railcar. "Congratulations, Ursaris," he said. He presented Etel and Margit each with a bouquet of flowers. Salvo and András received cigars similar to the one protruding from the corner of his mouth. An attendant followed with a tray bearing a bottle and five glasses, which he set on the small table in the middle of the car before being dismissed with a casual wave of Fisher-Fielding's hand.

Cole poured a golden brown liquid into the glasses and passed them out, two fingers for the women and three for the men. He raised his glass. Everyone followed his example. "To a long and happy partnership between the Fisher-Fielding Circus Company and the Magnificent Ursari Troupe," he said, downing the contents of his glass.

Salvo drained his glass too, rye whisky burning his throat and stomach. "Thank you, sir. We'll do our best."

Fisher-Fielding laughed. "I have no doubt of that. Carry on." And as quickly as he had come, he was gone.

Cole was more than a little preoccupied that evening. His control of the F-F was now threatened by a group he had christened "the Spouses." Originally, no official agreement of partnership had been made among the Fisher-Fieldings. When their brother Trevor, the third oldest, had died suddenly in 1920, lawyers were able to convince them of the need for a formal documentation of ownership. Since Trevor had never married and had no known heirs, they agreed to split the F-F's ownership seven ways, Trevor's former share being split between "the Respectables," the siblings that had not been involved in the circus. It was a point of contention, and Cole had argued against it, but the others won out. Now it was coming back to haunt him.

His eldest circus brother had produced one child, Martin Fisher-Fielding, who was a firm ally of Cole's. The second circus sibling, a sister named Mary, had borne two children, neither of whom had any interest in the circus whatsoever and had been content to sell Cole their share of the business. Here was where things got tricky for Cole. His sister Evelyn, his favourite sibling, two years older than him, had married a real-estate baron named Phillip Barnes against the advice of Cole, a fact that Phillip knew. His next oldest sibling, Winston Fisher-Fielding, had married a southern belle named Rebecca, and they'd had a son, Norris Fisher-Fielding. Following first Winston and then Evelyn's death, Phillip Barnes and Rebecca Fisher-Fielding married. Though it reminded Cole far too much of *Hamlet* for any degree of comfort, Norris didn't seem to mind his mother and uncle engaging in matrimony; in fact, he seemed enthusiastic about it. Rebecca, who had never much cared for Cole, and Phillip, who still begrudged the fact that Cole had advised against his marriage to Evelyn, now controlled two-sevenths of the F-F.

Cole's brother Peter had died nearly twenty years earlier, leaving his wife, Charlotte, with half his interest, and his son John with the other half. John, in an attempt to spite his mother, whom he deeply resented for an unhappy childhood, had always sided with Cole in the past. Charlotte was great friends with Rebecca Fisher-Fielding-Barnes and always voted with her interests.

As a result, Cole, between his shares and the support of his nephews Martin and John, controlled a fifty per cent share of the F-F, which was enough to swing any vote. A stipulation of the one-seventh share that the rest of the family controlled was that they didn't have any vote unless there was a tie, in which case they cast the deciding opinion.

Three days earlier, John Fisher-Fielding had been killed in an automobile accident. He was unmarried and hadn't left a will, and as a result his share of the F-F Circus Company would revert to his mother, his closest living relative. Now things had swung into uncertainty: Cole Fisher-Fielding controlled three-sevenths of the company, as did the Spouses. This meant that any vote would be tied, and the Respectables had the tiebreaker.

In the past, the committee of ten or so varied relatives that made up the Respectables had shown a complete inability to grasp the business of circus entertainment, concerned with nothing else than the financial rewards of their collective one-seventh interest. Cole was relatively certain that in the event of a tie, they could be easily lured into the Spouses' camp by the promise of larger profits. They neither knew nor cared about the intent or the feelings of the original siblings. Few could even keep straight in their heads who was who.

Fortunately, Cole had been elected to a five-year term as president of the Fisher-Fielding Circus Company in 1937 and would have four more years before he'd be in any real danger. Still, there would be a fight ahead, he knew.

The wire walkers, at rest in their railcar, knew nothing of the circus's politics. As they lay down for the night, they fell asleep: first András, then Margit, then Etel. Salvo, kept awake by fears of the dark, elephants, the future and the past, did not know that elsewhere Cole Fisher-Fielding was awake as well, with fears of his own.

ONE OF THE FIRST PEOPLE SALVO MET in the Extravaganza was a dark-skinned man named Emil Narwha. He might have been from India, or he might have been French, or he might have been from just down the road from wherever they were on a given day. Salvo had never asked Emil about his past and Emil had never asked Salvo, an unspoken arrangement that seemed to serve them both. For the first few weeks neither man spoke much. They stood and leaned against the side wall of the main tent, watching the bustle of the F-F pass them by, giving no indication of what they thought about it all. It was only after quite a while that Salvo discovered Emil was the head elephant wrangler, an exceedingly important position. He had held this post for over thirty years, long enough for the elephants to regard him as one of their kind, to look at the leathery old man as their father.

Salvo watched him work with the elephants, wondering how anyone could place his trust in a beast so large, something that could kill him without effort. Emil Narwha did just this, however, to Salvo's continual amazement. Gentle and patient Emil trained the elephants to do his bidding, and the elephants responded with their nearly complete cooperation.

After months of nods and abbreviated hellos, Salvo decided to ask Emil about what had been bothering him since he'd first discovered Emil's occupation.

Emil looked at him in surprise. "Afraid? That is an odd thing for a man like you to ask."

Salvo smiled and shrugged, feeling a little foolish. "I would walk the highest wire in the world before I would let an elephant touch me with its nose."

"Trunk," Emil said. "And you would never get me on any wire."

"But you are not afraid at all?"

Emil thought before replying. "Some people believe all animals are good. I do not believe this. I have seen an elephant stalk a man, always watching him with one eye, waiting for him to make a mistake, to get too close. And I have seen that elephant crush his enemy, and I would swear that the elephant enjoyed the man's screams and the crunching of his bones beneath his feet. I see that an animal can hold evil within it, and I've no doubt of that. But most are not this way; certainly none of my elephants. I treat them well, and they treat me well."

Salvo frowned. "How do you know if an elephant's evil?"

"Same as people. Easy to tell if you look properly."

Yet it seemed to Salvo that a great amount of evil was very well hidden. It could hide anywhere, in the hearts of strangers, loved ones, even in his own heart. It also seemed to him that hidden evil was the worst kind, and he envisioned it stalking him, huge and grey and shadowy. There was no escaping it, no running away.

"Cheer up, Ursari. Maybe one day you can ride on one of my elephants. Then you'll see."

Salvo shook his head no, and Emil chuckled as he walked back towards the menagerie. "You'll see one day. You will change your mind."

I doubt that very much, Salvo said to himself, but as he walked away he felt a certain kinship with Emil, a new admiration for the things he did not understand. As he passed the elephants, though, he could not bring himself to even look at them. He still remembered Good Bear the Bear, and to catch the gaze of a sorrowful camel or giraffe could move him near to tears. But the elephants were different, somehow. Salvo hated them. He felt that they were assessing him, plotting against him, and that if they ever got the chance they would do him whatever harm they could, a suspicion that had just been unintentionally reinforced. Sometimes on a certain cue from Emil, the elephants would join trunk to tail to trunk, marching wherever directed, and more than once in his endless moments before sleep, Salvo had visions of an endless train of elephants rushing towards him, relentlessly seeking to grind him into the earth, to tear him limbless. There were times when Salvo thought he might like to kill them.

ANDRÁS WALKED PAST THE BIG TOP, hoping to find a vendor who would give him a hot dog, or at worst, sell him one. A group of clowns went by, one of them a man András had seen vomiting outside their railcar several nights earlier. Today he looked miserable, his hands shaking and his walk hesitant. András noticed that several of the other clowns seemed to share this demeanour. He didn't know that the clowns had a reputation for being drunks, or that they often got into knock-down brawls with other performers, or the circus police. The clowns he had seen in Europe were not the same as these, that much he could tell at a glance. He had no urge to speak with or get to know them.

András had the same keep-to-himself attitude about most things the F-F had to offer. He enjoyed his life there immensely, loved the energy and the excitement, the continuous crowds and the travel. But he much preferred to be an observer than an active participant. He even thought, at times, that he would rather be in the audience than a member of the circus, but knew that for the audience it was a treat, not how things were every day, and that if he were not a performer he likely would never get to attend a show, so he did not feel overly sorry about his position.

None of the vendors were out yet. András's stomach growled dissatisfaction, but there was nothing to be done about it. He doubled back towards the big top. If he checked the rigging now, maybe there would be time for a hot dog later. He saw Etel standing beside the main entrance, smoking.

"What are you doing out here?" he asked.

Etel shrugged. "Margit is complaining again."

"About what?"

"Anything she can think of." Etel flicked the stub of her cigarette onto the ground, stepping on it. She quickly rolled and lit another.

"She does not like your smoking." András did not tell Etel it was because the smell of smoke reminded her of Tomas Skosa.

"That is too bad for her. I do not like her griping."

András shook his head. "It's not so bad."

"Why do you stand up for her?" Etel slashed at the air with her hand.

"Why do you attack her?" András's voice was raised, and he felt the muscles in his back tense.

Etel took a long drag off her cigarette, inhaling nearly half its length. "You are in love with her." It was not a question, but as soon as Etel said it she realized it was true.

András looked down at his feet, then brought his eyes up to meet his sister's. "What if I am?"

Etel's eyes were cold, her lips pursed. "You do what you like."

András turned and walked away from the big top. He was no longer interested in checking the rigging, no longer interested in hot dogs.

Etel dropped what was left of her cigarette. As she was about to grind it into the earth, a small clump of dried grass caught fire. Etel watched it burn, knowing she should stamp it out. After more time than was sensible, she finally brought her foot down upon the flame.

＊＊＊＊＊＊＊＊

WHEN WAR CAME TO EUROPE IN 1939, the troupe's decision to come to America was rapidly validated. This was before they even knew what was happening to Roma in the camps. However, in 1941, after the bombing of Pearl Harbor and America's entry into the war, they found themselves, as Hungarians, citizens of an enemy nation. Salvo, fearing persecution, contemplated shelving the act until the war was over, but he soon discovered that few people knew or cared that he was a Hungarian, just as few had cared that he was a Rom. As long as he walked the wire it seemed he could do no wrong. There were of course isolated exceptions. One man hired to help with their rigging was caught purposely slackening a guy wire during a performance. It turned out the man's brother had been killed the month before by enemy fire, which he somehow blamed on the Ursaris. The man was sacked, and though Cole Fisher-Fielding denied it when Salvo asked, Salvo suspected that the man was beaten up by members of the circus police on Cole's orders. Either way, András swore he saw the man being roughed up behind the menagerie. He did not attempt to interfere.

Salvo spent nearly all of his waking hours on the act, trying to devise new routines, new tricks, new techniques, anything to keep the act fresh and exciting. They were capable of performing nearly fifty separate manoeuvres and had four showstoppers, all variations on the three-level pyramid they had performed for their first crowd in America. Because they travelled to the same cities each season, Cole Fisher-Fielding insisted that the audience get to see different tricks from year to year, and Salvo readily complied. He enjoyed nothing more than the development of new feats.

The war brought increased crowds to the F-F Extravaganza. People's pockets were full of money, their minds eager for any kind of distraction, so the big top was very nearly always full, and attendance was at record levels. Their winter seasons were shorter, and the big top stayed on the road longer, despite rationing and a shortage of manpower. Citizens purchasing Victory Bonds received complimentary passes to the show. Anyone wearing a uniform was given free admission.

Early in 1942 the F-F had a three-day stand in the nation's capital. This stand also happened to coincide with the Fisher-Fielding Circus Company's annual general meeting; Cole's five-year term was up, and he would face for the first time serious competition for the top job in the form of Norris Fisher-Fielding, his nephew. The Spouses had not been idle since the balance of power had shifted in their favour. It was a toss-up as to who would rule the circus for the next five years.

On the day of the opening performance there was no matinee scheduled. Instead, the A-list performers were invited to a reception for the Respectables, an invitation that was not optional. Salvo, much to his disappointment and trepidation, was the only one of the Ursari troupe invited. He would be forced to mingle with the other performers, something he did not particularly enjoy.

Salvo never considered not attending, though. The majority of the performers respected and admired Cole, even if they didn't always like him, and most were more than willing to show their support for his leadership. Even those who were not disposed to like him had to admit that he was a better boss than Norris Fisher-Fielding was likely to be. Cole had built the F-F from nothing, whereas Norris was an Ivy League snob with a lazy eye and a voice that seemed to come through his nose. The choice was an easy one for most.

Salvo put on a brave face and left the railcar, heading towards the big top. He kept an eye out for Etel, who hadn't been in the railcar that morning. He wanted to tell her about a new move he had thought up, but he saw no sign of her. She was probably well hidden, he decided, knowing that she tried to avoid the hustle and bustle of the F-F as much or more than he did.

Salvo was halfway to the big top when he remembered that he had forgotten to ask András to double-check their rigging for that night. They usually took turns doing so, but Salvo wasn't sure if he would have time between the reception and that evening's show, and it was very important that someone confirm that the rigging was as it should be. Admonishing himself for forgetting, Salvo turned and jogged back to the railcar.

As he burst through the door, he caught a brief glimpse of naked flesh before it was covered by bedding. András peered up at him, his face red, and from under the covers Margit's voice called out. "What do you want?"

Salvo hesitated. He had suspected for some time that Margit and his brother had become enamoured of each other but had never been so boldly confronted with proof. "Can you recheck the rigging for me?" he asked András, who was now smiling.

"Sure."

Salvo nodded, backing out of the railcar. As he walked to the big top, he wondered how Etel would feel having to compete for her brother's affections, especially a brother like András who had raised her single-handedly and was not particularly generous with affection. On the other hand, Salvo decided, his brother was thirty-five years old, after all, and Margit was an obvious and, it seemed, willing partner for him.

ETEL WAS NOT JEALOUS OF MARGIT AND ANDRÁS. At least this is what she told herself over and over. She knew there was no way Margit could ever take her place in András's heart, and she derived a certain satisfaction from this knowledge. But on another level she was broken-hearted by the realization that András needed more than she could provide for him, that even a perfect sister has limitations. Etel spent long hours trying to fit things together, attempting to reconcile her emotions with her mind. She was most concerned when she understood that if an opportunity presented itself, she would in all likelihood be unable to resist taking steps to remove Margit from their lives.

Margit did not care what she thought, Etel knew. Margit was overwhelmed by András, and to a larger extent overwhelmed by the F-F Extravaganza. There was nothing about it she did not love. She loved the freedom, she loved the unspoken boundaries, and she loved the people, especially the dancers. In a candid moment she told Etel that their costumes made her dizzy, all the glitter and silk and colour. They made her think of glorious birds.

Etel thought this was silly. She did not understand how someone who had lived as hard a life as Margit's could be so easily swept away by glitz. She did not understand how it could be seen as anything more than a sham.

A TRUE SHOWMAN, Cole held his reception in the centre ring, under the big top. Fresh sawdust was laid, food and drink were plentiful, and spirits were high. Cole worked the crowd of Respectables, aware that he had enemies among these relatives, these nephews and nieces and second cousins. The de facto leader of the Respectables was a Canadian, the husband of Cole's deceased sister. Now in his seventies, Arthur Simpson had been five years younger than his Fisher-Fielding bride, something which had caused quite a stir at the time but now seemed quite irrelevant. His wife died giving birth to their third son. He remarried and his second wife also died, although the two had produced a daughter. Simpson went on to achieve a level of wealth and social standing that did not seem likely when he had first married. He had been the Canadian ambassador to Washington for some years and, now retired, was several times a millionaire. That it was rumoured his wealth was in large part derived from Prohibition did nothing to diminish his appeal to the Respectables. Cole felt fairly confident that if he could win Arthur Simpson to his cause he would prevail.

It would be no easy task. Simpson was not known to be a particular fan of the circus, or of entertainment in general. The only things that would interest him were the profitability of the circus and an assurance that he would not have to even think about the Fisher-Fielding Extravaganza for another five years. Working in Cole's favour was Simpson's respect for tradition. Cole hoped that the fact that he had made the F-F what it was and that he was one of the original seven would go at least some distance for him. He scanned the ring for Simpson and, after locating him, straightened his suit, put on his best smile and approached the man who owned his fate.

Salvo stood orphaned on the other side of the ring, feeling very unpopular and wishing he didn't have to be there. None of the other performers seemed interested in talking to him, and his English wasn't good enough to engage strangers in meaningful conversation, or so he thought. In reality, though he hadn't consciously tried to learn, Salvo's English was the best of any of the Ursaris, more than passable.

He took a sip of his iced tea, having refused the champagne the others were drinking on the grounds he was performing that night. In truth, the only time he ever drank was immediately following a show, and then only when Cole Fisher-Fielding, with his bottle of rye whisky, stormed into his railcar, which was fairly frequently. It was hot under the top, and the tea was good—bitter and refreshing. Several feet from him stood a very good-looking woman, maybe twenty-five years old. She was talking with a man whom Salvo did not immediately recognize, a man who was obviously one of the Respectables. After a second glance, Salvo realized that the man was Norris Fisher-Fielding. Salvo took several steps to his left, in the opposite direction. The woman, her back to Salvo, pushed Norris away with one hand, firmly, then turned and walked towards Salvo. Norris watched her for a moment and shook his head, before beginning a conversation with the person next to him.

The woman's eyes scanned the vicinity, looking for a familiar face and, finding none, rested on Salvo. Her eyes were a deep brown, almost black, and she appeared to assess Salvo for a moment before she approached him.

"Hello," she said, her voice and manner confident.

"Hello."

"Look, I don't really know many people here, and my cousin over there's having a problem grasping the parameters of the fact that we're sort of related, so can I stand here with you for a while?" She flashed him a smile.

"Yes." Salvo's palms began to sweat.

"You're in the circus?"

"Yes."

"Well, what do you do?" she asked.

"I walk the wire."

"Really? I've never seen the circus before. Is your act dangerous?"

Salvo shrugged. "Only if I fall."

The woman laughed at this, a sound pleasing to Salvo's ears. He hardly ever laughed. "You have an accent. Where are you from?"

"Transylvania. Hungary."

"You're Hungarian?"

"I am a Rom."

The woman paused. Salvo expected her to ask him if he was from Rome, which many Americans did. But she surprised him.

"Your people are not doing very well right now," she said.

Salvo nodded. "That is how it always is."

The woman took a drink of her champagne, Salvo of his iced tea. Someone passing by bumped into the woman, and she brushed against Salvo. As the person apologized, Salvo felt a buzz of electricity run up his arm where their skin had met.

"Will you be performing tonight?" she asked.

"Yes."

"Then I will see you." She made a move as if to leave.

"My name is Salvo," he blurted out.

The woman smiled. "Nice to meet you, Salvo. My name is Anna. Good luck tonight." She walked away, disappearing into the crowd. Salvo looked away from where she had been just in time to see Norris Fisher-Fielding glaring at him. He looked down at his feet, and when he looked up Norris was gone.

At the other end of the ring, Cole concluded his conversation with Arthur Simpson. The man was hard to read, and from what he could tell, it didn't appear that he had made up his mind either way. Cole was relieved that at least he hadn't decided to throw his support to the Spouses and was somewhat confident that upon viewing the Extravaganza that evening, Simpson would lean towards Cole. The circus could move even the most stoic of souls, he knew.

In the time before he would have to walk, Salvo tried his best to put Anna out of his mind. It was obvious that she was of a different class and from an entirely different world. He had to concentrate on that night's show, not think about some girl he'd probably never see again. On his way back to his railcar he passed the elephants, and he swore that one of them was glaring at him the same way that Norris had glared at him. He suppressed a shiver but was unable to relax in the hours that followed.

It was another sell-out night, the big top packed to bursting. Salvo waited outside with Margit and Etel while András checked the rigging on the opposite side of the tent. Etel smoked three cigarettes in rapid succession and was in the process of rolling a fourth. Margit's hands fidgeted with the folds of her costume, and Salvo rhythmically clenched and unclenched his fists. András returned only moments before the cat act went into its final movements, and together they silently entered the big top and ascended to the wire.

Cole watched from his seat as the Magnificent Ursari Troupe began their act. On his left was his loyal nephew, Martin, and to his direct right sat Arthur Simpson, his daughter, Anna, from his second marriage, and then Cole's nemesis, Norris Fisher-Fielding. The Spouses and various Respectables rounded out the row, everybody pretending that this was simply an amiable trip to their beloved circus, no one openly stating the animosity that flew back and forth between the two camps. Feeling his nerves begin to race, Cole discreetly popped one of the glycerine tablets he had been prescribed for his heart into his mouth and resolved to appreciate the rest of the performance. If the vote tomorrow didn't go his way, this would be his last show as F-F president. If that was the case, he didn't want his last show to pass unenjoyed.

With the rest of the audience he craned his neck skyward as Salvo stepped onto the wire. As usual, the Ursaris started with a simple crossing, building gradually in sophistication. But this time something different happened. When Salvo was three-quarters of the way across, he noticed a moth. There was nothing special about it; it was one of many that attempted to eat away at the untreated side walls of the canvas. But it didn't matter. Even though it was never within five feet of Salvo, it was as though he'd been confronted by the angel of death, and he backed up, visibly frightened. For a moment it looked as though he would fall, his back foot missing the wire, his balance lost. The audience gasped, fearing the worst. But then, and he didn't know why, his mind told his head to turn, and he found his gaze locked into that of the woman Anna. She returned his gaze, and unlike everyone else in the big top, she was not the least bit alarmed. She was calm as a newborn, her face serene and reassuring. He could see that she knew he would not fall, and so he did not. As if he had total control over the laws of physics, he easily regained his balance. Everyone, including Cole Fisher-Fielding, breathed a sigh of relief. Salvo tipped his pole in salute and continued to the end of the wire. Arthur Simpson glanced at Cole and smiled approval. Cole believed that Salvo's salute had been intended for him, and he felt a rush of pride. He was certain the vote would go in his favour.

When Salvo reached the platform András shot him a look of fright. "What happened?"

"Nothing," Salvo answered. "I'm fine. Let's get on with it."

András knew he was lying, but now was not the time to go into any detail. Salvo didn't doubt that he could continue with the act, but he knew he would feel the full weight of his mistake once he was on the ground.

Anna Simpson had never seen anything like Salvo's act before, and he was unlike any person she had ever met. How he walked that wire she didn't know, but she suspected it was magic. When he had looked down at her she'd felt as if he had looked right into her, through her clothes and her skin and flesh, all the way to her spine, to the marrow in her bones. She wondered what his life was like, what he looked like when he slept, what he smelled like. She had stood next to him that very afternoon, and she could not remember if he had smelled of anything. Anna resolved to find out.

To Salvo, the rest of the act passed in a daze. It was only after they were back in their railcar that he snapped out of his stupor.

"What was that?" Margit asked, angry.

András was equally upset. "You almost fall on an easy crossover and then you expect us to trust you with our lives?"

Etel stayed quiet, but he could see she was disappointed in him.

"Nothing happened. I didn't fall. I wasn't even close. Leave it alone."

Etel got up and left the railcar.

"Don't tell us nothing happened," András said. "We have eyes, we see."

"It won't happen again. I worry about myself. You do the same."

Margit threw her hands in the air. "He's like a stone," she said to András. "I need some air." She too left.

András followed her, pausing as he exited. "We need you to be the best of all of us," he said. "We cannot put ourselves on the wire if you can't be trusted."

"I know. I'm sorry." Salvo rubbed the back of his neck.

András nodded slowly, then followed after Margit. It was still quite warm, even though the sun had gone down hours ago. Etel and Margit stood together at the edge of the rail area, Etel smoking furiously, Margit's arms folded across her chest. Neither spoke until András approached.

"That was bad, there," Margit said.

"It has passed. He's good now," András said.

"Can you guarantee it?"

András paused. "No."

"Yes, you can," Etel said. "He will not fall, and he will not make us fall. If you can't see that, you should not go on the wire."

"I saw him *nearly* fall," Margit said, "and that's more than enough to make me nervous."

"You saw nothing. He was not even close to what it would take for him to fall. If it were one of us, we would have fallen, but not him."

"What makes him different than us?" Margit asked, her tone mocking.

"He is better on the wire," András said.

"He is more than that," said Etel. "We are wire walkers, it is our job. Salvo lives for the wire. Salvo and the wire are the same thing. We will never be like that."

No one spoke, both András and Margit knowing Etel was right. Etel threw out the nub of her cigarette, heeling it into the earth. "We should not be so quick to judge him."

In the railcar, Salvo was being far harder on himself than any of the others ever could have been. He knew that he would not have fallen, that he was nowhere near falling, but that did not matter. His concentration had been shattered on the wire, and that was something that must never happen.

But what perplexed him most was how, when he should have been focusing all his attention on restoring equilibrium, he looked to the audience instead, straight to the one thing he had told himself to ignore, straight to Anna. How he'd known where to look he had no idea.

There was a knock at the railcar. Expecting it to be Cole Fisher-Fielding, Salvo didn't answer, knowing the door would fly open without any effort from him. But the door didn't move, and after several seconds there was another knock. Salvo answered it. Anna stood there, accompanied by a nervous-looking porter.

"Hello again, Salvo Ursari," she said.

"Hello, Anna." Salvo became instantly aware that he smelled of that night's performance.

"Thank you for your help," she said to the porter, dismissing him with a tip. She looked at Salvo, who stood dumbfounded. "Would you like to take a walk?"

Salvo nodded and stepped out of the railcar. They walked towards the midway. In an attempt to behave like a gentleman, Salvo offered her his arm, which she accepted.

"I enjoyed the show tonight."

"It has gone better."

"No, it was good. The people loved you."

Salvo stopped, turning towards her. "You knew, after I saw the butterfly, that I would not fall."

"I didn't see a butterfly."

"Maybe it was a moth. I can never tell the difference. But you knew I would not fall."

Anna turned her head to one side. "Of course." She took a short breath. "If you fell, the world would fall with you. And I knew the world would not fall."

They continued walking. Later both of them would remember this as the moment they fell in love.

THE NEXT DAY ANNA WAS IN THE STANDS to see Salvo walk in the matinee, a walk that passed without incident. Neither her father nor Cole Fisher-Fielding were sitting with her, however. Both were in attendance at the Fisher-Fielding Circus Company's annual general meeting.

The financial officer reported that profits were up since the war, that record crowds were coming in, and that, in short, the F-F had never been in better shape. Nevertheless, Rebecca Fisher-Fielding-Barnes insisted on challenging Cole's leadership, attacking his character, his business sense and his ability to run the show. It was a speech for the Respectables; everyone else knew how they were voting. When a vote was called, Cole and his nephew Martin voted for his continued presidency, and Rebecca, her husband, Phillip, and Charlotte Fisher-Fielding voted for Norris Fisher-Fielding. Because Cole's vote counted as two, the result was a tie. The Respectables would, for the first time in F-F history, control the fate of the circus.

As Arthur Simpson stood to cast a vote on behalf of the dozen or so assembled relatives, Cole tried in vain to swallow the lump in his throat. Arthur Simpson calmly winked at Cole, then cast the deciding vote in his favour. He would remain in charge until 1947, at which time there would have to be another vote. Cole had dodged a bullet for now. He thanked the Respectables for their support, promising them that the F-F would continue to thrive under his direction. Norris sulked in the corner, not appearing at all pleased with the token position he was elected to later in the meeting.

That night, as they watched the show, Martin and Cole were in high spirits.

"Did you see the little weasel's face?" Martin said, laughing.

Cole snorted but said nothing.

"Shot you a look that could kill. God help us if he ever gets his greedy hands on the F-F."

Cole hardly heard Martin. He was busy noting Anna Simpson's rapt attention to the Ursari act, Salvo in particular. He knew she had been to the matinee and that this was the third consecutive show she had attended. From the way she looked at Salvo, he could tell why she was there. Cole was grateful that the vote had already happened; Arthur Simpson would more than likely not have thrown his support to Cole if he had known that his daughter was swooning over one of his performers. Even so, he could sense trouble brewing.

His feelings proved correct. When the circus pulled out of Washington late the next night, after a third sold-out evening performance, Anna Simpson was aboard the Ursaris' sleeping car. Cole received a furious call from Arthur Simpson the next day, but there was little he could tell him that was of any relief to the man. Both Salvo and Anna were adults, after all, and Cole knew from experience that when a person decided to run away with the circus there was nothing anyone else could do.

Salvo could not believe what Anna had done. That he was in love with her was no surprise, but that she could love him back baffled and amazed him. When her father threatened to disinherit her, he told her she should go back. She refused, saying she would only leave if he didn't love her, and he could not tell her that, so she stayed. It was hard for them at first; the circus was not a place that afforded young lovers much privacy, and it seemed that András or Margit or Etel were always around, which they were. But they managed somehow, and nine months after they were married in the ring, Anna gave birth to identical-twin daughters. For a long time after that, Salvo would sleep soundly.

By the time the 1945 edition of the F-F Extravaganza pulled into Boise, Idaho, it was already dark. It was the middle of summer, and though the sun had been down for hours it was still hot enough that windows of houses were left open in hopes of catching some of the faint breeze that blew listlessly across the empty streets. The big top went up quickly and relatively silently; everyone was tired and wanted to get to sleep. Corners were cut where they could be, and no time was wasted. Even the elephants, who always seemed tired, appeared more languid than usual. It had been a long, hot tour, and the summer was nowhere near over.

Forecasters had predicted rain for the last week of July, but it was already the third of August and no rain had fallen. It didn't look as if any was on its way, either. No one much minded; it was summer, after all, and things were good. The war was all but won, people had jobs, loved ones overseas would be home soon. And the Fisher-Fielding circus was in town.

As performers, the Ursaris were not required to help with the set-up of the big top, but with the shortage of labour that the war had brought, Salvo and András preferred to do their own rigging rather than trust it to someone who might not know what they were doing and make what could be a costly mistake.

Anna stayed in the railcar with their daughters, Mika and Elsabeth. They were two and a half years old now, and though each had her light skin, auburn hair and small mouth, Anna saw more of Salvo than herself in her children. They looked back at her with green Ursari eyes, eyes that could melt and infuriate her in the same instant. It secretly pleased Anna that she was the only one who could tell them apart without any effort whatsoever, though she knew it bothered Salvo that he could not. Fathers and daughters, she thought, shaking her head.

The fact that she and Salvo had been formally married meant little to her father. She knew how it infuriated him to see his only daughter run away with an immigrant circus performer, turning her back on the life he thought should have been hers. Arthur Simpson had forbidden her half-brothers to have any contact with her upon pain of disinheritance, a punishment she had already suffered. Her brothers were not pleased, but there was little they could do; Arthur controlled their money, and thus controlled them. When her middle brother's RCAF fighter plane had a mechanical failure and spun into the Atlantic, Anna's eldest brother had defied their father and telegraphed her the news. Anna had refused to attend the funeral in Ottawa, seeing for the first time how she was not unlike her father.

After this estrangement she began to wonder if she hadn't made a terrible mistake. She could not deny that she loved Salvo, or their children, but she also knew that she did not love the circus. She tried to push these thoughts to the back of her mind, attempting to focus on other things.

Gradually, Salvo had taught her the wire. She had hesitated at first, not sure if she wanted to learn or not. She had eventually capitulated to Salvo's eagerness and her own curiosity. There was not much opportunity for Salvo to teach her, however; most of their time was taken up with the show and the girls. But what little time that remained was spent on the wire.

GREEN EYES SEEMED TO INDEED BE a dominant Ursari trait. Though they had not married, Margit had become pregnant and, in the final year of the war, gave birth to a child, János. No one had to ask who the father was, and the boy bore the Ursari name with no shame. As far as András and Margit were concerned, they were married. Neither was very religious, and they saw no reason to engage in the bother of a civil ceremony.

It was Etel who picked up whatever slack needed reigning in between the two couples and their children. She dealt with the children quietly and efficiently, never missing a beat, never making a mistake. Margit often complained that János smelled horribly of smoke after spending any amount of time with his aunt. Though it also bothered Anna, she never said as much out loud. She tried not to be dragged into Margit's jealousy. It took her a long time to understand how a person could be jealous of a sister-in-law, yet there was something about Etel that Anna could never quite get comfortable with. She had a silent, severe way about her that made Anna wary. When Etel did speak, her works were often harsh, and usually correct.

Since the Pearl Harbor attack, the government had restricted the number of people the circus was allowed to employ, and the labour shortage had driven wages through the roof. Where before the war the F-F employed over fifteen hundred men and women and drew trains of 130 cars, they now employed barely nine hundred people and drew eighty-five cars.

Because of their late arrival and the extra work necessary to erect the big top, both András and Salvo were exhausted for the next day's matinee. They spent the hours before showtime attempting to sleep, but the bustle and noise of the circus proved too much, and they emerged from the railcar bleary-eyed and irritable.

It was going to be another hot day. The lot they were playing in was smaller than usual, size having been sacrificed for proximity to rail lines. The big top stood in the back of the lot, enclosed by woods on three sides. On the street side of the main tent was the midway and the sideshow tents, as well as various hot-dog and soda tents. The red wagons that sold tickets were parked in various strategic locations. Directly beside the big top was the animal menagerie, where beasts of all ilk resided.

For this season the F-F had mounted a modified three-ring circus. In the middle of the big top was a large ring, floored with sawdust, flanked on either side by stages raised three feet off the ground. Here the clowns and riders and various other earthbound acts performed. On the far ends of the performance area were two caged rings, where the dangerous-animal acts took place. These animals were brought in and out of the rings through two barred chutes that ran from each ring to the exterior of the tent. The elephants, camels and other more docile performing animals were brought in through the main entrance.

The matinee was a sell out, and many were turned away, told to come back for the evening show or the next day. It was stifling inside the big top, people everywhere fanning themselves with programs. To squinted eyes, the stands looked like the fluttering feathers of some giant bird. Some people bought Cokes or lemonade from the vendors, others smuggled in their own drinks. In the front of one of the bleacher sections, a group of nurses had bought a block of tickets and the women came fresh off their shift, white uniforms standing out amongst the crowd.

The show started late, there being some confusion between the general manager and the ringmaster regarding the order of the acts. Normally the cat act was near the end of the show, directly before the Ursaris went on, but their trainer had asked to have the act moved up, claiming that the heat made it difficult for him to get his cats to respond. As a result the cat act and the elephant ballet were switched, much to Salvo's consternation. He avoided the elephants as much as possible and usually didn't have to see them while in the big top, but now there would be no way to miss them. He hated the elephant ballet. It was ridiculous, he thought. Elephants in giant tutus were paraded around the ring, appearing to dance, when in fact it was the band who was playing to the elephants' movements. People didn't seem to mind; the elephant ballet was one of the more popular acts in the F-F show that year. Salvo could not understand why Emil would allow his beloved elephants to be presented so foolishly.

The Ursari troupe climbed to the platform as the ballet started, and Salvo tried to ignore both his fatigue and the elephants below, wishing hard to be on the wire soon. Salvo was the first to the top, followed by András and Margit. Anna was next, though she would not be going on the wire today. She was not ready to perform in public, and Salvo felt she would learn more on the platform than she would on the ground. Besides, her hands were needed to help with harnesses and bicycles and balancing poles. The girls and János were on the ground, being looked after by one of the other performer's wives. Though it took him to a moment to figure out what was wrong, Salvo realized that Etel was not on the platform.

"Where's Etel?' he asked András.

He shrugged, looking down the ladder. "There's a little time. Maybe she had to use the toilet."

Afraid that she would not make it back in time, Salvo began revamping the act in his head. He dismissed his efforts moments later; as the elephant ballet ended, he spotted Etel beginning the climb to the platform. He picked up his balancing pole and wait-ed for the band to play him onto the wire.

Out of the corner of his eye, he caught a glint, a streak of light, but he had by then achieved the rapt concentration needed for walking and paid it no heed. As he stepped onto the wire he heard a commotion from the far end of the tent, and behind him he heard András shout to him.

"Come back, Salvo. The big top is on fire."

Salvo turned his head and saw a line of fire shoot across the canvas, travelling fast. He pivoted around and leapt back onto the platform.

"My God," Anna said. "This can't be happening."

Below, the audience seemed stunned. People sat in their seats, as if refusing to believe that they were in danger. A few got up and ran to the exits, mainly those in the direct vicinity of the fire, but most people stayed where they were, as though they expected the fire to be put out and the show to continue.

The fire spread with a terrifying speed. What the crowd did not know was that the canvas of the big top was waterproofed with a mixture of gasoline and paraffin. It kept the rain out, but it burned fast and hot.

Etel was the first down the ladder, followed by Margit, András and then Anna. Salvo was last, having debated whether to try and save one of the bicycles. He too had underestimated the fire's speed. Once on the ground he looked up and saw flames on the portion of canvas directly above the wire. He felt as though standing in front of an oven door.

The fire had started on the side wall of the tent, an area not waterproofed. It had been slow to spread, and several ushers had attempted without success to beat it out. In their haste to finish the job the night before, no one had set out the fire extinguishers. Once the ushers realized that the fire could not be subdued, they set about pulling down the side wall so that the fire would not spread to the rest of the big top. They were not quick enough. A small spark of flame had ignited the treated canvas and all was lost.

It took precious minutes for people to realize that the big top was burning. All at once they swarmed towards the exits, finding them clogged with like-minded individuals. Panic ensued. Salvo saw one man fighting his way through the crowd, punching men and women and children indiscriminately until he lost his footing and went down under the throng. Some people, knowing they were trapped and unable to go forward, instead went up the bleachers and jumped the fifteen feet down to the ground, only to find their escape thwarted. The bottom of the tent was staked firmly into the ground to prevent people from sneaking in. No one had ever considered people getting out. Those who had pocket knives sliced slits in the tent. This worked for some, but not all; in certain sections the side walls were supported by a grid of iron rails that were nearly impossible to squeeze through.

The ringmaster pleaded over the PA for people to leave their seats in an orderly fashion, but if anyone heard him no one heeded his words. The band didn't move and had begun to play "The Stars and Stripes," a circus code for disaster.

Cole Fisher-Fielding had not been under the big top when the fire started. He was out at the red wagons checking on the day's receipts when the alarm was raised. Once he realized the big top was on fire, he ordered the side walls torn down. Workers rushed to comply but were prevented by the crowd. The pressure of people against the rails made it impossible to lower them, and the people in front were being crushed by those behind. In a few places they finally succeeded, but it was not enough.

Salvo held Anna tightly by the arm. He knew that if he let go of her they would be separated by the crowd, and if one of them fell they would be trampled. He did not know where Etel and Margit and András were. He had lost sight of them as soon as they reached the ground.

It was obvious to Salvo that there was no way to get out of any of the main exits. To even attempt it was out of the question. Directly in front of them, people were being ground into the bars of the animal chute. The noise was deafening, and he could feel the full heat of the fire. He looked at Anna and saw that the exposed skin on her neck had blistered.

They forced their way through the throng to one of the steel rings and climbed up the bars. A few people saw what his idea was, and some of them followed him. They made their way towards the chute, intending to crawl along its roof and out of the tent. Salvo hoped that there were no cats in the chute.

They reached the chute, and pushing Anna ahead of him, Salvo looked towards the exit. It was mayhem; people were screaming, pushing, shouting, and the roof of the big top was nearly completely engulfed in flame. The big top had become a furnace, sucking cool air in the sides of the tent and up to the roof, where it became superheated.

András had pulled Margit and Etel in the opposite direction. He briefly considered scaling the other animal chute, but the fire had burned hotter there and the bars were too hot to touch. He opted instead to try for one of the exits near where the fire had started. When people had seen the fire, they had instinctively gone in the opposite direction, which was partly why they were being crushed over where Salvo was, but this impulse afforded András, Margit and Etel a greater chance of escape. If they could run the gauntlet of the flames, they would be able to pass through the exit relatively easily.

They ran as fast as they could, first Etel, then Margit, then András. When they were halfway to the exit, one of the sections of bleachers collapsed, sending chairs raining down on them. András was knocked to the ground, and when he got up he saw Etel lying in front of him, unconscious. He picked her up and continued towards the exit. He did not know that his shirt was on fire, and he could not see Margit.

Outside, Cole Fisher-Fielding could tell that the big top was about to come down. The canvas itself had not burned through yet, the fire still feeding on the flammable waterproofing. Once the support rigging that held the canvas aloft burned, the canvas would fall as a sheet of fire. Then Cole heard someone shout that the fire had spread to the menagerie. The animals were trapped.

He knew the trainers would rush to the menagerie right away, but he himself did not budge from his task of trying to help people through the side walls. People came before animals.

Inside, the fire had spread to the ground. The chairs and seat wagons, thick with years of coats of paint, ignited quickly and burned hot. Salvo and Anna were nearly out, three-quarters of the way down the chute. Its barred roof was seven feet off the ground, and they scuttled across it as though climbing a horizontal ladder. The cries of those pressed against the bars of the chute were drowned out by the roar of the fire and the commotion of the crowd. Salvo wanted to help those trapped, but there was nothing he could do. If he tried to pull them up onto the roof, he himself could be pulled down.

A hand grabbed his foot, he shook it free. Then, suddenly, a child's face was in front of him. He looked down to see a young woman, trapped against the bars, holding the child up to him. Without thinking he took the child, a boy, maybe five years old. There was nothing he could do for the mother. He continued, close behind Anna. He was slowed by the boy, losing the use of one hand, and Anna got further ahead of him, and then she reached the end of the chute. Here the canvas was secured to the metal of the chute with rope-ties. Anna loosened the knots and squeezed under the canvas to freedom. Salvo was seconds behind her. Holding the boy like a sack of potatoes he breached the tent and fell to the ground.

He got up and ran away from the tent, catching up to Anna. He collapsed to the ground beside her and looked back, just as the fiery canvas descended upon those still inside. The boy in his arms was crying. The menagerie must be on fire also, he thought, mistaking the screams of humans for the trumpeting of elephants.

András had emerged from the tent, moments earlier, and he quickly saw that Margit had not made it. He carried Etel to safety and, finally realizing that his shirt was on fire, dropped to the ground and rolled, tearing the shirt from his body. He smelled burning flesh, unsure if it was his own. People ran by, some trailing flames, others untouched by the fire. Ten feet from him a man lay unconscious, smouldering.

András struggled to his feet, summoning strength to go back into the tent. He suspected that Margit had been felled when the chairs toppled on them, and that she could be lying just inside, maybe under a chair. People were streaming out of the exit, and as he attempted to go in someone bumped into him, sending him flying. When he got up he saw Margit being helped out by a man in a sailor suit. He ran up to her, helping the sailor lift her to a safe distance.

"I called to you," she said, "and you ran past me." She passed out, her ankle jutting to one side, broken.

Cole Fisher-Fielding was still trying to get more people out when the big top had collapsed. A shroud of flame descended on those still inside, intensifying and then silencing the cries of the trapped. It had been only twelve minutes since the fire had started, and it was all over. A singed giraffe ran by him, falling down awkwardly. Cole ran over to the menagerie, hoping something of use could be done there.

Most of the animals were still locked in their cages. Elephants, zebras, camels, lions, panthers, giraffes, gnus, deer, ostriches, horses, apes—they were all still inside. The elephants that were in the ballet had been saved, and the giraffe Cole had seen had somehow managed to jump out of its enclosure, but the rest were trapped. Handlers worked furiously to get the animals out. Some of the elephants obeyed their trainers and went through the flames, but many of the other animals refused to be moved, stubbornly afraid. One old elephant, startled and disoriented, ripped the arm off a man who was trying to lead it to safety. The beast remained in the elephant pen, its trunk wrapped around the dismembered limb, and not even Emil Narwha could convince it to come out. Several of the dangerous cats were pulled to safety, their cages mounted on wheels and easily rolled free of the fire. A pygmy hippopotamus knew enough to submerge itself in its pool, and if the water didn't boil, Cole thought, she would probably survive.

Cole and the animal handlers worked as fast and as long as they could. When scraps of canvas began to fall, igniting the straw on the ground, he ordered everyone out of the menagerie. One man who worked with the apes wept without shame as his animals burned. Emil Narwha had to be forcibly restrained to prevent him from going back in after his remaining elephants, but he broke free of his captors and bolted into the tent. He never came out.

Anna Ursari's first thought after escaping the big top was for Mika and Elsabeth. She was so concerned for their safety that it was a long time before she even noticed that Salvo carried a wailing boy in his arms, and even then she didn't pay this much heed until they had located the girls, safe in the care of their circus guardian.

When fire crews arrived there was little they could do to save anyone. Later they began the grim task of recovering bodies. This fire was not like a normal fire. Usually, people died of smoke inhalation. Here, they were roasted alive. More than one veteran firefighter could be seen retching at the edge of the woods. It was even worse in the makeshift morgue; people attempting to identify the bodies of loved ones were forced to hold perfumed handkerchiefs to their faces.

In total, 112 people and fifty animals died. The sound of gunfire could be heard from the area where the animals had been moved. Salvo saw one elephant, its skin half peeled from its flanks, being led in the direction of the shots, and several minutes later he heard three successive blasts of a rifle. He felt sorry for the creature and would never again look at an elephant with hatred in his heart. Salvo did not yet know that his friend Emil was dead. When he found out hours later, he would collapse to the ground, his hands beating futilely at the trampled earth.

András and Etel were at a ramshackle infirmary, receiving treatment for their wounds. Margit had been taken to the hospital to have her ankle set, and would undoubtedly wait there for quite a while, as her injury was not life-threatening. Etel had a large bruise on her head, and she, András and Anna all had minor burns and blisters. Salvo was the only one of them who had managed to escape unscathed; not a hair on his body was harmed.

The same was true of their rescued boy. After seeing that the others were being attended to, Salvo took the boy around to the various aid stations and meeting places that had sprung up. He hoped he would be able to find someone who knew the boy's family. He had little hope of finding his mother. Already they had begun to bring bodies out of the area where the chute had been.

The boy could be of little help. Aside from his name, which was Daniel, he didn't or couldn't say much. He didn't appear to know the names of either of his parents, or his last name, or where he lived. Salvo supposed the boy was in shock and assumed that he would remember this information later. Either way, he was unsuccessful in locating anyone who knew the child, and he didn't want to take him to the police. He had saved this child, and it was his responsibility to see that he ended up in the proper place. Where that was, he wasn't sure, but he didn't trust the police here any more than he had in Budapest, and he wasn't about to just hand the boy over. This was, however, exactly what Anna thought they should do.

"He is not our child," she said, when he returned.

"What would you have me do?"

"He must have parents."

Salvo looked at Daniel, who was fast asleep on the floor. "I think they are not alive."

Anna swallowed. "He is not our responsibility."

Salvo nodded, but they both knew that he was.

Elsewhere, Cole Fisher-Fielding was attempting to ascertain the extent of the disaster. He did not yet know exactly how many people had been killed or injured, but he knew that there had been nearly ten thousand people under the big top that afternoon, and he knew that a significant number of them hadn't got out. So far, he hadn't heard whether anyone from the circus had been killed in addition to Emil Narwha. Not everyone was yet accounted for, but many were, a consolation that did little to alleviate his worry. He knew that there would be tough questions in the days ahead, and that things were going to get worse before they got better. He also knew this was very likely the end of the Fisher-Fielding Circus Company.

THE F-F WAS IMPOUNDED—neither performer nor equipment nor animal permitted to leave town. After extensive interviewing and an exhaustive investigation, the cause of the fire was still unknown. Arson was suspected, and the women's toilet area was assumed to be the starting point, but investigators had no solid evidence and no suspects. Soon their questioning turned to those who ran the show. Where were the fire extinguishers? Why weren't there sufficient exits? Most importantly, why had the big top burned so quickly?

When they learned that there had been no extinguishers, the men whose responsibility it was to set them out were arrested on charges of criminal negligence. When they learned that the canvas of the big top had been waterproofed with paraffin and gasoline, they arrested Cole Fisher-Fielding on the same charge. He protested; the F-F had applied to the army for permission to use non-flammable waterproofing and had been refused. Materials were in short supply, and military needs took precedence over the circus.

The Ursaris could not believe what was happening.

"I do not understand," András said, "how these Americans can drop bombs like that on Japan and hold no one responsible, but for this accident they will put an old man in jail."

"It is as always," Salvo answered. "People want someone to blame."

"Cole Fisher-Fielding did not start the fire," Anna said.

"People are angry," Salvo said. "Their anger will lessen, and they will let Mr. Fisher-Fielding go."

Etel looked up from her seat on the floor of the railcar. "It burned so fast."

No one spoke. After a while Anna picked up Mika and Elsabeth and left for the cookhouse. Salvo and Daniel stayed behind for a bit, then followed.

Etel stayed in her place on the floor, saying nothing. No one had yet noticed that she hadn't smoked a single cigarette since the fire. András was lost in his own thoughts, János asleep on the bed.

When Anna and Salvo returned to the railcar, Margit was back from the hospital. She had been there a week with her broken ankle. She was packing her suitcase, hastily throwing her meagre belongings into it.

"Margit, be reasonable," András implored.

"There is no reason to you. You left me to die. I want no part of you any more."

"I did not know you had fallen." András tried to place a hand on her arm, but she pulled it away.

"You never looked to see. I watched you. You fall, get up, look only for Etel, run right by me."

"I didn't see you."

"I called out. I screamed loud as loud can be. You did not turn."

"I didn't hear you."

"No, you did not want to see or hear me. You made your choice, András. You left me to die. You are dead to me." She threw her suitcase out the door and hobbled past him.

"Margit—" Salvo began.

"I will go with you no more, Salvo Ursari. Thank you for all you have done for me in the past, but I go with you no more."

"What about János?" Anna said. "He is your son."

Margit looked at the boy, appearing as though she might soften or even break her resolve. Then her face hardened. "Very little of him has anything to do with me. He is his father's son. Let him bear this." She continued out the door.

"Go after her, András," Anna said.

András did not move.

"András?" Salvo said.

"Yes."

"She is leaving."

"Yes." András's voice broke.

"Aren't you going to go after her?" Anna asked.

"No."

"Why not?"

"Because she is right." András turned to face the wall. "I did not see her. But if I had, I would have done what she accuses me of." He would not look at them. His shoulders shook, but he made no sound. Salvo and Anna backed out of the railcar, children in tow.

They went to a shady section of grass and let the four children play. Salvo sat leaning against a tree, and Anna rested her weight on his side, her head on his shoulder.

"If I went, would you come after me?" she asked.

Mika laughed as Daniel threw a handful of grass into the air. Elsabeth was sniffing the earth like a dog, and János the baby lay on his back staring up at the sky, gurgling contentedly.

"You would never go," Salvo answered, finally.

"No," she said, "I wouldn't."

They learned the next day that Margit had gone to Los Angeles with one of the vendors. They were both charged with obstruction of justice, as performers were under orders not to leave town, but the charges were eventually dropped.

Two months after the fire, the trial of Cole Fisher-Fielding began. Three others, the men whose responsibility it had been to set out the fire extinguishers, had already been found guilty, receiving jail sentences ranging from six months to two years. It seemed certain that Cole would be acquitted; he had papers proving that his request for the non-flammable waterproofing had been refused, as well as a certificate of inspection from the city's permit office. He had broken no laws, his lawyers asserted, and therefore was guilty of no crime.

It had taken a month for officials to complete their investigation, at which time the F-F was permitted to leave town. Some people wanted to disband to winter quarters, to lay up the show, but Cole knew that if this happened, the chances of it ever starting up again were slim to none. It would be difficult to keep going; they had no big top to play under, and many of the acts had lost some if not all of their equipment. The reputation of the F-F was severely tarnished, and the only way to repair it was to show people something good.

Cole called in every outstanding favour owed him, made some promises of his own and managed to scrounge up enough gear to keep the show touring. There was no time to get a new big top made, and even if there was, there would still be no adequate way to waterproof it, so Cole booked the F-F into arenas and halls in a much-scaled-down version. The important thing was that the show stay on the road. He only wished he could accompany it. He left his nephew Martin in charge, instructing him to watch out for Norris. If the Spouses could, they would use the tragedy as an excuse to seize control of the circus.

The first two days of his trial went well. There was no real evidence against him, and it was fairly clear to those in the room that some scapegoating was taking place. On the third day, however, things took a turn for the worse.

Added at the last minute as a witness for the prosecution was Norris Fisher-Fielding. Reporters scribbled furiously, and people whispered to each other. Cole's lawyers looked at each other, puzzled.

Norris took the stand calmly. When he spoke his voice was soft, and for the majority of his testimony he came across as a reluctant witness, offering nothing incriminating against Cole, let alone damning.

The prosecuting lawyer chose that moment to make it clear why he had called Norris.

"Mr. Fisher-Fielding, let me ask you this. To the best of your knowledge, had the Fisher-Fielding Circus Company made any inquiries with any private companies concerning the availability of non-flammable waterproofing?"

Norris swallowed, appearing nervous, and mumbled, "Yes."

"Could you speak up, sir?"

"Yes."

"And what was the result of this inquiry?"

"It was determined that it would be possible to purchase this waterproofing from a private interest."

"And was this done?"

"No."

"Why is that?"

"It was determined to be too expensive."

Cole's lawyers scrambled, demanding that Norris provide proof of this statement, which he could not, but the damage was done. Closing arguments were made, and the jury went into deliberations. The trial was over.

Free on bail, Cole returned to his hotel. He was freezing cold but sweating profusely, and had been experiencing a shooting pain in his arm all day. As he climbed the stairs to his room, he keeled over, clutching at his chest.

He was rushed to the hospital in one of the ambulances that had removed the injured from the circus lot. Doctors worked frantically to save him, and though he was twice pronounced dead, he managed to survive. He had suffered a massive heart attack and would be in the hospital for some time.

The next day the jury delivered a guilty verdict. Cole was sentenced to three years' imprisonment. Because of his health the sentence was commuted, but nonetheless Cole was now a convicted felon. He knew that his days of running the F-F were over; the Respectables would never vote him in again.

He was correct. An emergency vote was held, and Norris was elected interim president of the Fisher-Fielding Circus Company. When Martin told him the outcome, Cole wept openly. Three weeks later he died.

The Fisher-Fielding Extravaganza was playing in Sacramento when they received the news. Norris refused to allow the flags to be lowered to half mast, and forbade the ringmaster to announce his uncle's passing. He could not silence the performers, however. The Ursaris performed in black and carried an empty chair across the wire. The band played Cole's favourite songs. The whole circus came to a halt for an entire three minutes, paying silent tribute to the passing of the last of the original Fisher-Fieldings and the last great showman of the American circus. Then the show went on.

IT BECAME CLEAR TO ANNA that if Daniel had any memory of his life before the fire, it was not going to resurface any time soon. Beyond his own name, the boy seemed to have little awareness of anything. He was a good natured child, kind to Elsabeth and Mika, who had taken to him immediately. It was not that Anna did not like this boy; she simply didn't feel that he belonged with them.

"He isn't our child," she said, many times.

"Whose child is he?" Salvo answered.

"That's not the point. Someone might be looking for him."

"No one is looking. His picture was in the paper. No one came forward."

"We aren't responsible for him."

"I took him from his mother's arms. I am responsible."

"We cannot keep him."

This was how this discussion ended every time they had it. But they never gave him away. Anna knew Salvo would never agree to it, and Salvo knew she would never do it without his agreement. Anna pronounced judgment knowing nothing would come of it. Daniel was soon as much a member of their family as anyone.

An orphan in the circus was never an orphan. Children ran in packs like dogs, toddlers were herded like sheep. So it was with János; when Margit left, János was not allowed to suffer his mother's absence. Etel picked up the majority of the maternal duties, but while the troupe performed, the children were in capable hands. The Fisher-Fielding Extravaganza could be a lonely place for adults, but it was never such for children.

If Norris Fisher-Fielding could have found a way to keep the performers' children at home, he would have done so. He felt that there was no place for children in the circus, a view seen as antithetical and tyrannical by most, if not all, of the F-F staff. In addition to this affront, Norris set about removing many of Cole's signature acts, a seeming attempt to erase his nemesis's mark upon the show.

One of the first acts to get the axe was the elephant ballet. Though Salvo had never liked it, he was sorry to see it go, knowing that the people who came to the show had enjoyed it, and having reversed his position on the loathsomeness of elephants in general. He had seen them in pain during the fire, just as people had been, and somehow their mutual pain had made them less threatening. He missed his friend Emil Narwha, who was perhaps the only real friend he had ever had, and so did the elephants. Their grief was shared. Even Salvo could tell.

Had Salvo thought more about himself and less about the elephants, he might have realized that the Ursari act was in jeopardy. They had been discovered by Cole, championed by Cole, and Salvo had been a good friend to the man. In addition, Anna's roundabout relation to Norris and spurning of his romantic intentions, only to marry a lowly performer, had left him with little love for her.

Anna had seen this fallout coming and had tried to warn Salvo, but he had not listened. He believed that the act was all that mattered, and he knew people still loved it, so he was disinclined to fully appreciate how precarious their situation was.

Then, just when the indoor dates were beginning to draw crowds again, Norris made a move that surprised everyone and likely made Cole roll over in his grave. With a full month and a half left in the season, Norris ordered the Fisher-Fielding Extravaganza back to winter quarters in Florida. They were done for the year. This was in reaction to a recent court decision ordering the Fisher-Fielding Circus Company to pay restitution to the victims of the fire, a sum totalling nearly five million dollars. Norris argued that it would bankrupt the circus, a claim no one believed. In an effort to back up his claim, Norris ordered the circus off the road.

Salvo hated Florida. He hated the heat, hated sitting around for weeks at a time without performing. The others looked forward to the break, but for Salvo it was like going to jail.

In an effort to talk Norris out of an early hiatus, he went to see him in his private railcar. Norris beckoned him in, his face cold. "I'm afraid I have no choice," he said after hearing Salvo's request. "But I'm glad you came. I was going to send for you anyway."

"Why?" Salvo asked, not liking the tone in Norris's voice or the slow sneer that had crept across his face.

"Mr. Ursari, it is my unfortunate task to inform you that the Fisher-Fielding Circus Company is releasing you from your contract at this time."

Salvo was stunned. "We're fired?"

"If you want to put it that way, then yes, you're fired."

"What for?"

"You act is not what it once was. It has become stale."

"That is a lie."

"I assure you, Mr. Ursari, it is not. But, further to that, there has been some suspicion among my police staff regarding your sister's involvement in the fire, and—"

"What?" Salvo staggered back, unable to believe what he had heard.

"We have reason to believe that she may have been the one who started the fire."

"That is a lie."

"Is it? She was seen in the area where the fire started only moments earlier, is known to be a smoker and has been described by others as somewhat suspicious."

"None of this proves anything."

"No, it doesn't. That is why I have not passed this information on to the federal investigators, and why I do not intend to unless you provide me with no alternative. I would hate to think what an accusation of this kind would do to your family, be it substantiated or otherwise." Norris opened a lacquered wooden box that sat on the table beside him and removed a cigar. He clipped the tip and lit it, taking a tentative puff.

"This is not right," Salvo said, his mouth dry.

"I am afraid I have no other choice. Let me say, for the record, that your contract is not being renewed because of the poor quality of your act. The fire has had no bearing on this decision. That is for the record. Off the record, let me tell you the following: As long as I am head of the Fisher-Fielding Circus Company, no Ursari will set foot under a roof my show is in, let alone perform in one. My cousin was a fool to get involved with your kind, and I will see no more harm come to my interests as a result of you."

Salvo was speechless. He stood there, unable to move, unable to speak.

"Our business here is completed. Please be off the lot in a maximum of twenty-four hours. Keep in mind that you are being watched closely. Good day." Norris rose from his chair, motioning towards the door.

As Salvo walked back to his railcar, he tried to understand what had just happened. He knew that Anna had been right, that Norris was out to ruin them. But he didn't know what to make of Norris's accusation that Etel had started the fire.

What he remembered frightened him. Etel had been late for that performance. And she had been at the women's outhouse, where the fire had apparently started. And how many times had he seen Etel throw a cigarette onto the ground? A sickening feeling turned in his stomach. He knew that if Etel had started the fire, it would have been on purpose. He knew that with the rapt attention she always paid to fire there was no room for accident.

Still, he did not believe she would be capable of arson. She would not have done such a despicable thing, he told himself. She had no reason to. But a tiny part of him was not sure. A fragment admitted that it was possible that his own sister had burned the Fisher-Fielding big top to the ground.

He needed to talk to Anna. She would know what to do. He quickened his pace and leapt up the three steps into their railcar. Inside, Etel and András sat huddled around Anna. Anna was clutching a piece of paper, and her eyes were wet and red.

"What is wrong?" he asked, wondering if they knew his news already.

Anna rushed to him, tears flowing freely.

"Her father is dead," András said softly.

Salvo comforted her as best he could, but he had a hard time remaining focused on his task. Eventually, he released her and took András by the arm, ushering him outside. "I will be only a moment," he said. Anna nodded.

"She seems very upset over a man who disowned her," András said when they were outside.

"She loved him," Salvo answered. He tried to think of a way to tell András what had happened, what had been said. He could think of no way to soften the blow. "We have been fired." The words seemed alien and incomprehensible.

András said nothing. The sentence simply did not register.

"Did you hear me?"

"Yes. We are fired." András kicked lightly at the ground.

"They say the act is no good."

András shook his head. "How can they say that?"

"There is more," Salvo said.

"The act is good, no matter what Norris Fisher-Fielding says." András remembered the crowds, how they had cheered for them. He knew there was nothing wrong with the act. They would find work elsewhere.

Salvo exhaled sharply. "They say Etel may have started the fire."

András's jaw clenched, his face hardening. "Who says that?"

"Norris Fisher-Fielding, for one. Is it true?" Salvo's voice was tentative. He did not know if he could bear the question's answer.

András grabbed Salvo by his shirt. His face was inches from Salvo's. "Do not ask me that. She is our sister. She would do no kind of thing. How do you even think to ask if she would?" He could feel the blood pounding in his temples.

"I'm sorry." And he was. But he had to ask. There had been no choice.

"You should not even think such things. She is our sister." András released Salvo and backed away. It was all he could do to contain his rage.

"Norris says he will not tell the police what he thinks. He is a powerful man, and if he said that Etel started the fire, it would not matter if she did or not."

"There is no *if*. She did not." Like the snapping of a twig, András's anger gave way to a sob.

Salvo knew he must be strong, or else they would both be in tears. Others were depending on them to keep things together. "Yes. But we must leave the Fisher-Fielding."

"Where will we go?"

Salvo shrugged. "I don't know."

AFTER MUCH DISCUSSION IT WAS DECIDED that they would go to New York. András and Etel would go first, and Salvo and Anna would join them after attending Arthur Simpson's funeral in Ottawa. Many people who Salvo had thought did not like them came to wish them well, many saying that they thought it was a travesty that they were being let go. No one spoke of the suspicions surrounding Etel, if they even knew of them. Etel knew nothing of the allegations; András had made Salvo promise not to tell her. He said nothing to Anna, either. She was under enough stress as it was.

Arthur Simpson's funeral was an elaborate affair. Anna refused to sit at the front of the church with her brothers. Instead, she sat at the back by herself.

"Please, come in with me," she had asked, nearly begged Salvo before entering the church. And though Salvo desperately wanted to help her, to be with her when she needed him, he could not bring himself to cross through the door.

"I cannot," he said, pulling her close. "God is not welcome in my house, and I am not welcome in His. That is our arrangement."

"God did not kill your parents," Anna said. Salvo did not argue with her. Now was not the time. He released her from his embrace and held her hand.

"Once God came to a village. He was very tired, and a Rom and his wife invited Him to stay the night. God slept well and awoke refreshed, grateful to the Rom and his wife for their hospitality. And He said to the wife, 'You have been kind to let me stay in your house, so when you die you will come and stay in heaven with me.'

"To the Rom, He said He would grant three wishes. The Rom chose his wishes carefully. 'For my first wish, I want that anyone who sits in my chair has to stay there until I say they can get up. For my second wish, I want that anyone I tell to get into my iron pot must do so. Finally, I want that wherever I lay my coat, no one can make me move from that place.'

"Well, God thought these to be strange wishes, but He had made His promise to the Rom so He granted each in turn. The Rom lived a good long time, but eventually the angel of death came to take him. 'Please allow me to say goodbye to my wife first,' the Rom said. 'You can sit in my chair while I do so.' The angel of death sat in his chair, and found he could not get up again.

"'Let me live until my wife dies, and I will let you go,' the Rom said to the angel. The angel agreed, and the man lived another twenty years. Three days after his wife died, the devil came to see him.

"'I have heard you are sly, Rom,' said the devil. 'But now you must come with me.' The Rom smiled. 'Yes, I will come with you gladly. But first you must get into my iron pot.' And the devil found himself doing exactly that. When the Rom placed the lid on the pot, the devil became frightened and cried out. 'Let me out, and I will leave you be forever!'

"The Rom let the devil out, and in another three days the angel of death returned for him. He took the Rom down to hell, but the devil refused to let him in. So the angel of death took him to heaven. But God wouldn't let him in. 'Just let me have a quick peek,' the Rom pleaded. 'My good wife is in there.' So God opened the gates of heaven a crack. The Rom threw his coat inside, and because of His promise, God had to admit the Rom, and there he still resides with his wife."

Anna smiled slightly. "Does this mean you'll come inside?"

Salvo shook his head. "No. But I will not be far away. I will wait right here."

He released her hand, and she entered the church. Salvo watched as the doors closed and the funeral began, and he wished he could have gone inside. Anna deserved that much.

ARTHUR SIMPSON HAD BEEN TRUE to his word, and Anna was not mentioned in his will. Her half-brothers, however unable to stand up to their father while he was alive, resolved to defy him in death. They each gave her a portion of their own inheritance; while it was not as large as the share she would have originally received, it was a noble gesture on their part. They presented her with a trust substantial enough to provide her with a modest annual income, as well as forty acres of land in British Columbia's Fraser Valley that had been purchased during Prohibition for its proximity to the American border. In addition, they left her their one-seventh of one-seventh share in the Fisher-Fielding Circus Company, even though she had no Fisher-Fielding blood in her.

Their share was worth little now, the circus all but bankrupt, but it was a symbolic gesture. Unlike their father, they did not look down upon Anna's husband, or her lifestyle. In a way, they admired her. It was for this reason that Anna accepted their gift. If she had for a second thought it was given out of pity, she would have refused it.

When they arrived in New York, Salvo immediately set about attempting to find work with another circus. He found none; the Fisher-Fielding had been the biggest and best circus around, and the industry was hurting, not only as a result of the fire. Since the end of the war no one had been going to the circus, and it appeared as though the days of the big top were numbered. Where ten years ago there would have been work, now there was none.

Salvo despaired. He hated New York, hated the bustle, everyone in a hurry, everyone looking miserable. When Anna suggested that they go and live on their land in Canada, though, he initially refused.

"I am a Rom," he said. "We are not farmers."

"You are many things. And you don't have to farm if you don't want to."

"András and Etel will not come."

"Then they can stay here."

Salvo was quiet. Anna took his hand. "This city is no place to raise children. We've always done what you wanted. But the circus is over. I want us to do this. We need a new start."

Salvo could not refuse her. He didn't want to go, but he would. He owed Anna that much. When he told András and Etel, they didn't understand, and he couldn't explain it to them. János cried as they left, and Salvo's brother and sister waved goodbye stonily. He did not think they would see each other again soon.

After they boarded the train, Salvo began to feel a little better. He let Daniel sit on his lap and look out the window. The further west they went, the flatter things got, until they began to climb into mountains. He remembered his journey from Transylvania to Budapest twenty-six years earlier. These mountains were much higher.

They arrived at night. It was cold, and they were tired and hungry. It was all Salvo could do to get a fire started in the wood stove that would heat their small farmhouse. Daniel cried all night, and Salvo and Anna took turns forsaking the warmth of their bed to comfort him. Near dawn, on his way back to sleep, Salvo looked out the window and saw their land for the first time. It stretched around the house, a large barn on one side, the rest open field. The hayfields reminded him of the fields of his boyhood, and although he would later be unable to recapture whatever it had been that made the two places seem similar, he would always recall thinking it was very possible that he was finally home.

———

SIX

Anna frowned, seeing that she had left their oatmeal unattended for too long. Now there would be a blackened crust on the bottom of the pan, and it would be no small job getting it off. Elsabeth and Daniel rumbled down the stairs, still in their nightclothes, and pulled their chairs up to the table. Daniel rubbed his face, bleary-eyed. Anna wondered if he'd slept enough the night before, knowing that he shared Salvo's insomnia.

After the fire, Salvo again lost the ability to sleep. Anna had no trouble sleeping herself, but with both a husband and a son who did not sleep, she felt that there should be something she could do to help them. But she was powerless against their insomnia, and nothing irritated her more than a lack of control.

"Where's Mika?" she asked the children, only to have her question answered by Mika's appearance at the table, fully dressed and ready for school. "You're eager to get to school today."

Mika nodded. "Field trip."

Anna had forgotten that the girls' teacher was taking them into the city for the day, to see Stanley Park. None of the children had been to Stanley Park before, and Mika had been looking forward to it for weeks. Typical of the other two, Elsabeth didn't want to go—something about squirrels—and Daniel was jealous because his class wasn't going. Anna sometimes wished that the excesses of each child could be pooled to make up for the deficiencies of another; Mika's enthusiasm and Daniel's pride and Elsabeth's reserve mixed into three perfect children. Presto.

"Oatmeal?" Daniel said, peering at the stove.

Anna took three bowls from the cupboard and began spooning the mush of oats into them. Overcooked, she thought. "It will make you strong, like your father." She knew that Daniel didn't like oatmeal, but he would do anything to be like Salvo, who was still asleep upstairs and would be for several more hours.

"I already am strong," he said with confidence, as Anna placed their bowls on the table.

"Can we have sugar?" Mika asked hopefully. They usually weren't allowed, except for special occasions.

Anna took a canister of brown sugar off the shelf and placed it on the table. "One spoonful each, no more." She watched as each child took their sugar. Mika's spoon was first in, taking a heaping load and dumping it into her bowl, stirring the golden lump through the grey mush. Daniel took a slightly smaller spoonful, choosing to sprinkle his across the surface of the oatmeal. Elsabeth paused, considering how much she wanted, then extracted a perfectly level spoonful and placed it at the side of the bowl, portioning a little sugar with each spoonful lifted to her mouth. Anna saw how if she had been asked ahead of time to guess how each child would react she would have said exactly what they had just done. They were perfectly, utterly, wonderfully predictable. She loved them for it.

"Hurry up," she said. "You don't want to miss the bus."

For the first five years the Ursari farmhouse had been more a cabin than a house. Built around the turn of the century, it was in its time a respectable dwelling, never comfortable but nothing to be embarrassed about. Were it up to Salvo, the house would have stayed as it was; by his standards, it was more than adequate. Anna had higher standards, however.

The entire building was jacked up, and a proper foundation was built underneath it. A septic field and indoor plumbing were added. The woodstove was replaced by an oil-burning furnace, and finally, in 1950, a second storey was added on to the building, making it a fine dwelling by anyone's estimation, and a palace by Salvo's.

None of this elevation in their living conditions had come about as a result of Salvo's skill as a farmer. Salvo was a horrible farmer, a fact known by him and everyone else within a five-mile radius. On the rare occasions that he went into town for supplies, he could feel people laughing at him, everyone thinking it hilarious how a man who could balance on a thin wire high above the earth could not bring a field of corn to harvest.

They kept no animals. There was no point; Salvo was too frightened of animals in general to deal with them on a regular basis, and there would be absolutely no question of him ever slaughtering a beast. Anna had not forced the issue, feeling much the same. They kept a small field of corn and had a modest vegetable garden that yielded a variety of foods, enough for their family but not enough for a commercial enterprise.

Surprisingly, Salvo did not mind being a farmer. He didn't like that he wasn't very good at it, and he was frustrated with his inability to grow even the simplest of crops, but despite all this he enjoyed the relative peace and quiet. He thought he did, at any rate. There were times when he wasn't sure whether his feelings were genuine or a masterful self-deception. He knew he wanted to be happy, if only because any fool could see that Anna was happy.

In the spring of 1951 Salvo hired a local boy named Jacob Blacke to help him on the farm. It wasn't so much that there was more work than Salvo could handle. Salvo had simply accepted the fact that, as an ex-circus-performing Rom, he knew little about making things grow. Jacob Blacke knew a lot in that regard, so Salvo hired him.

Jacob was a handsome boy, eighteen years old, with youthful but rugged features that bore the marks of hard work and early mornings. He lived a mile down the road and drove a rusty truck that Salvo could hear coming for most of the way. That spring they had planted seven acres of corn, and Salvo was confident that he would see results this year, finally.

"The growing's not so hard, Mr. Ursari," Jacob said. "You'll get used to it."

Salvo nodded, but he wasn't sure he believed him.

"It's a real nice piece of land. You're lucky to have good soil. Our soil's not so good."

"It matters?"

"Sure it matters. Better the dirt, better the corn." Jacob smiled a wide smile that made Salvo smile too.

Anna approved of Jacob's help. It had been her idea, at first. She had subtly suggested and prodded until Salvo had thought that it would be a good idea too, and had presented it to her as his innovation, which she readily endorsed. She knew that this was the best way to get Salvo to do something.

With three children, she was a master of organizational manipulation. Daniel, whom they guessed to be about eleven years old now, was easy; the boy rarely disobeyed either of his parents, was an amiable older brother to the twins and was not nearly as loud or boisterous as other boys his age. He sometimes seemed to have a maturity that was far beyond his years. At other times, though, he would stare up at Anna with blank eyes, looking for all the world as if he hadn't a clue where he was. She often wondered whether there wasn't something seriously wrong with the boy, but she had long ago resolved to love him like a son, and her wonderings were appropriately tainted with a mother's affection.

Salvo recognized the look in Daniel's eyes for what it was: fear. He tried to do what he could for the boy, understanding all too well what it was to go through life with your fears following right behind you, but as he had never discovered a way to quell them himself, there was little he could do. Overall the boy seemed happy, and that was good enough for Salvo, who knew that it was quite possible to have a less-than-perfect childhood and still be a happy adult. Considering what Daniel had experienced so far in his life, Salvo considered it normal that the boy should not be entirely without dread.

His girls, however, were the opposite of Daniel. If they had demons that haunted their sleep, they never showed it. They were identical in appearance to the point where Anna was the only one who could always tell them apart. Salvo still, on occasion, could misidentify them; he felt bad after doing so, chastising himself for being a poor father.

Errors only happened when a cursory glimpse of the girls was all he had to go on. If he looked for even a second longer, he would know for sure who was who; Elsabeth and Mika were so different in personality that their facial expressions gave them away more accurately than if they had been wearing name tags.

Elsabeth was like Salvo in many ways, mostly in ways that Salvo liked. She had somehow managed to escape inheriting his many neuroses, which was no small relief to both him and Anna. Mika, on the other hand, reminded Salvo of what he imagined his wife had been like when she was eight years old, although he never said as much to her. Mika was charming, funny and kind, but both her parents knew that there was a performer in her. Salvo thought this a good thing; Anna did not.

Both girls were, as far as Salvo was concerned, quite beautiful. As a parent he knew he was obliged to believe this, but most others were inclined to agree, also noting that Salvo and Anna were attractive themselves, though it was generally agreed that Salvo looked much younger than his forty-one years, while Anna looked older than her thirty-five. Other than Salvo's history with the Fisher-Fielding Extravaganza, little was known about either Ursari by their neighbours, and little information was volunteered on the rare occasions that Salvo and Anna fraternized with those surrounding them.

They led, all things considered, a happy life, or so Salvo believed. Therefore he was both puzzled and frightened when, in the late spring of 1951, the panic and fear that had plagued him for most of his life intensified unexpectedly, making the hours before sleep nearly unbearable.

"ONCE," SALVO BEGAN, "THERE WAS A FAMILY of Roma who left all that they knew and went to a strange land. They did not speak the language, and they knew no one. But they were brave, and they were proud, and they could walk high in the air, where no one else could walk, and for this people grew to love them."

The three children sat at his feet, enraptured. Anna had gone into town for groceries, and as soon as she had left, the children started in on Salvo, first asking then begging for a story. Though Salvo often told them stories, he did not tell them nearly as many as they would have liked. His stories were by far their favourite thing about their father. He almost turned into a different person, a person they thought was maybe not even their father but someone else from a strange and exciting world they had never before experienced.

"From all over, people would come to see these Roma perform their feats of daring, always leaving amazed and pleased with what they had witnessed. The Romany family became heroes.

"Then one day there was a horrible fire. It was hotter than the sun herself. The Romany family was trapped, but because they were strong and brave they found a way to escape. And on their way, a boy was snatched from the jaws of the lions, and the Romany family brought him out of the fire and made him one of them."

"That's me!" Daniel whispered, incredulous. He had heard this story before, but Salvo always told it slightly differently, and Daniel always appeared surprised about his inclusion in the tale.

"Did the family of Roma have any other children?" Mika asked, nudging her sister. Elsabeth smiled and they both looked expectantly at Salvo.

"Of course they did. Roma always have many children, because they can never get enough of them. But their children were not in the fire, because Romany parents always keep their children safe."

"Will you always keep us safe?" Elsabeth asked.

"As long as I am breathing, no harm will come to you. Your mother and I have taken a vow."

"A secret vow?" Daniel's eyes shone. He was currently fascinated by secrets and liked to pretend that he had a great many of them to keep.

"A very secret vow. But I can say no more about it. I have already told you too much."

Mika was not interested in secrets. "What happened after the fire?"

Salvo's face became serious. "After the fire, the family of Roma did not want to walk across the sky again. They knew they must protect their children, that they must live as others do. So they went to a quiet land and made their home."

"Were they happy?" Elsabeth asked. "Did they miss their old life?"

"Yes, they were very happy," Salvo said. "And they did not miss their old life at all."

His voice was convincing, and there was nothing in his manner to suggest he was being less than truthful. Still, each of the children was left feeling that perhaps there was more to the story than they were being told, though they never said as much, either to each other or to their father.

New York had not been a welcome place for András and Etel. After Salvo and Anna left and it was apparent that there would be no work with any circus, András set about getting himself a job. He could neither read nor write, and though his conversational English was good, he had an accent that to many sounded German, which was an unspoken but definite barrier to employment. He eventually got a job working for a man who owned a number of hot-dog wagons throughout the city. The pay was not good, but after Etel got a job cleaning the rooms in a dive hotel they were able to scrape by.

When they left the F-F, Etel had known that there was more behind their departure than she was being told. She did not press the matter initially, assuming that she would be told once they were gone. Hours before they left, though, Martin Fisher-Fielding had approached her as she waited in line for the washroom. She could feel a chill from other performers towards her, and it made her uncomfortable. When Martin approached, many abandoned their places in line and pretended to be otherwise occupied, trying to avoid being seen in Etel's general proximity and at the same time remain within earshot. Martin made it hard for potential eavesdroppers, leaning in close to Etel's ear.

"For the record," he said, "I do not believe you started the fire."

Etel was too dumbfounded to speak. She shook the hand that Martin offered, and watched as he turned the corner out of view. First slowly, and then with exponential acceleration, she realized what was happening. Why, she wondered, have András and Salvo said nothing? Then she knew they stayed quiet because they thought she might have done it. And she became angry.

Six years later she was still angry. She had said nothing to another soul about the fire, and even András did not suspect that she knew the whole story. As time went on, her anger crested and fell and rose again, and several times she almost leapt from her seat and attacked her brother with her fists. But her rage always abated just before she broke, bottoming out before it steadily began to rise again.

Her anger had become a burden, she knew. There were times when she would catch András giving her a long, assessing look and she knew that he was wondering whether she had done it. She wanted to scream that she had not, but if András needed to be told, then she did not want to tell him.

She felt betrayed and she hated her brothers for it. But they were her family so she stayed quiet, and she knew that she would always stay quiet. Things are not perfect in this world, she told herself, and wishing changes nothing.

Most nights András arrived home late, Etel and János already asleep. They rented a two-room apartment in the Bronx, Etel and János sleeping in the bedroom and András sleeping on the sofa in the main room. János was nearly seven, an age where he was getting to be too old to share a bed with his aunt, and there had been discussion lately of them perhaps looking for a larger apartment, which András knew they could not afford. He would make himself a sandwich in their tiny kitchen and open the door to the bedroom, looking in on his son and sister. Etel would be snoring loudly, her back to the door, and János would be barely visible under the covers. And András would shake his head sadly. This was no good.

He had no idea Etel knew about Norris's accusations. He had, however, noticed that she had not smoked a single cigarette since the fire, and while she had once been somewhat lax with her personal hygiene, she now washed with a ferocious regularity, smelling of soap where she had once smelt of smoke. In his weakest moments, András did wonder if there could be any truth to Norris's allegation. He tried very hard to not have weak moments.

It was no great secret that Etel missed the wire. "Once," she would tell János, "we walked high above the ground on a wire no thicker than your little finger. We were loved by all. No Rom has been more loved than your father, or your uncle, or myself." Often late at night she would ask András if he missed the wire, always looking a little disappointed when he shrugged and said there was no point to missing what is over.

Though János bore a startling resemblance to his mother, András tried to stop himself from thinking of Margit. When he did, he remembered her face when she had first emerged from the burning tent, and remembered how he had saved his sister over her, and he knew that his choice had been made then. It upset him that life had placed him in such an untenable position; how does one choose between the woman one loves and the sister one has raised from a baby? It was impossible, he knew, and although he wished he had never been made to choose, he did not think he had done anything wrong. Etel was, he suspected, a far better mother to the boy than Margit would have been. But still there were nights when he could barely hold in his tears, when he felt so lonely he might implode.

When he had seen all he could take, András would ease the door closed and collapse into the sofa. He would check his watch and, seeing that he was due back at work in a few hours, try to sleep. The street outside was always alive with the sound of cars and people, no matter what the hour, but it never stopped him from falling into a deep slumber that could have lasted for weeks.

On the other side of the city, a power struggle was taking place that would affect the future of the American circus. When Cole Fisher-Fielding died, he had willed his share of the Fisher-Fielding Circus Company to his always-loyal nephew, Martin, which had left Martin with a three-sevenths interest in the company, the largest stake any one person had ever owned. The Spouses, between Charlotte Fisher-Fielding and the unholy union of Rebecca Fisher-Fielding and Phillip Barnes, controlled an equal share, with the Respectables once again possessing the tie-breaking vote. Norris Fisher-Fielding's presidency was up for renewal in the spring of 1952, and it was no secret that Martin intended to challenge his cousin.

Norris's position was precarious; many still viewed his decision to take the F-F into winter quarters before the season ended in 1945 as irresponsible, and others were upset with how he had attempted to remove all traces of Cole Fisher-Fielding from the Extravaganza. Specifically, people pointed to the firing of the Ursaris, although they were not the only ones to be let go, as the act of a petty, vindictive man, not at all the sort of leadership the circus needed.

As if this weren't enough, the cold, hard numbers showed that the Fisher-Fielding Circus Company was losing business. Whether this was a result of Norris's stewardship or not was debatable; all over the country, circus attendance was dwindling. Many big-top circuses had gone out of business, and those that had survived had moved to indoor venues. By 1950, the Fisher-Fielding Extravaganza was the only major circus still playing under a canvas tent. Aside from playing Madison Square Garden in New York and the few indoor dates that had followed the big-top fire, the F-F had always played under canvas. Even Norris Fisher-Fielding was reluctant to make the switch indoors.

Martin Fisher-Fielding proposed to do exactly that. He was less inclined to revere history as he was to celebrate showmanship, and he knew that if the F-F were to go on, it would have to change with the times. He believed his uncle would have agreed; the F-F's survival was more important than the big top. He had, compounding this belief, more personal reasons for wanting to move the show indoors. He was there the day the big top had burned, and though he never told anyone, he had since then been unable to force himself to enter any tent or anything that resembled one. He had not been into the new big top the F-F had purchased for the 1946 season, nor did he think he ever would.

Although he didn't know it at the time, Martin was not alone in his phobia; among the survivors of the F-F fire there were many who could not enter a building without checking first for fire exits, and many who would not enter a tent of any kind. These people stood in the rain at weddings and picnics, did not attend fairs or outdoor shows and never, ever went to the circus.

The vote was close, and for a while it looked as if Martin might win. But in the end Norris successfully placated the Respectables, and he was given another five years. Martin resolved to bide his time. Five years was not so long.

~~~~~~~~~~

On a sunny day in June 1953, Salvo stood in the middle of his cornfield, the corn nearly as high as his head. With Jacob Blacke's help it appeared as though he would get a substantial crop, and he was pleased. He was tired and could not stop yawning, in spite of all the coffee he'd drank that morning. Sleep had eluded him in the preceding weeks, and he did not expect it to come easily that night. He was once again mortally terrified of the dark, though he would not leave a light on for fear that Anna would find out. He spent hours lying on his back, his heart racing, sweating through his nightclothes, waiting for disasters that never came. It left him exhausted, cranky and ashamed. Why he who had once walked a high wire should be such a coward on the ground was something he did not understand.

He was suddenly seized by an impulse he couldn't describe. Before he could identify the source of this feeling, he found himself walking towards the barn. In the past it had held both livestock and hay, but as Salvo had neither of these, it was empty save for a few farming implements that leaned up against the far wall. When his eyes came to rest on a fifty-foot length of quarter-inch cable, he knew why he was there. With a ladder he drove a spike into the main vertical beam of the barn, sixteen feet off the ground, and secured one end of the cable to the spike. Then he climbed the hayloft at the other end of the barn and wrapped the cable tightly around a support beam. If he'd had extra cable, he would have put in a perpendicular guy wire.

He leapt onto the wire. The barn's sloped roof offered him barely enough clearance to stand fully upright. He could feel cobwebs pulling at his hair, and he could smell the wetness of the exposed wood. If he'd wanted to, he could have reached out and touched the roof, but he didn't. Salvo's feet travelled steadily and without hesitation, and his balance was true. When he reached the middle of the wire he stopped and stood perfectly still. This was the first exercise he'd learned on the wire: the quest for immobility. He stood motionless, and gradually the barn began to recede from his eyes, and a calm radiated through his body. Outside, the branches of a willow tree brushed softly against the side of the barn.

Daniel came into the barn hours later, sent by Anna to tell Salvo to come in for dinner. At first he didn't see his father, but he instantly knew that someone else was in the barn. He froze, preparing to run, and then he saw Salvo above him on the wire, motionless, his eyes closed. Daniel was unsure what he should do. He didn't want to startle Salvo, perhaps causing him to fall, but on the other hand he needed to get his attention. He decided to wait it out, and as quietly as he could, he lowered himself to a seated position.

After many minutes, Daniel knew that Salvo wasn't going to give this up any time soon. He rose and, in a voice that he intended to sound much calmer than it ended up being, called out to his elevated father. "Hello?" he said, instantly wishing he had thought of something better.

Salvo's eyes snapped open. Much to Daniel's relief, he didn't fall. Salvo looked down at him and blinked. "Daniel?"

"It's time to eat."

"Yes. I will be there soon."

Daniel nodded and moved to the door.

"Daniel." When he turned around, Salvo was no longer on the wire. He stood at the edge of the hayloft.

"Yes?"

"Please say nothing of this to your mother. You are a good boy, and it would be a favour to me."

Daniel's heart leapt. He had never had a secret to keep before, and he felt privileged to be given one. "I won't tell," he squeaked.

"Thank you." Salvo climbed down the hayloft's wooden ladder and put his arm around the boy. Together they walked to the house.

Later, as they ate, Anna could not understand why the usually melancholy Daniel beamed with such joy. She resolved to ask Salvo if he knew anything of this mood swing, but her husband fell asleep immediately after eating, his snores evincing a deep sleep that she had not heard from him in a long time. By morning she had forgotten her question.

Salvo knew that he had not achieved immobility. He knew this because he knew that immobility was impossible, yet he felt that he had come as close as he ever had, and that was enough. He could now see that the previous eight years without the wire had been an illusion of happiness; only his family—their love for him and his for them—kept him from that knowledge.

During his near immobility he had envisioned the most daring, most elaborate, most fantastic wire trick the world would ever see. It had built itself before his very eyes, and though there was a part of him that wondered if it were technically possible to perform, Salvo believed that if it were possible, he would be the one to make it happen.

To this end he began to train in earnest. Anna rarely came into the barn, so he had little danger of his wire being detected. He elected to keep his intentions a secret for the time being. Salvo knew his wife was not looking to return to the wire.

He had not lost as many of his skills as he first suspected he might have. He was rusty, and those muscles not used on the ground needed reconditioning, but he made good progress and was confident he would be able to return to his previous form in a reasonable amount of time.

Salvo's training was rigorous, far more intense than he had ever undergone at the hands of Tomas Skosa. He allowed himself no mercy and gave himself no room for error. If he were to succeed he would not only have to be perfect himself, he would have to be able to make others perfect.

So focused was he upon his training that he failed to notice the three sets of eyes that peered up at him through a crack in the wall at the rear of the barn. Daniel had suitably impressed upon Mika and Elsabeth the importance of complete silence, and when they had seen what their father was doing, their attention was so rapt that the possibility of sound was non-existent.

To the children, Salvo was performing the impossible on a continuing basis. As soon as he left the barn, they crept up into the hayloft and stared out at the wire, wishing they were brave enough to venture out onto it, wishing they were like their father. They held for him a reverence they had never known before; they had always emulated Anna while at play, unknowingly admiring her strength and clarity, thinking their father to be weak and indecisive.

Eventually, Daniel worked up the nerve to step onto the wire. "I'm not scared," he said.

"Go out there, then," Mika said. Both she and Elsabeth knew he was lying.

"Fine." Daniel stood at the edge, then focused his eyes on the end of the wire like he'd seen Salvo do. He took a step, feeling the wire under his feet for the first time. His balance held.

Mika grabbed her sister's hand, too frightened to speak, too excited not to. "He's doing it," she whispered. It was fantastic.

Elsabeth's mouth dropped open, but she said nothing. He's brave, she thought. I wonder why I'm not that brave. Maybe he can make me brave.

Daniel took two more steps—slowly, carefully—then, like someone pulling a cloth out from under a set table, the wire was gone from under him, and he was falling. Just as he realized he was falling he hit the ground, his feet first, then his back, then his head. For a moment his vision blurred, red flooding his eyes, and he felt disoriented, like being dizzy in both directions at once, and his head hurt. He tried to stand and found he could, and he saw his sisters standing in front of him, worry on their faces.

"Daniel? Are you okay?" Mika tentatively placed a hand on his shoulder.

"We're going to be in trouble," Elsabeth said.

"No we're not. Only if you tell."

"I'm not going to tell."

"Are you okay, Daniel?"

For a minute Daniel didn't answer them. His hand rose to touch the spot of his head that hurt, and when it lowered there was no blood on it. He tested his movement and found that he was all right.

"Daniel?"

He smiled. "I'm fine. I'm going to try again." He climbed the ladder and stood at the edge of the wire, about to step on it again. A sharp, searing pain lanced through his temple and he stepped back, unsure of where he was.

"Maybe we should stop for today," Elsabeth suggested.

Daniel nodded. "Yeah, I guess so."

"We'll try again tomorrow?" Mika's eyes were glued to the wire.

"Sure. Tomorrow."

They crept out of the barn and into the house, watching very closely to make sure that neither of their parents saw them, especially their mother. They had heard her speak of the high wire before, and although she never said as much, her voice betrayed a tone of dislike that they easily picked up on.

That night, Daniel's head ached so badly he thought he was going to die, and he threw up twice. The next day he didn't throw up, but his head still hurt. Anna kept him home from school for three days; she attributed his symptoms to a flu. It was almost a week before he felt well enough to even think about the wire again.

In the spring of 1957 the Fisher-Fielding Circus Company would again decide between two cousins. Martin Fisher-Fielding had long known that he did not have the support of many of the Respectables. They identified him with his uncle, an association Martin was proud of and had done nothing to discourage. Some of the Respectables, however, still blamed Cole for the fire and its subsequent effect on revenues. This sentiment was fostered by Norris, who knew that the Respectables were the key to his power. Norris had been concerned when he had first learned that Anna's brothers had given her Arthur Simpson's block of the F-F, but there was little he could do. His alarm had diminished greatly when no Ursari had shown up at the 1952 vote, and he had little reason to think that they would ever appear. Martin, on the other hand, saw the opportunity he needed. If he could get Salvo and Anna on his side, then there was a chance that the Respectables might vote in his favour.

The trouble with this strategy was that the Ursaris were difficult to get in touch with. They had no telephone, and Martin knew that if he were to win over Anna, he would first have to win over Salvo, and there was no point in sending him a letter; as far as Martin knew, Salvo might not even read English.

He was thus faced with a difficult choice. He could either stay in New York and work on somehow gaining the support of the other Respectables, who though scattered were much easier to raise through conventional means, or he could travel across the continent and speak with the Ursaris. If he failed to gain their support, or if their support did not sway the Respectables, there would be no time to try anything else. It was a huge gamble, but Martin had a little of his uncle in him, and he decided to risk it. He made arrangements to travel to British Columbia.

Salvo did not immediately recognize the well-dressed man who walked up his driveway. He knew the man looked familiar, but it took him a long time to realize that it was Martin Fisher-Fielding. He was not someone Salvo had ever expected to see at his farm.

Martin strode confidently up to Salvo, who was replacing the broken handle of a shovel. He extended his hand, and Salvo shook it.

"Welcome," Salvo said, wondering why Martin was there but not knowing how to ask him.

"Thank you. This is beautiful country here."

Salvo looked around, as if to verify what he had said. "Yes, it is."

"I'll get to the point, Mr. Ursari—"

"Salvo."

"Yes. Salvo, I need your help." He explained the situation to Salvo, who though not ignorant of Fisher-Fielding politics had no idea how precarious the balance of power was. When Martin was done pleading his case, Salvo spoke.

"I will help you. I do not know if Anna will go along, but I will try. Norris Fisher-Fielding is not someone Cole would have wanted running his circus."

"Thank you."

"But if this works, if the F-F becomes yours, then I will need you to help me."

"Of course. Anything I can do."

Salvo hesitated, aware of the implications of what he was about to say. "I want to return to the wire."

"The Fisher-Fielding Extravaganza should never have let the Ursaris go. If I become president, the first thing I will do is reinstate your contract."

"I will hold you to that, Mr. Fisher-Fielding."

Martin nodded. Salvo was a reasonable man, he thought. Norris was a fool to have made an enemy of him.

"My wife is in the house. We will go and see what she says." Salvo motioned to the house, and they walked up the path towards it. Before they entered, Salvo put his hand on Martin's forearm. "It would be better if we did not mention the wire yet," he said.

"Right," Martin said, and they entered the house.

Anna listened to Martin's pitch, her face betraying no expression. She had known that eventually someone would want to try and unseat Norris, but she had not thought it would be so soon. At any rate, her mind had been made up before Martin had even arrived.

"I have no love in my heart for Norris," she said slowly. "I hope you can get the circus out of his hands. I'll help you in any way I can, but . . ." She paused. Martin's face dropped, knowing that there was more coming and that it would not be good. "But I will not go to New York to vote, and I won't deal with the others. I want no part of these politics."

Martin's heart sank. He was defeated, he knew. Salvo sat silently in the corner, trying to think of something to say to Anna that might change her mind.

"Let me ask you," Anna said, "how much do you think my share of the F-F is worth?"

Martin shrugged. "Right now, not very much. Perhaps thirty or forty thousand dollars, at best." Salvo's eyebrows raised. That sounded like a lot of money to him.

Anna nodded. "That seems about right. Here's what I'll do. You can have my share of the F-F, Martin."

Martin frowned. "I'm afraid I can't, Mrs. Ursari. You aren't allowed to sell your share. That was one of the conditions of the original agreement. The shares of the Respectables—" He stopped at this, unsure whether Anna was familiar with the name given to her group, but she did not appear fazed—"these shares cannot be sold."

"I know. But they can be given away. And I'm giving them to you."

Martin blinked. "You are?"

"Yes. The Fisher-Fielding Extravaganza is a special thing. It's where I met my husband, whom I love more than anything. We aren't rich, but we don't need money. Nor do we need to own part of something that's not ours."

Martin stood, his face beaming. "Thank you, Mrs. Ursari. Thank you."

Anna took his hand, and she smiled. Salvo fetched his bottle of rye whisky and they drank a toast to Cole Fisher-Fielding, and another to seal their deal. After Martin left, hurrying to the nearest lawyer's office to have the necessary papers drawn up, Salvo asked Anna why she had done it.

"Etel did not start the fire," she said, "and it was wrong of Norris to say she did. My father would have voted against Norris, and he would have got others to do the same. And," she put her hand on Salvo's cheek, "without the F-F, we would never have met."

Salvo smiled, feeling guilty for deceiving her.

That night Anna lay in bed, wondering if she had made the right decision. She knew that a return to the wire would put an end to their way of life, and she hated to leave it, but she had known for some months now that there would be no other way.

She could even trace back to the date when she had realized that it would be nearly impossible to keep Salvo off the wire. It was 1950, their wedding anniversary, eight years since they had been hastily wed in the ring of the Fisher-Fielding Extravaganza, everybody in a hurry because they had just finished a matinee and there would be an evening performance in a couple of hours. She had not at the time of their marriage yet begun to hate the circus, and if asked at that moment she would have sworn she never would.

One of the first things Anna learned when she joined the F-F was that the circus meant different things to different people. Some of the performers were there because they were good at something that only the circus would pay them to do. Others were there because they had always been there, the children of performers or workers; they knew of no alternate way of life. Still others were there because that was all that was left for them, the circus being the only place that would give them a warm meal and a job. Some, like her, had come running from elsewhere.

When she met Salvo Ursari, Anna knew full well that he was the exact opposite of the kind of man her father wanted her to marry. And her father was pushing her to marry someone, anyone, of the sort that he approved. She knew it was only a matter of time until she found someone among that crowd whom she did not loathe, and that would be it. For her there would be a life of luxury, privilege and infinite, immaculate boredom. For her, at age twenty-six, the sort of life promised her was barely better than death.

When she had looked up that day in the crowd, and she had seen Salvo nearly fall and then look straight to her, she knew two things: She knew that a life with this man would never be boring. And she knew that he needed her, like no one she had ever known needed her. When their gaze met his eyes spoke to her. Save me.

She had not at the time realized that this was exactly what would happen, that she would feel compelled to remove Salvo from the wire, to save his body as well as his spirit, but this is what she had done. And she hated him for it, for making her love him so much she would feel it necessary to keep him from the one place he was alive.

All during the time after the fire, and even in the months preceding it, she knew that she must get Salvo away from the wire. She believed that if he saw another side of life he would not need to walk, that he would grow used to a different life.

On the night of their last anniversary, Salvo gave Anna a framed photograph of herself on the wire. She remembered when the picture was taken but had not known that Salvo had a copy. It was after her first walk across the wire on her own. She was standing on the platform with a goofy grin plastered across her face, her arms raised in victory. Looking at the picture, she thought she looked like an idiot, and said as much.

"No," Salvo said. "That is the most beautiful woman I have ever seen."

Anna looked at him and saw that he meant it completely. A terrible twinge set off inside her. Slowly, over the next few days, she began to see what she had done. She was jealous of the wire, resentful of all the things that it gave Salvo that she could never give. A part of her had reasoned that if she could remove the wire from his life, then she would be the most important thing. A wave of guilt washed over her, but still she could not bring herself to speak to Salvo about it. So when Martin Fisher-Fielding showed up at their house, she knew immediately what she must do.

Lying awake that night, though, she began to second-guess herself. Had she romanticized the wire yet again? she wondered. Did she forget so easily what life with the F-F was like? She wondered until light began to come in the window, and would continue to wonder in the weeks to come.

WHEN NORRIS FOUND OUT WHAT had occurred, he was furious. There was nothing he could do, however, and when he lost the vote for the presidency he refused to take a lesser position, much to Martin's relief. The news of Martin's victory was met by those in the Extravaganza with much pleasure. Martin was well respected as a man who was a capable manager and someone who understood the values that had made the F-F great. As the show ended its tour in the fall of 1957, people looked forward to the next year's run with great anticipation.

The time had come for Salvo to take the next step towards returning to the wire. He was confident that his training had reinstated his skills, and he needed to assemble a troupe capable of pulling off the act he had envisioned. First, though, he required Anna's approval. He waited until the children were in bed. They sat in front of the fireplace in the front room, Anna listening to the radio.

"I have something to tell you," he said. He tried to appear calm, but he could hear the tension in his voice.

Anna nodded. "I was wondering when you would."

Salvo was surprised. "What?"

"I'm not a fool," she said, "and I go into the barn from time to time." She turned her gaze onto him, her face cold.

Salvo said nothing, ashamed.

"You want to go back to the wire."

"Yes."

"This life isn't enough for you? You have to have the crowds, the applause?" Anna's voice rose, and her brow was furrowed.

"Our life is more than enough. For ten years I have loved our life. But without the wire, I cannot enjoy it." It shocked Salvo to hear himself say such a thing, because he had not realized it before, and because he instantly knew it to be true.

"Then walk the wire in the barn."

"It is not the same."

"You have a family now, Salvo. What if you fall?"

"I will not fall."

Anna looked him in the eyes. "If I say no, will you go anyway?"

Salvo considered this question. "No. If you say no, I will stay here and grow corn."

Anna stood, moving to the window. "If we do this, there will be conditions."

His shoulders slumped ever so slightly. "I understand." Salvo tried to contain his excitement. He could not believe Anna was softening her position.

"I mean it. It will be done a certain way." She tried to sound resolute, but she knew her resolve was already seriously weakened.

"Yes. It will be done right."

"I pray to God I don't regret this decision."

"You will not." Outside it began to rain, lightly at first, then heavily, the drops sounding like bells as they struck the roof's metal gutters.

ALL DAY LONG ETEL WAITED FOR JÁNOS, who was a few weeks past his thirteenth birthday, to come home from school. A letter had arrived, and Etel had opened it, surprised when Canadian money had tumbled out, a lot of money. But though she could speak English well enough, she could not read most of what the letter said. She recognized her brother's name, though, and she could hardly sit still. When János got home he would read her the letter, which, while short, said much.

Late that night the door opened, and András, wilted, trudged through the doorway. He was working nights as a bouncer at a nightclub and days at the hot-dog stand, and he was exhausted. He was startled to see Etel sitting up. A multicoloured pile of money was arranged on the table, and a piece of paper was clutched in her hands.

"From Salvo," she said, thrusting the paper towards him.

"What does it say?" he asked.

"He is going back to the wire." A smile spread across her face.

"How?" András could not bring himself to believe her. Surely there was some misunderstanding.

"Norris Fisher-Fielding is gone, and the F-F has invited him back."

"What is the money for?"

Etel's smile lessened slightly. "He wants us to come to Canada."

"Why?" András groped his way into a chair.

"He wants us to walk again."

András paused. He had not thought he would ever return to the wire. "What do you think we should do?"

Etel's green eyes shone. "I think we should go."

András looked at the couch he slept on, the dingy apartment they lived in, and thought how in six hours he would have to be back at work so that they could afford even this squalor. He thought of János in the next room, of the future the boy would likely have if they stayed in New York, and his decision was made. "Then we will go."

They left the next day.

To perform the feat Salvo had conceived, the troupe would have to consist of eight people. When András and Etel had resumed training and Anna took to the wire, they were four. They trained through the winter, and by spring of 1958 they were very good. But they were still four bodies short of eight, though no one besides Salvo knew it. Salvo knew that once the act started back with the F-F in several weeks, it would not be hard to find performers willing to join them.

The Ursari house was crowded. János and Daniel shared a room, as did Elsabeth and Mika, leaving a room for András and Etel to share, and a room for Salvo and Anna. With the four teenagers, there was a constant battle for use of the house's one washroom, and many mornings Salvo resorted to using the old outhouse behind the barn rather than wait his turn.

It was on one such morning that Salvo woke and from the other side of the door heard the shower running. He pulled on his shoes and went outside. As he passed the barn he noticed that the door was open. When he reached out to close it, he saw a glimpse of leg just inside the door. He entered the barn.

János stood in his pyjamas, his back to Salvo. Elsabeth and Mika were up in the hayloft, similarly dressed. They all watched the centre of the wire, where Daniel stood, motionless. At first no one saw Salvo. Finally Mika did, nudging her twin, whose face flushed when she looked down at him. János turned around and ducked his head, knowing they had been caught. Daniel had seen nothing, still standing.

Quietly, so as not to startle the boy, Salvo spoke. "Come down, Daniel."

Daniel looked down, and pivoting with surprising technique, walked back to the hayloft. He was first down the ladder, followed by Mika and then Elsabeth. They stood in a line beside János. János and Elsabeth looked frightened, almost ashamed, but Mika and Daniel were stony-faced, defiant.

"You should not be up there," Salvo said.

None of the children spoke.

"The wire is not a place for play."

"We weren't playing," Mika said, her voice high.

"You have no training."

"We've watched you," Daniel said. "We can do lots."

"You are children."

"We aren't so young."

Salvo considered this assertion. Daniel was approaching eighteen, which was indeed not so young. Mika and Elsabeth would turn fifteen in a few weeks, and János was a year younger.

"We could do more if you taught us." Mika had spoken, but all the children's eyes flickered at the suggestion.

Salvo shook his head. "Your mother would never allow it."

"You could convince her."

"At least try," Elsabeth said.

Salvo again shook his head. He turned and left the barn, closing the door behind him. He had not considered this possibility. It could give him the eight people needed for the trick, but these were his children. Anna would not approve.

It took Salvo a week to work up the nerve to tell Anna what he had seen. As he had guessed, she was less than enthusiastic.

"They were on the wire? They're children!"

"They are older than we like to think."

"Have you been teaching them?" Her tone was accusatory.

"No. But they have our blood."

"Not Daniel." As soon as she said this, Anna wished she hadn't.

Salvo did not say that he often felt that Daniel was the most like him of any of the children. "But the others . . ."

Anna ran her hand through her hair and chewed at her lip. "They think the wire is romantic. They don't know the truth."

"You once thought the wire romantic."

Anna prickled. "I didn't know the wire, just like they don't."

"The wire is not a bad place."

"No, but it is a hard place, and it is a dangerous place. Do you really want that for our children?"

"I do not see how we can stop them. We can tell them no, but they will do it anyway, and they will not always be children."

Anna considered his words. "Then we must tell them what the wire is really like."

Salvo suspected they would have different versions, but he agreed.

ANNA AND SALVO SAT ON THE LOVESEAT in the corner of the front room. Daniel, János and Mika sat on the larger sofa opposite them and Elsabeth sat on the floor, leaning against Mika's legs. András sat in a chair to the side, and Etel stood. She could have sat in another chair that remained empty, but she choose to stand.

"Either way," Salvo said, "whether I will teach you or not, you are never to go on a wire by yourselves again."

"You will teach us?" Mika asked.

"That remains to be seen," Anna said, displeased with the excitement in Mika's voice. "You need to know some things first."

"We're listening," Daniel said.

Salvo began. "The wire is not like any other place. One mistake on the wire and you are dead. You are dead, your troupe is dead, we are all lost. That is a big responsibility. You cannot take it lightly."

"Many die," András said quietly.

"We know all of this," Mika said.

"You cannot know any of it." András's jaw was firmly set.

"Has any of you ever fallen?" Elsabeth asked.

"No," Salvo said. "That is why we are alive. But every time we go on the wire, we accept that we may die."

"Then why do you do it?" János, who was the smartest of the children and said little, had asked the very question each of them had secretly hoped no one would ask. There was no answer that would keep these children off the wire.

"Why do you do it?" János repeated, his voice insistent, eyes squarely on Salvo.

"I do it because I must," Salvo answered. He did not like his answer, but there was nothing else he could tell them.

"For the money?" Mika asked.

"No. For my life."

"Then you understand why we want to walk," Daniel said. He sounded more like an adult than he ever had. Salvo knew then the argument was over. How could he deny his children access to the very thing that made his life worth living?

Anna remained unconvinced. "It is not a way of life I would wish upon you children."

"If we don't like it, we can quit, right?"

"Few do."

Etel, who had remained silent until now, spoke quietly. "I was almost your age when I learned the wire. If you begin now, you will never stop."

"Why would we want to stop?" Daniel asked.

For this only Anna had an answer, but she said nothing.

All was quiet for several minutes. Then, András spoke, his words directed to János. "I am against this way of life for you. But if you choose to train, I will not stop you."

János looked to Etel. "Your life is yours," she said.

He next looked at his cousins, then at Salvo. "Will you teach me?"

Salvo nodded. "Yes."

"And us?" Daniel asked.

Salvo looked to Anna. "I have no objections. But it is up to your mother."

Anna stared at the floor, her hands clenched together, knuckles white. After a long time she looked up, into the faces of Elsabeth, then Mika, then Daniel. She exhaled sharply. "I never wanted this life for you. Are you sure it is what you want?"

"Yes," each of them said in turn.

"Then you may do it. There's too much of your father in you for me to prevent it."

The children twitched with excitement, in spite of the gravity of Anna's words. Salvo hushed them. "This will not be easy, and it will not be fun. You will work until you think you cannot work any more, and even then we will not be nearly finished. You will do as I say, because I will not allow you to perform unless I have complete confidence in you, unless I am certain you will not fall. If I do not have this confidence, or I lose it, you will not go on the wire."

"Don't worry," Daniel said. "I was snatched from the lion's den. I will not fall."

Salvo smiled at this remark. "You need to sleep now," he said. "Tomorrow we begin."

That night, none of the children slept. Neither did Anna, Salvo or András. Only Etel slept soundly; the others could hear her snoring through their doors.

SALVO WAS TRUE TO HIS WORD, a stern taskmaster who accepted nothing short of perfection. In the mornings he trained the green walkers—Daniel, János, Elsabeth, Mika and Jacob Blacke, who upon learning that they were going back to the wire had begged Salvo to teach him, and because he could use another person, Salvo agreed. A spare walker would always come in handy on the road. János had the most natural talent of all of them, but Elsabeth and Mika were very good as well. Jacob Blacke was not bad. Daniel was the least talented but was arguably the hardest worker, and as a result he was able to progress, if at a slower rate.

In the beginning Salvo had them do only exercises that would train the muscles they would need on the wire. He could tell they did not like these drills, finding them boring and tedious, but they did not complain, and eventually he let them onto the wire. The first thing he had to do was unteach them what they thought they already knew. What they had learned of the wire they had learned by watching Salvo, and this was not a good way to learn. Too much of what looked easy was not—details were missed. Daniel in particular had horrible technique, and Elsabeth and Mika had a tendency to bow their legs. János was not as damaged, and Jacob, never having been on the wire, needed no retraining.

When Salvo was satisfied that he had erased their misconceptions, he began to really teach them. They learned immobility first, all five of them on the wire at once. If one fell or broke concentration they were all forced to leave the wire and begin again. After they had mastered this lesson to Salvo's approval, they walked.

Salvo lowered the wire to a height of about four feet off the ground, and he had them walk from one end to the other, over and over again. As they walked in one direction he corrected them, pushed them and prodded them, told them what they were doing wrong and what they were doing right. When they reached the end they walked the other way, and he left them alone, watching their progress.

After several months each of them could cross the wire three times and back without Salvo correcting them. János could do it many times. Salvo then placed all five of them on the wire and had them walk together.

He snapped his fingers, and they each took a step forward. Watching, he saw that Daniel was a fraction of a second behind the others. "You're slow, Daniel," he said.

"Sorry, Father," Daniel said.

"Do not be sorry. Just walk with the others." He snapped his fingers, and this time Jacob was slow. "Jacob, now you're off."

Jacob nodded. He knew better than to apologize.

Salvo snapped his fingers, and this time they all stepped in sequence. He clapped his hands once, and Mika and Elsabeth pivoted 180 degrees. "Watch your outside leg, Mika," he said. "It's too wide. You cannot bend it so much. See?" He pushed her lightly with one hand, and her balance was gone. He grabbed her arm to steady her, so she would not fall. Above all he did not want them to learn how to fall.

"If I don't bend it, I can't pivot," Mika said.

"Yes, you can. It's harder, but you will not fall, and that is the important thing. Try it again."

Mika pivoted, this time with her leg in the correct position. "Good," Salvo said. "Again." She repeated the pivot once, twice, three times. The others stood, motionless.

Salvo clapped his hands twice, and Daniel, Jacob and János pivoted 180 degrees. "Very nice, János. Good, Daniel. Jacob, crisper. It must be crisper." He wasn't sure about Jacob. He was adequate most of the time, but he would never be brilliant.

"That's enough for today." Salvo watched them walk to the end of the wire and step down, then file out of the barn without saying a word. He suspected that they would complain about his methods once out of earshot, but he didn't mind. Their hard work would pay off, eventually.

Salvo sighed. The 1958 version of the Fisher-Fielding Extravaganza was due to begin its tour in only three weeks, and he knew that the children were not ready to perform. But if they did not join the show, Martin would be forced to hire another wire act, and they could potentially lose their spot. Though Salvo did not believe that Martin would go back on his word to give the Ursaris a contract, he knew enough about the circus to know that when an opportunity presents itself you do not pass it up, so he decided that their training would continue on the road.

The act they would perform was much the same as the act they had performed prior to 1945, with Anna taking Margit's place in some of the tricks, Etel in the more difficult ones. On opening night in Madison Square Garden they performed the act flawlessly, but received only lukewarm applause where once there had been ovations. Salvo was puzzled.

"What is wrong with the act?" he asked out loud, once they had reached the ground.

"There is nothing wrong," András said. "We did it perfectly."

"But the people did not cheer."

"They have seen us before," Etel said. "Maybe we no longer excite them."

Salvo considered this for a moment. He had never thought such a thing possible. "Then we will have to find a way to make them care," he said, his jaw setting with a firmness that would have frightened Anna if she had seen him.

In general, interest in the circus had declined. Competition with movies, television and professional sporting events had reduced attendance to a fraction of what it once had been. The show had been much pared down as a result, and although the acts were still all top-notch, there was a certain amount of spectacle missing. The F-F had been the last circus to move indoors, marking the end of an era. Yet it was, as Martin pointed out repeatedly, better than bankruptcy.

When the F-F finished the run and went to winter quarters, the Ursaris returned to their farm. After a week off, Salvo held an intensive three-day training session in the barn, with all nine of them present. He put them through every technique, move, trick and manoeuvre they knew, keenly observing their slightest movement. They all met his approval, including the children. They were ready.

When he told them of his plan, of the act that he believed would transform the wire, they were dumbfounded.

"It can't be done," András said.

Salvo laughed. "It can. And we will do it."

The others followed Salvo's lead, except Anna, who said nothing.

IN THE AFTERNOON DANIEL COULD feel it coming. He could tell when it was near because he could smell sunflowers. He didn't know how he knew the smell was sunflowers, as he could remember sunflowers having no particular smell—he just did. He quietly excused himself and went outside, walking quickly around the barn and into the barren field behind it. He stood and waited, and just when he thought he might have been wrong, it arrived. His body froze at first, his muscles tense, refusing to respond to his brain. It was as if he were encased in concrete. He did not know how much time he passed in this state. It could have been seconds or minutes; there was no way for him to tell. Then he started to shake, slightly at first and then more violently, until he was on the ground thrashing like a fish in the bottom of a boat. His brain pulsated, and he felt like he was being struck by lightning over and over again. Then, without warning, it stopped. He was himself again. He was tired and wet and muddy, but he was himself again. He got up, wiped spit from his chin, touched his hand to his tongue and saw blood, and headed back to the house. He snuck up to his bedroom, changed his clothes and returned to the front room, where his father, uncle, aunt and cousin sat watching television while his mother and sisters bustled in the kitchen. Daniel sat beside his father and closed his eyes. He said nothing to anyone. It had been worse than the last time; each of the four seizures he'd had since his fall had increased in severity. Months would go by without incident, and he would almost allow himself to believe that he was better. If he did not get better, someone would find out, and they would take away the wire. And that was something Daniel could not let happen.

****

They worked on the act all winter long. First they did it on the ground, then on a wire strung a foot high. For a long time they could not do it successfully. Many bruises and scrapes and twists occurred when it did not work, and many times András and Anna lobbied for them to give up, but Salvo never wavered and neither did Daniel, which was enough to convince the younger ones to keep trying. Then, only two weeks before the F-F began its 1959 tour, they did it without incident two, three, four, five times in a row. From then on they never fell. They had done the impossible, and even András and Anna were unable to prevent themselves from feeling proud and thrilled and excited.

The F-F would open at Madison Square Garden, as it did every year. The Ursaris would perform their new act, one they were sure would make circus history. Upon seeing the act in the dress rehearsal, Martin Fisher-Fielding ordered that they shelve it immediately. Furious, Salvo stormed into his office.

"Why are you doing this?"

"It's too dangerous, Salvo. I can't have this risk."

"It is not too dangerous."

"Are you kidding? I've never seen anything like it."

"I know. And that is why people will come to see it."

"Salvo, I—"

"Remember that I helped you once. You made me a promise. Keep it now."

Martin Fisher-Fielding rubbed the back of his neck and paced the floor. "Will you at least use a net?"

"No," Salvo said. "That would make it truly dangerous."

Martin shook his head in disbelief. "All right. Have it your way. But remember that I voiced these concerns."

"You will change your mind after tonight," Salvo said. "Thank you."

As he walked away, Martin thought that this Ursari was either a genius or a madman, or both. He continued this line of thought as he sat in his seat that night, waiting nervously for the Ursaris to go on. Finally it was their turn, and as they took to the wire all eyes shifted skyward.

The first part of the act he had seen before. The crowd responded with mediocre enthusiasm, and he could hear chatter throughout the stands. Then, as the final trick began, silence descended. This was something no one had ever seen.

They walked in unison onto the wire, a three-level, eight-person pyramid. There were four on the bottom, each pair connected by a harness supporting a pole. Salvo was in front, connected to Etel. Behind them, András was connected to Daniel. Standing on the pole between Salvo and Etel was Anna, with János on the pole between András and Daniel. Anna and János were joined like the others, and on their pole stood Elsabeth and Mika, a foot apart. Jacob Blacke had scrambled down the ladder from the platform they had begun on and was on his way up the other side, towards their destination.

All Martin could hear was the heavy breathing of the man sitting next to him. The pyramid moved as if it were a single entity, stepping forward, pausing, stepping again. They all moved with Salvo, as perfectly as if there were strings pulling their bodies with his. When they reached the midpoint of the wire, they stopped. At the top of the pyramid Mika, who was the further back of the twins, pivoted to face the way they had come, the opposite direction of the others. Then both she and Elsabeth lowered their torsos and, placing their hands on the shoulders of Jacob and Anna, slowly lifted their legs from the pole, into the air, upwards until their feet met—a handstand at a sixty-five-degree angle. The effect was such that it appeared as though there were a three-storey house on the high wire. The crowd let out a collective gasp.

The girls held their handstands for ten seconds, then brought their feet back to the pole as the pyramid began to move again. The crowd came to its feet, and by the time the Ursaris reached the platform, the applause was so loud and so fervent that Martin was afraid they would riot. For fifteen minutes they continued unabated—even after the Ursaris returned to the wire to acknowledge and bow four times—ignoring the band when it began to play, unwilling to watch the next act, which began and gave up twice. From them on, the Ursaris were always the final act, and Martin thanked his lucky stars that he had let Salvo talk him into letting them do "the House."

By the end of the 1959 run, the Ursari name was forever etched into the minds of circus-goers across North America. They were on the covers of magazines and newspapers, the subject of television documentaries, and there had even been talk of a movie based on their lives. Salvo shielded the younger ones from as much of this publicity as he could, doing most of the interviews by himself or with Anna. The girls were particularly vulnerable, he figured, and he tried to make life as normal for them as possible.

After the show went to winter quarters they returned to Canada, even though the rest of the circus went to the sunny weather of Florida. People laughed at them, unable to fathom why they would prefer a harsh Canadian winter to a tropical one, and no one believed Salvo when he told them that the weather in the Fraser Valley was anything but harsh. It rained a lot, and Salvo liked the rain. He supposed he liked it because of his memories of the drought in Transylvania, but there was more to it than that. He liked how it washed everything clean, how you could go out in the rain and be a part of it, and then how you could go into your house and feel like you were safe in a nest while outside the world flooded. He never got that feeling in Florida, unless there was a hurricane blowing through, and the constant drizzle of home was preferable to a hurricane by far.

In their farming community, no one cared that they were the Magnificent Ursari Troupe. While they were not exactly treated like ordinary people, they were certainly not regarded as celebrities. For the most part they were left alone. The odd person would get a little annoying, but nothing like the people in New York or Chicago or Los Angeles.

The Ursaris were, for maybe the first time since they had left the F-F, truly happy. Salvo revelled in the success of the act, not only able to sleep without trouble but passing most of his days without worry. His only concern was keeping everyone on top of their wire skills, ensuring that no one slacked off and jeopardized the act, but everyone was good about working hard and taking direction from him, so there was little problem in remaining in prime form. They were professionals, after all.

András and Etel remained reserved, as usual, but when remembering the applause of the crowd they glowed. There were times when neither of them could believe that where they had once been hungry, unloved and despised, now they were celebrated and lauded wherever they went. András took this knowledge in stride, but Etel was sometimes suspicious of their success; surely it could not last forever. Sooner or later, someone would stand up and point out that they were, after all, merely humans, and that it was only a silly wire act. But it had not happened yet, and the longer things went on, the less Etel thought it would.

Daniel Ursari had much of Salvo in him. He lived for the time they were performing, for the sound of the people below, to hear the complete silence of their attention and then the complete mayhem of their approval. He never thought about falling, about how the people below felt that at any minute their House would tumble down. That was not why he walked. He walked because when he was on the wire, he was not a socially awkward orphan of a circus fire, with bad skin and cowlicked hair, he was Daniel Ursari, aerialist, master of gravity. He was a living superhero. There was no feeling like it he had ever known.

János, the best on the wire of the younger ones and probably better than Anna, too, would probably have been happy no matter where he was. He was able to be quietly content almost anywhere, equally at ease on the wire as he was on the train or at a restaurant. He did not seem to care where he was, so long as he was with his family, and so long as everyone else was happy.

Elsabeth and Mika, so similar in appearance, both loved the wire but for very different reasons. Mika liked people looking at her, the attention she received, and being able to do something that few people could do. And there was a way that some people looked at her, usually men and in particular Jacob Blacke, that she especially liked. Elsabeth didn't care whether people looked at her, and she didn't really even care whether they liked the act or not. What she liked was the Fisher-Fielding Extravaganza, the circus atmosphere, all the other acts and the people and the sights she had never seen. She would have been as content to go to the circus as a spectator as she was to be a performer.

Anna did not love walking the wire. She did not love the attention the act had received, and she did not love the circus. Yet when she saw how much joy their success had brought not only Salvo but also their children, her heart could not help but swell, and her grin was large and genuine. She was always happiest when they were not performing, and winter hiatus was her favourite time of year by far. She looked forward to Christmas with their family, to a tree and presents and a few days away from the wire. They got a tree, and though she was not much of a cook, she knew enough to pull off a turkey and trimmings, and this she was determined to do.

Christmas morning the household woke early, and the children (who were hardly children) rushed to the tree to see what was under it for them. Salvo and András and Etel had never really understood many Western Christmas customs, but they couldn't help but be excited. They all chattered away as paper was ripped, Elsabeth and Mika squealing with delight as they opened tiny boxes from their parents. The boxes contained sterling-silver pendants in the shape of their initials; Salvo had ordered them all the way from Montreal, months in advance, and had a hard time resisting the temptation to give the gifts early. He felt a certain sense of regret that these were the first personally meaningful gifts he had ever given them. They would turn seventeen in a couple of months, and it would not be long before they would be of an age where children often left their parents. He hoped that the act would keep them close, but there was no way to be certain. The girls gave Anna and then Salvo tight hugs in thanks, and Salvo squeezed Anna's hand. Anna smiled. She was having a moment she would never forget, and she knew it.

<hr />

For six years the "Ursari House" had been the premier act in the Fisher-Fielding Extravaganza, which was once again the undisputed heavyweight of the North American circus world. By 1964, however, gate receipts were falling, and attendance was the lowest it had been since the post-fire years. The big cities still packed the houses, but in the mid-sized cities it was not unusual to play to half-full arenas. The F-F no longer went to smaller cities; since the big tops disappeared, no circuses did.

Despite this downturn, things were good for Martin Fisher-Fielding. Since his coup in 1957 he had faced no serious threats to his leadership. Norris Fisher-Fielding had all but abandoned his hopes of regaining the helm of the F-F; with Martin's control of the majority vote, the only way he could ever outvote him was if one of the Respectables gave him their shares, which was not likely to happen. The Respectables did not tend to give things away. He had tried to purchase their shares through a third party, but the deal had been closely scrutinized, and in the end it was ruled to have violated the original agreement and was nullified.

It was midway through the season, and the F-F had just closed out a show in Columbus, Ohio, heading to Cleveland for a three-night stand. On the train Mika Ursari sat, trying to think of a way to tell her parents the news of her engagement. She had for three years now been seeing Jacob Blacke behind her father's back, and she knew full well he likely would not approve of her marrying him. He was, after all, ten years her senior, but that wasn't what would bother her father. For some reason Mika could not understand, Salvo looked down on Jacob because he was a farmer. Everyone, including Salvo, knew that this made little sense, but it remained a fact. Mika didn't care, and she didn't care what her father said. She was twenty-one and could do what she liked.

Mika asked her mother for help, and Anna set Salvo up. He didn't notice when the railcar emptied in a stream of various excuses, leaving only himself, Anna and Mika present. Jacob, timid as ever, had declined to be present. Mika could not understand why he was so afraid of Salvo, but she agreed to tell them herself. He was her father, and she would deal with him.

The best way, she decided, was to get right to the point, to lay things out as they were. "Jacob and I are getting married" is what she told him, her voice steady and her face composed.

Salvo reeled, unprepared for any sort of grand announcement. "You're what?"

"Jacob and I are getting married," she repeated.

"Jacob Blacke?"

"Yes."

"When was this decided?"

"A while ago."

"I see." Salvo's eyes narrowed, as they always did when he was angry.

"Salvo," Anna began, her voice low and calming, "Jacob is a fine man. He has always done well by you."

Salvo nodded. "He is a good man, and I am glad to have him in my troupe. But I will not allow him to marry my daughter."

"I suppose you have some reason for denying us," Mika said, her voice rising a little.

Salvo was silent. He stared at Mika, noticing not for the first time how much she resembled her mother in both appearance and temperament. "You can do better," he said finally.

"That is for me to decide," Mika said. She stood up and went to the door. "I will marry him, and you can either agree or I can disappear. It's up to you." She slid the door open and stepped out.

"You will do as I say," Salvo shouted after her, anger in his voice. The door closed.

Salvo leapt to his feet, but Anna stopped him from following her. "What have I done?" he said. "Why do I get such defiance from my children?"

"They are adults now," Anna answered. "We can't tell them what to do."

"They will listen."

"No, they won't."

Salvo slumped into his chair, suddenly looking very tired. Anna sat beside him, reaching for his hand. "Why do you disapprove of Jacob?" she said.

"He is not good enough for her."

"That," Anna said, "is what my father said about you."

Salvo looked at her, rubbed his forehead, and exhaled a long breath.

"She'll do it anyway, so you may as well make peace."

Salvo nodded. She was right; she had learned this lesson hard. "I will speak to her."

Anna squeezed his hand. "It's no fun getting old."

"We're not old."

"I'm not. But you've been younger."

Salvo laughed. If someone had told him in Budapest that he would someday be fifty-four years old, he would not have believed them. Now he felt as though he would live another fifty years and still be a child.

They arrived in Cleveland in the early afternoon and had a couple of hours to rest before that night's performance. Salvo was never able to nap before a walk, so he went to the arena to check the rigging. He was surprised to see András and János there, sitting side by side under the wire. They both wore grave looks, watching him approach with obvious trepidation.

"What is the matter with you two?" Salvo asked jokingly. Neither of them answered him, and Salvo asked the question again, this time seriously.

András looked at János, then at Salvo. "He has lost his nerve."

"Who, János?"

"Yes."

"What do you mean?"

"I cannot go on the wire, Uncle," János said, shame on his face.

"Of course you can. You are a wonderful wire walker."

"I can't," he said, shaking his head.

"I do not understand."

242

"I can't explain it. Something inside me has broken."

"If he walks, he will fall," András said. "He is afraid. He should not walk with fear."

"We all have fear," Salvo said. "It is what keeps us careful. A little fear is a good thing."

"It is not a little fear." András put his arm around the boy. "The thought of going up makes him shake. It is best for everyone that he stops."

Salvo looked at János, who had tears streaming down his face, and he knew that András spoke correctly. Still, the boy was one of the most gifted walkers Salvo had ever seen, and he did not like the thought of him quitting. "All right," he said. "Why don't you take a break, sit out a couple of days, and then see how you feel."

János nodded. "Okay. But I don't think this will get better."

Salvo smiled. "Wait and see. Maybe you'll surprise yourself."

András and Salvo moved out of János's earshot. "He's lost it completely," András said.

"He should sit out. But he should not make any final decisions. He can assist on the platform for now."

András looked back at János. "I do not think he will change his mind."

"Maybe not. But you can never tell. Jacob can work his spot, and if he wants to come back, there will be a place for him."

András nodded. But he knew János would not be back.

ELSABETH AND MIKA SAT ON A BENCH in the performers' area. Mika slumped, dangling her arms, stretching them out. Elsabeth slowly rotated a sore wrist, watching her sister out of the corner of her eye. She wished that Mika had waited until the winter break to tell their father about her engagement. The wire was hard enough without having people mad at each other, and it was stressful for everyone to have disagreements going on while they lived in such close quarters. If only everyone could get along, things would go smoothly and easily. How much happier we all would be, she thought.

Elsabeth was bored. She was bored with her entire life, bored of herself. She had no idea what to do about it, and hadn't told anyone else of her feelings, not even Mika. She knew most people would laugh at her; how could her life be boring? She travelled across the continent with the circus, performed death-defying feats and was famous. What could be boring about that? she wondered. And yet it was.

She had never really had a friend, she supposed. Mika was a friend, but she was her twin sister so it was different, and other than that there were only Daniel and János, who were kind enough and dear to her, but they were relatives too, not friends. Being a Ursari had isolated her from other people her age, and it wore her down. Elsabeth was always tired, even when she slept for hours and hours, and nothing could stop her from yawning all day long. She wondered whether she would ever wake up.

"I don't understand why he has to be this way," Mika said, snapping Elsabeth out of her thoughts.

"It's just the way he is."

"That's not an excuse."

Elsabeth shrugged. "What can you do?"

"Nice attitude," Mika said. "This affects you too, you know— or one day it will. Unless you plan on marrying the president, or God, no one will be good enough."

"I don't see it coming up anytime soon. I don't even know any men. Unless I marry Daniel or János."

"I wonder if Dad would allow that."

"Gross."

The girls laughed at this conjecture. Then Mika's face hardened and she clenched her teeth. "It isn't funny. Sometimes I really hate him."

Elsabeth said nothing. She didn't hate their father, but she thought she might if she were Mika. Elsabeth had never experienced an emotion as strong as hate, and wondered what it was like. She was almost jealous of her sister, and it made her feel pathetic.

ETEL CLIMBED THE LADDER to the platform, the second last to do so. Salvo went first, as he always did, then Anna, the twins, Daniel and Jacob, András and finally Etel. Usually János went before András, and Jacob usually went last, but tonight János was going last because he would be the one to set up the gear for the House, and would not be going on the wire. Etel was sorry for her nephew, but she could not understand how the boy had lost his nerve so suddenly. Such comprehension was not within her.

Already on the platform, Salvo cast his thoughts back to his conversation with Jacob a quarter-hour earlier. He had first explained that János did not want to walk for a while, and that Jacob would be doing the House. Jacob did not normally do the House, but he knew it and had done it in practice many times, as well as having filled in when someone was sick. Salvo had confidence in him, not nearly as much as he had in János, but confidence nonetheless. Then, before he left, Salvo had extended his hand to Jacob, and told him that he would welcome him into the Ursari family as a son-in-law. Jacob had taken his hand and promised him that he would treat Mika well, and Salvo had believed him.

As Mika gained the platform she shot Salvo an angry look, and he knew that she had not yet spoken with Jacob. He smiled to himself, knowing she would feel ashamed when she found out, and he resolved not to tease her too badly. It would be a happy time later tonight, and he would break out a bottle of rye, maybe two. You are a lucky man, he said to himself. He looked down and saw that the juggling act that preceded them was nearly finished and began to mentally prepare himself.

He willed his mind blank and envisioned himself performing the act flawlessly, felt his muscles flow across the wire. He did this for several minutes, then he heard the band play the jugglers off, and it was time for the Ursaris to start.

Salvo stepped onto the wire, his balancing pole gripped firmly in his hands. He crossed the wire by himself, doing a handstand in the middle, wavering slightly to sell it. Then he returned to the platform, and András, Daniel and Mika went out. András and Daniel held a pole between them, and Mika braced it around her midsection and spun around it, once, twice, three times. The crowd liked this one, and showed their approval loudly. The Ursaris did the bicycle tricks, followed by Etel's blindfolded solo walk. Then Salvo lay on his back in the middle of the wire, and Anna walked across, stepping on his stomach as she crossed over him. He winked up at her, and she smiled.

As Salvo reached the platform, he noticed Daniel had the strangest look on his face—he was white as a ghost—but he didn't ask him what was the matter. It was time to build the House. He joined himself with Jacob, who had switched places with Etel, who usually walked directly behind Salvo. When they were harnessed together János passed them their balancing poles, and they stepped forward four feet onto the wire. Behind them, András joined himself with Daniel, the last one on the bottom row. Then Anna leapt onto the pole between Salvo and Jacob, and Etel between András and Daniel. János passed Etel and Anna a harness, which they placed over their shoulders. There were no straps in these harnesses; a U-shaped piece of metal went over each shoulder, and the pole joined a crosspiece at chest level, in the front or back depending on what the performer's position was. Anna and Etel took their balancing poles, and Mika and Elsabeth mounted the pole between them. Salvo received a signal from János that all was ready. With a tilt of his head they started out.

Immediately János began the climb down the ladder to the ground, where he would rush to the other side of the stage and then climb back up to the far platform in time to help the others disassemble the House. This was normally Jacob's job, and he was pretty good, but he usually only barely made it. Salvo wasn't sure if János was as fast going up and down the ladder as Jacob.

He did not think about this prospect as he crossed the wire. He concentrated on timing his movements to the exact moment that the others would move; even though they followed his lead, he tried to anticipate their emulations. When they reached the centre of the wire he stopped, and he could tell by the crowd that Elsabeth and Mika were upside down. They held this longer than usual and Salvo wondered whether they weren't buying János some time. When he saw that János was nearly halfway up the ladder he knew that the boy would make it, so he decided instead that Mika was probably making some kind of point. He heard a sigh from the crowd when the twins were down, and to make a point of his own, he delayed several seconds before starting forward again.

Salvo felt a slight tug at his harness, an indication that those behind him were not following. He stopped, but it was too late. The wire jolted underneath his feet and the House collapsed.

They were falling. Hands released balancing poles, reaching out—some finding reward and others not. Salvo fell straight onto the wire, wrapping his legs around it, ignoring the pain as his right leg bent beyond its normal capacity. Knowing what had happened, he blindly reached out and grabbed Anna as she fell past him, his grip poor at first, better once he had a chance to adjust it. Etel hung onto the wire beside him, leaning her waist over it, her left hand clutching the wire, her right reaching out to steady herself. Further back, András dangled by his fingertips; he was having a hard time holding on. Jacob was beside him, almost sitting, and he moved to help András better his grip. Below people were screaming hysterically, and Salvo wished they would be quiet. He looked down and only then did he see Daniel lying on his back, his body flailing wildly, like he was being electrocuted. Not far from him lay Mika and Elsabeth. Neither of them moved. Between them spread a puddle of what he knew could only be blood. Anna tried in vain to look down, but it was impossible for her to see them from where she was, and her efforts were compromising Salvo's grip on her arm.

On the ground circus staff scrambled to erect a makeshift net for those still on the wire. By the time Anna and then András dropped into the net, medical staff had already strapped Daniel onto a gurney and taken him to the hospital. They did the same for Mika and Elsabeth, but there was less haste. Once Anna and András were safe, Jacob was able to make it to the platform on his own, as were Salvo and Etel. János was there waiting, his face bloodless and his hands shaking. They rushed down the ladder, Jacob running in the direction they had taken Mika, and Etel and János following Salvo to the net.

Salvo took Anna in his arms, holding her tightly before he allowed the paramedics to take them all to the hospital. Anna wept fiercely, knowing that Elsabeth and Mika were dead and that Daniel was near to it, if he wasn't dead already. She did not have to tell Salvo that the world had fallen.

SALVO WAS THE ONLY ONE of them who was not injured. Anna's shoulder had dislocated when Salvo caught her, and her knee was badly twisted. Jacob pulled both his hamstrings, and András had been hit in the head by Daniel's pole, bruising him badly and giving him a concussion. Etel had internal bleeding, having hit the wire hard. Even János was hurt; he sprained his ankle going down the ladder.

Daniel's injuries were the most serious. His spine was broken in three places, but miraculously he was not paralyzed. He had slipped into a coma, however, and it was unclear when or if he would regain consciousness. There were internal injuries as well, but the doctors were not sure exactly how serious they were.

In three days' time there would be a funeral for Mika and Elsabeth.

THE DAY AFTER THE FALL, Salvo went to see Martin Fisher-Fielding. Martin was sombre, obviously shaken by what had happened. He felt partially responsible, having known how dangerous the act was and still letting them do it, because it was good and it sold tickets.

Salvo tried to reassure him. "It is not your fault. We would have done it in a different circus if you had said no."

Martin bit his lip, knowing Salvo indeed would have. "What happened up there?" he asked.

"I don't know. Someone made a mistake, I guess. I don't know who."

"I'm so sorry, Salvo."

"I know."

"If you ever want to come back, there will always be a place for you in the F-F."

"Thank you. I think we will need some time off to recover. But I will walk tonight."

Martin stopped short. "What?"

"I know it is a solo walk, and that it is not so good an act. But I want to walk tonight."

"Salvo, I don't think—"

"I would consider it a favour."

Martin looked at Salvo and saw he was determined. He knew it was not a good idea, but he could not deny him. "All right. But be careful."

"Thank you." Salvo turned and left, not closing the door behind him. His mind was preoccupied and his heart heavy.

That night Salvo walked, and for the first time in his life, the world did not recede when he stepped onto the wire. He knew that this walk was different. He was not walking for himself, and he was not walking for the wire. Salvo walked for his girls; it was the only way he knew to honour them.

He used no pole and the band played no music. The audience watched silently, everyone aware of what had happened the night before, aware of what it must be costing this man to be on the wire. As he reached the spot where they had fallen, Salvo Ursari knelt, placing his hands on the wire. The audience did not know that in his mind Salvo was touching their eyelids, gently forcing them closed, a task someone else had done before he had reached them. He stayed kneeling for a very long time, but no one below moved an inch. Finally he rose and continued, his tears dropping from the wire and soaking into the sawdust on the ground without a sound. As he finished and collapsed to the floor of the platform, the audience applauded tentatively, aware that they had witnessed something they did not fully comprehend. Though in later years Salvo's memory of that day would be blurred by fatigue and grief, no one down below would ever forget it.

SEVEN

The second half of the 1964 circus season brought the lowest attendance figures in the Fisher-Fielding Extravaganza's history. Whether this was a result of the Ursaris' fall or whether it had been coming anyway was a matter for speculation, but either way there was little denying that the glory days of the F-F were at an end. Martin was unable to think of anything that would bring them back; at the end of it all was the cold hard fact that people just weren't interested in the magic that made the circus great. There was no way to reverse this change, it seemed. He doubted even Cole himself could have made things any better, but he often wished the old man were still alive so that they could try.

That year the Fisher-Fielding Circus Company barely broke even, and it was more than likely that it would lose money the following year. Many within the organization wanted to sell the show; despite the seeming futility of going on, there had been substantial offers made by outside interests for the company. But since Martin owned a controlling share there was little anyone could do until he made a move.

Martin considered his options long and hard. Were this not a family business, the life's blood of his father and his aunts and uncles, he would have sold long ago. Instead, he decided to push forward. When Charlotte Fisher-Fielding died, Martin immediately bought up her one-seventh of the company. Neither Norris nor his mother and stepfather had the money to do this, and even Martin had to borrow heavily to make the purchase. A provision in the original partnership agreement allowed him to nullify the clause that had prohibited the sale of Respectable shares; the founders had stipulated that once someone controlled more than four of the seven F-F holdings, they could change the company charter. Nearly all of the Respectables were willing to sell him their shares, seeing, as everyone else did, that the circus would never again be as profitable as it had once been. This development further infuriated the remaining Spouses, but they had little recourse. When the dust had settled Martin controlled just under five-sevenths of the Fisher-Fielding Circus Company, with only Rebecca Fisher-Fielding-Barnes and Phillip Barnes holding a remaining seventh each, and one stubborn old Respectable holding on to his fractional interest because he liked the idea of owning part of a circus. Many wondered why Martin was going to such pains to take control of an obviously failing business, and his sanity was even questioned in some circles.

For eight weeks Daniel Ursari lay unconscious, and then, just when the doctors thought it unlikely he would ever wake up, he opened his eyes and rejoined the world. It would take another year for his bones to heal, but he would live. He would never walk the wire again, doctors said. His heels had been shattered so badly that it would always be painful for him to put weight on them, and certainly he would never be able to meet the physical demands of the wire. He said nothing when they told him this news. Though there was nothing physically preventing him from speaking, he had not uttered a single word since regaining consciousness.

Anna went to visit him every day, and finally when he was well enough to be moved they took him back to the farm, installing him in the upstairs room he once shared with János. From his bed he could see the door to the room that had been his sisters', and as he lay recovering, he tried hard not to look in that direction, but always his eyes found their way to the empty space of the entrance.

The fall was never mentioned, nor was the wire; when Salvo came to see him he, too, did not speak. Salvo sat beside the bed, as silent as Daniel, and hours would pass without either of them moving. When Salvo left he would gently squeeze Daniel's arm before going.

Every day Salvo went through the fall in his mind. He had seen so little, his back being turned to the others, and he could not figure out what had gone wrong. That he had no idea what caused the fall troubled him greatly; if the source of something could not be identified, there was no way to prevent it from happening in the future. And despite all that had happened, Salvo had every intention of returning the House to the wire. It would not be the same without Mika and Elsabeth. The thought of them would always bring him pain, but there was nothing he could do to change that. His feelings were simple, and they had been steady throughout his life. The dead die and are buried, and the living go on. He was not cold about their passing. He felt the girls' deaths as deeply as anyone, except perhaps Anna, but he could not let their deaths kill him too. The wire was his life and he would walk again.

Anna vowed she would never again set foot on the wire, and no one doubted that she meant it. She refused to even speak of the wire and removed all photographs of the family performing from the walls, placing them in a box in the attic and never looking at them again. She was angry—a slow, hard anger that seeped its way into her every thought and action—and after a while she forgot how to *not* be angry. Most of all she was angry with Salvo. It was he who had put them on the wire, he who had thought up this needlessly dangerous trick, he who had talked everyone into performing it. They had enjoyed a good life on their farm, and were it not for Salvo's unbending selfishness, they would still be enjoying it. Now her girls were dead, and she was left with this crippled orphan son who was not really even hers. Though she had never thought it possible, she sometimes wondered if she hated her husband.

WITH THE MONEY THEY HAD MADE IN THE F-F, András and Etel bought a small house several miles down the road from Salvo and Anna's farm. András was fifty-six years old, and a hard life was beginning to catch up with him. He spent his nights coughing, and in the days he sat in a chair in the front room and listened to records, any Romany music he could find. He knew he had turned his back on his heritage, that he had all but become a *gadjo*, and for this he felt a pain that nothing seemed able to soothe. He had done what he could, he knew, raising Etel and then János, and knew that if he had stayed in Europe, he would likely have died in Hitler's camps like so many other Roma, but this fact did little to console him. When he realized that he and Etel no longer spoke to each other in Romany, and that János spoke only English, he knew that with himself and his siblings would die a thousand years of Ursari Roma. The name and blood would live on in his son, but this boy was a Canadian, not a Rom, and what was more, it was a good thing for him that it was such. János knew of their stories but never told them to others, and András doubted he would live to see his grandchildren to tell his stories to them. András knew this would make his father turn in his grave, and he felt shame.

Etel, who had no memory of either of her parents and knew them only in story, felt none of this disappointment. In fact, she felt nothing. Etel Ursari was completely devoid of emotion, and she knew it, and she did not care. She believed herself a ghost, a machine, and though every night in her sleep she saw images of the fall, she was completely detached from it, as if she were watching a movie that had failed to engage her. She had been turned off and had no desire to be turned back on. She spent her days cleaning a house that did not need cleaning.

For whatever reasons, both András and Etel failed to notice that János was acting strangely. Maybe it was because the change was gradual, or maybe it was because there was no one thing that marked a transformation. Either way, János's entire attitude towards life had shifted. He was easily disturbed or excited, and he was getting more and more reckless as time went on. He bought a car and drove it with little or no regard for his own safety, putting it in the ditch several times in the first month he had it. He was not harmed in any of these minor mishaps, which had an unfortunate impact: János believed he was invincible.

János was alone. Of the four children who had grown up on the Ursari farm, he was the only one who was not killed or severely injured in the fall. That it was largely because he had the sense to quit the wire at the right time did not factor into his thinking. After the fall, there was nothing that could harm him. Death was obviously not interested in claiming him. It had touched everyone else. He could see how his father and aunts and uncle were faring, and Daniel's condition was not getting better. Only János, in his own mind, was untouched by the fall. If anything, it had made him stronger.

In the spring Salvo decided that he would put in some corn. Since they had begun performing the House he had not been growing crops, but now he felt he should be doing something, and tending to the farm seemed as good a thing as any. He telephoned Jacob, hoping he would help him with the seeding, but no one answered the phone at his parents' farm. After several days of attempting to reach him by phone, Salvo got into his truck and drove to the Blacke farm.

As he got out of his truck, the front door of the farmhouse opened, and Mrs. Blacke came out. She was a small woman, older than Salvo, her hair thin and white. She came down the front steps and stopped ten feet from him.

"Go away," she said.

"I need to speak to Jacob," Salvo said soothingly, thinking the old woman was likely a bit senile.

"You are no friend of his."

"Yes, I am. I am Salvo Ursari."

"I know who you are." The woman spat on the ground and stared at him defiantly.

Salvo was taken aback, not knowing what he had done to anger this woman or make her hate him so. As he wondered what his course of action should be, the door to the house opened again and Jacob stepped into the doorway.

"Jacob," Salvo called, and was surprised when he didn't respond. Jacob looked awful. He appeared to have aged ten years in the three months since Salvo had spoken to him, and under his eyes, which were red and blinked as they came into the light, there were black bags. "Jacob," Salvo repeated.

"Why are you here?" Jacob asked, his voice raspy.

"I need your help with some corn."

"What?"

"Corn. I'm putting in some corn."

"And you think I will help you?" Jacob was incredulous.

Salvo paused. "I was hoping—"

"I'm all right, Mother. Please wait for me in the house." Mrs. Blacke hesitated, then retreated into the house, placing a hand on Jacob's shoulder as she passed him in the doorway. He stepped forward and pulled the door closed. "I would sooner piss on your grave than help you," Jacob said.

Salvo could not believe his ears. "What have I done to you?"

Jacob laughed a sarcastic laugh. "That you don't know speaks volumes."

"I do not understand."

"You wouldn't."

"I didn't cause the fall."

"I'm only going to tell you this once: Get away from me, and don't ever come back. I don't ever want to see your face again. Understand?"

"Jacob—"

"Go. Now." Jacob went into the house, closing the door behind him.

Salvo stood there for a moment, then got into his truck and drove home, stunned.

All day long Etel had known something bad was going to happen. The feeling had crept into her bones like a draft, and nothing she did would shake it. When the call came, she was almost relieved.

She and András rushed to the hospital where János was in serious but stable condition. Drunk at two o'clock in the afternoon, he had driven his car into a telephone pole, destroying both the car and the pole and badly injuring himself. The police were at a loss to explain the accident; witnesses reported that he hadn't been going particularly fast, and he had made no attempt whatsoever to avoid the pole. It was assumed he had passed out and lost control of the car, something neither Etel nor András believed.

Etel called Salvo and Anna from the emergency room, and the four of them sat together while János underwent surgery to repair a lacerated kidney and a punctured lung. It was the first time the four of them had been together for any length of time since returning to Canada. At first no one spoke much. For three hours they sat in near silence, until Anna could bear it no longer.

"Why do so many bad things happen to this family?" she said, standing up.

"We are Ursari," András answered. "It has been happening forever."

"I am not Ursari," Anna said.

"Then it must be your own bad luck."

"We have made our luck," Etel said. "And it is not all bad. Once we were the best wire walkers in the world."

"Look where that got us," Anna said.

"We could be the best again," Salvo said.

Etel looked incredulously at Salvo. "You don't actually believe that, do you?"

"I am not sure," he said.

"I will never step on a wire again as long as I live," Anna said. She jammed her hands in the pockets of her coat and walked down the hall towards the cafeteria.

"Nor I," András said when she was gone

Salvo began to speak, but András cut him off. "This is not your decision, Salvo. For thirty years I have walked the wire with you, and always I let you be in charge. Most times you were right, but there were times when you were not, and bad things happened. I am not saying these things were your fault. Probably they were not. But it is time for me to be the one who says what I do, and I say I will not go back to the wire. I have no love for it left. The price has been too high."

Salvo turned to Etel. "And you?"

"I could walk again," Etel said. "I was always happy on the wire, and I do not regret what we have done. Bad things happened, but bad things happened before the wire and they will happen again. But I do not think I will walk any longer. I am not young any more, and we will never be what we were. I will miss the wire, but it is done for me."

"But what about—"

"You must understand," András said, "that the wire has never been for us what it is for you. Any fool can see that on the wire you are a different person. There is where you are alive. But we are not like that. We can live on the ground. We don't need the wire the way you do."

Salvo leaned back in his chair and thought about this, trying to understand what András had said. "Why did you walk all these years?"

"Because it was better than not walking. It was exciting. We were famous, people loved us, and we made money. That is not bad for an orphaned Rom," András said.

"But you would have walked for free," Etel said.

Salvo knew this was true. He had never much cared what the F-F had paid. "I am sorry," he said.

Etel smiled. "Do not be sorry. We are not complaining. We are simply stopping."

Anna returned with a tray holding four cups of coffee just as a doctor arrived, holding a clipboard and looking very serious. "András Ursari?" he asked, looking at the three of them.

András stepped forward, fear washing over his face. "Yes."

"Your son is out of surgery. The operation went well, and he should be awake in a few hours. You may see him then."

"He will live?"

"It's too soon to say for sure, but it looks like he will recover."

"Thank you."

The doctor smiled a slight smile, then retreated behind a set of swinging doors.

Etel shook her head. "That boy is lucky," she said.

"He will not think himself lucky when I get a hold of him," András said. "There will be no more of this foolishness."

Salvo and Anna left soon after that; Daniel could not be left alone in the house for more than a few hours at a time. On the way home, Salvo told Anna that the act was over, that the others would not walk any more.

"I will not pretend that I am sorry to hear it," she said.

"They are not angry. They are simply finished."

"I am not angry either," Anna said, but neither of them believed her. They drove the rest of the way home in silence.

ONE MORNING WHEN ANNA RETURNED from a trip to the grocery store and began to fill the cupboards, Salvo looked up at her from the kitchen table, where he sat, motionless. She was shocked when he suddenly burst into tears, burying his hands in his face. "What is wrong?" she asked.

"Daniel hates me," he said, collecting himself. "That is why he will not speak."

"He does not hate you," Anna said.

"Yes, he does," Salvo said. "And so do you."

"No," Anna said. Her voice surprised her with its lack of conviction.

"Yes. It is not hard to see. You just don't know it yet."

Anna considered this theory, and as she considered it, she knew it was true. "They are dead," she said.

"Because of me."

She wanted to tell him that he was wrong, but she could not. Anna nodded, swallowing. "And because of me. It is both our faults. Maybe I do hate you. But I hate myself too. We have done an awful thing."

Salvo was on the verge of tears again. "What are we going to do?"

"I don't know," Anna said. She did not move closer to Salvo. She picked up her cup of tea and went into the other room.

Salvo followed her. "I'm sorry," he said.

"It doesn't matter how sorry you are. Of course you're sorry. But that doesn't change anything, does it?"

Salvo said nothing.

"Maybe you lived for the wire. That's your problem. But I never did. What I lived for was you, and the children. So tell me, what's left for me?"

Salvo wanted to tell her that he was left, but he couldn't. Instead they sat in silence, until finally it was time for Anna to give Daniel his food and medicine. She left Salvo alone. He sunk his head into his hands and wondered if things would ever be good again, if there was any way to recover.

Then Salvo had a moment of unusual clarity, struck with an understanding he had never reached before. When his parents were killed, when the F-F burned, when the House had collapsed, though others near him had always been hurt, even killed, he had always managed to escape physical harm. He had stood on the steeple of a doomed church, and he had cast out his soul. He tried to live a life without pain. And though his body remained unscarred, he had caused and received more than one man's share of sorrow in his life and, until the death of Elsabeth and Mika, had tried to feel nothing. But this, he thought, is something I can no longer do.

For the first time since 1919, Salvo turned his eyes heavenward. What he offered up was not a prayer, not yet, but it was close.

I have lived for a long time, God, thought Salvo. It has taken me until now to see the things I have done. I have been on the wire and I have not fallen, and it does not matter. A man who is not alive cannot die. I was never invincible. We are all glass soldiers.

ONE SUMMER MORNING ANNA went into Daniel's room and he was not there. What she would think odd later was how her first thought was that he must have ascended to heaven. She rushed out of the room and found Daniel leaning heavily on the wall, working his way towards the stairs. When he saw her he fell, and after she got him back to his bed, he refused to give her any clue as to what he had been trying to do.

If he had spoken, Daniel might have told her that he was trying to get away from them. He would have told her that he was an epileptic, and that he'd hidden the fact from them, at first out of shame and then because he knew he would not be able to walk the wire if his problem were known. He would have told her how he'd had a seizure on the wire, first freezing, then, after he hit the ground, full on. He was surprised he hadn't had one since the fall; he supposed that the many pain medications he was on somehow prevented them.

After Salvo, the wire had meant the most to Daniel. His adopted father had been like a god to him for as long as he could remember, and Daniel had wished for nothing more than to be like him. Whenever he was on the wire, Daniel had pretended he was Salvo, and that was what had given him the courage to walk the wire.

Now everything was ruined. That no one knew he had caused the fall made it worse, because he knew he could never tell them, and he knew that for the rest of his life he would live in fear that they would find out. Combined with this painful secret was the certain knowledge that he would never walk the wire again, and that he had killed his sisters and ruined his father and mother. He had smelled sunflowers. There had been time for him to back out of the House, but he had gone anyway, because he didn't want to give up his secret. It needn't have happened, he knew, with a pain worse than any broken back.

Daniel resolved that as soon as he was able, he would go far away and never come back. If there was a way short of suicide for him to get away from himself, he would do that too.

IT WAS ALWAYS LITTLE THINGS that began it. Earlier in his life Salvo's fears had been recurring ones, but now they could be found in things he had never given two thoughts to before. One sunny Sunday he and Anna took a drive into Vancouver, and they had a picnic on the beach looking out on English Bay and the Pacific Ocean. Salvo had seen the ocean a hundred times in his life. He had crossed the Atlantic to come to North America, and even though he had been seasick the entire way, he had never been afraid of the ocean. But as they sat on their blanket looking out at the freighters anchored in the bay, Salvo was overcome by the irrational belief that a giant wave would at any minute sweep them off the sand and carry them under. The very idea of the vastness of the ocean—an idea that Anna had remarked only moments earlier was an appealing one to her—caused the muscles in his calves to contract so hard that both his ankles made a cracking noise. He sat paralyzed, and sweat began to run down his face and into his eyes and mouth. He tasted its saltiness and it reminded him of the ocean, and this compounded his fear.

Anna had seen Salvo's panic attacks before, and she knew something of his insomnia, though they had never discussed it. She had written it off as nerves, and since it disappeared sometimes for years, she didn't give it much thought. This time, however, she noticed it was happening, and she took in the full scope of his terror and saw that no matter how hard she tried to calm him, to convince him that everything was okay, he would not or could not listen. All that could be done was to wait for it to pass, and this took longer and longer each time. There were occasions when she thought that it was likely he was losing his mind. Salvo, too, secretly wondered this. He could not tell if his wondering was part of his affliction or the part of him that remained, so he did not know whether to believe it. He did not know much of anything.

In the fall of 1968, Martin Fisher-Fielding pulled the trigger on a deal he had known for nearly ten years would have to be done. In so doing, he sealed his fate in the annals of circus history. For the princely sum of 111 million dollars, he sold his seventy per cent stake in the Fisher-Fielding Circus Company to a Dutch entertainment consortium, and the show that had revolutionized the industry and made his family a household name passed out of Fisher-Fielding hands forever. By all but the few who knew that he had no other choice, that the circus was on its knees and waiting for a death blow, he was vilified. People spat on him in the streets, and friends of forty years did not return his calls.

His only consolation, aside from the money, was that the Spouses had got a raw deal in the whole arrangement. After he had sold his share of the F-F they had little choice but to sell as well and had received considerably less for their twenty-eight per cent than it was worth, a relatively paltry fourteen million dollars. The remaining Respectable, whose sliver of the company amounted to less than two percent of the circus, waited the entire deal out, and then got nearly seven million, half as much as the Spouses. The Dutch consortium had wanted to own the entire company, and was willing to pay handsomely for total control of the name that had become synonymous with the circus.

It pained Martin greatly to see the F-F pass from family hands, and as much as he loathed the Spouses he would rather have seen them control the show than sell it, but there had been no other way. If he had waited another five years, they would have been bankrupt, and then it would have been worth nothing. At least this way they made some money. He only wished that others could see it in these terms. They did not. Martin bought a castle in Scotland and left the United States a bitter man.

It was not long after the F-F was sold that Anna woke up one morning and discovered Daniel was gone. She was not surprised. He had been nearly completely physically recovered for almost a year, and in that time Anna had seen him have several large seizures. After the first one, she had known without a doubt what had happened on the wire. She did not tell Daniel that she had seen him in the field behind the barn, and though she desperately wanted to, she did not run to help him on the subsequent occasions she saw his seizures. She was sure that Daniel would leave if he knew his secret had been discovered.

Likewise she had said nothing to Salvo. The guilt kept her up nights, so much so that she was often still awake after Salvo had frightened himself into sleep. She knew that he still blamed himself for the fall, but she did not want to tell him that it was not his fault because she was afraid that if she did he would return to the wire. Slowly, though, the guilt wore her down, and she knew that soon she would have to tell him everything. The consequences would be hers to bear.

Daniel left no letter, taking only his bank book and a small suitcase. Most of his clothes were still folded in their drawers, and he had even made his bed. Anna lay on his bed and stared at the ceiling. Slowly she felt something inside her rip itself free from her chest and float away from her body, and when she sat up she was no longer angry. At first she didn't know what was different; she had been angry for so long that she had grown used to the feeling, until it felt like anything else. Then she realized what had changed, and she went downstairs and out into the fields to find Salvo.

She found him sitting cross-legged in the field behind the house, staring up at the sky. There was fear in his eyes, and he was stiff like a corpse. Anna pried him off the ground and took him into the house, sitting him at the kitchen table. They sat across from each other, Anna's hands over Salvo's. After he had passed through whatever had frightened him, she told him that Daniel was gone, and that he would probably not be coming back. Salvo nodded, like he too had been expecting this to happen.

Anna swallowed hard, her heart racing. "It was him who caused the fall."

Salvo stared at her blankly. "Daniel?"

"Yes. He had a seizure on the wire."

Salvo was dumbfounded. "How long have you known this?"

"Several months. I was afraid to tell you."

"Why?"

"Because I knew he would leave."

"He has left anyway."

Anna bit her lip. "And I knew you would go back to the wire."

Salvo shook his head. "I will not go back. It does not matter whose fault the fall was."

Anna got up and went to a drawer. She opened it and took out a stack of letters. She placed them on the table in front of him. "I think you should go back," she said. "I won't walk with you, but I think you should go back."

"What are these?" Salvo fingered the letters, not opening them.

"Offers to walk. Skywalks, mainly."

"You have kept these from me?"

"Yes. I'm sorry."

Salvo stood. "I can't go back."

"Yes, you can. It's the only way that your fear will stop. I don't understand why, but it is the truth."

Salvo looked into Anna's eyes, and he knew she was right. But he did not know if he could return to the wire. He did not know if it could be the place it had once been. And he did not know that he would not fall. "I will think about it," he said.

Neither Salvo nor Anna slept any sooner than normal that night, but for the first time in a long time, each found comfort in the other's arms, and they did not miss the sleep.

<hr />

Daniel got off the bus and blinked as the light brightened. Toronto. It had taken him a while to get there, and as soon as he stepped off the bus he knew he would not stay for more than a few weeks. It had nothing to do with Toronto; it was simply a feeling that this was not the end of his wandering.

His father had told him a story when he was small, and since the accident it came to him often, interjecting into his thoughts like a rude companion.

"Once, long before you were born, there was a group of Roma who found a boy standing on the side of the road, all alone. They looked high and low for his parents, but no one could find them. Finally it was time for the Roma to move on, and by then everyone liked the boy, for he was a very smart and likeable boy, so they decided to take him with them.

"Well, time passed and the boy grew up, and his adopted family was very proud of him. He had learned to play the most wonderful music and was a gifted smith, and he could even cast magic if he needed to. But he was curious about the world of his ancestors, and about *gadje* life, so he vowed he would leave his Romany brethren for one year. After the year was up, he would return and tell them all he had learned.

"He went for the year and was taken in by the *gadje*, who also liked him for the same reasons as the Roma. He lived with them and was treated like a prince, though he never said anything of his past.

"When a year had passed he returned to the Roma, but his mind was poisoned. 'I am told that you Roma steal babies. Was I stolen?' he asked. Many were insulted by that question, but they knew the *gadje* said these things, so they answered him. 'No, no. We found you on the road with no one and nothing, and we took you in like our own.'

"He looked skeptical and asked another question. 'They say that the Roma lie and cheat. Is that true?' Well, many others were insulted, but they answered him the same. 'No, no. We do the same as anyone else. No better, no worse.'

"He did not appear convinced. 'I do not understand,' he said. 'I have lived with the *gadje* for a year, and I do not understand why they would lie. They are far smarter than the Roma.'

"Now the Roma were really insulted. To think that he whom they had raised, whom they had fed and clothed and taught all they knew to, would say such things about them and take the word of the *gadje* over theirs, well, that was too much for them. Though they loved him dearly, he was cast out and told to stay away until he felt differently towards the Roma.

"He was only too happy to be gone. 'Good riddance,' he said to himself. 'I am not a Rom anyway.' And he went back into the city. However, when he met a family he had known only days before, they did not seem to remember him. 'I will show you,' he said, and he picked up a fiddle to play them a song he knew they loved. But when he played, the most horrible sounds came from the fiddle. He did not understand why, but he was undeterred. He saw a pot that had a hole in it and said, 'I will fix this pot, as I have many pots for you before, and you will know from the job I do that it is me.' But try as he might, he could not fix the pot. 'Go away, you, and quit hurting our ears and damaging our pots,' the family said to him. They threw him out of their house and shut the door tightly behind them.

"The man was very angry. 'A curse on this house,' he said, 'and all that inhabit it.' But nothing happened. His magic was gone as well.

"From then on he was a beggar, and in only a few years he was no longer handsome and looked like an old man. Then one day his old Romany friends came through the town, and they recognized him at once. 'How do you like living as a *gadje*, brother?' they asked him. 'I cannot play music. I cannot fix things. I have no magic,' he cried. 'Of course not,' they told him. 'Those are Roma things.'

"At once the man saw the error of his ways, and he begged to be taken back in. The Roma laughed. 'Of course, of course. You only had to ask. All is forgiven.'"

Daniel knew why this story found its way into his memory so often. But he did not believe in the ending. He would never be able to go back. They would take him back without hesitation, he knew this. But what he had done could not be erased, and above all he did not deserve their love. He would never again allow anyone to love him, would never take that kind of chance. Killers do not deserve forgiveness.

He picked up his suitcase from the side of the bus and walked through the bus station, intending to find the closest rooming house, where he could collapse into a long sleep. He hoped that when he arrived wherever he knew he must go, he would realize he was there.

~~~~~~~~~~

In the summer of 1969 a man named Jim Carter was arrested in connection with a string of fires set in San Francisco, California. Upon further questioning, the forty-two-year-old alcoholic confessed to a wide variety of crimes ranging from petty theft to arson. Among the arsons for which Carter claimed responsibility was the Fisher-Fielding circus fire.

Investigators were initially suspicious. Carter claimed that he had been employed by the F-F during the summer of 1945, and that he had started the fire by holding a match to the side wall of the big top in the area of the women's latrine. Circus records showed that he had indeed been employed by the show during the time he claimed, although his whereabouts for the day in question could not be accounted for one way or the other. What finally convinced investigators that Carter's story was true was when he told them of his lighting not one but two matches, the second one several feet from the first. It had never been released to the public, either during the initial investigation or the subsequent inquiry, that the fire had two incendiary points. So, the police promptly charged Carter with the Fisher-Fielding fire.

A court judged him insane, and he was committed to an asylum where he died some years later.

When news of the arrest reached the Ursaris, Salvo didn't know what to do. Although he had never really thought that Etel had started the fire, he knew that there had always been doubts in his mind. For a long time he could not even bring himself to look at Etel, and finally he felt he had no choice but to confront her. András suspected he might do this, however, and so he intercepted him.

"What are you going to say to her?" he asked.

"I will tell her I am sorry. That I never should have doubted her."

"How will that help her? She knows nothing of these accusations. Finding out now will only hurt her."

"I think she knows," Salvo said.

"Are you certain?"

Salvo considered this. "No."

"Well, unless you are certain, you should say nothing."

"I owe her an apology. And so do you."

"No. An apology is a selfish thing sometimes, Salvo. If we tell her, we will feel better, but she may feel worse. We owe to her that our shame be kept to ourselves."

Salvo nodded. András is right, he thought. I will say nothing. Time will take care of our transgression.

TIME HAD DONE LITTLE to ease the mind of Etel. Twenty-four years had not made the day of the fire any less vivid in her memory, and the smell of smoke or the sight of flame still bothered her. It never occurred to her that this might have as much to do with her experience as a baby as it did the F-F fire. After Carter's arrest, however, the thing that bothered her even more than the fire was how good it had made her feel to see the guilt in her brothers' faces when they had realized they had grossly misjudged her. She thought she had long ago forgiven them for their doubts, but when she felt her heart leap at their misery, she knew it was not so. Etel resolved to try harder to forgive them, exasperated when she found that if you have to work at forgiveness it will not come. Many days she was sure it never would.

SALVO'S DECISION TO RETURN TO THE WIRE was not made as easily as it had been at other times. This time he would be alone, and though Anna had said she would support him in his endeavour, he knew that she did it only because there was no other way, and that her heart was not behind it. If there had been any alternative, Salvo would have stayed on the ground.

He made a deal with himself. In 1975, six years' time, he would be sixty-five years old. That was the age that people in North America retired, and that would be the age that he would give up the wire for good. Before, he had always assumed that he would walk indefinitely, and he thought that maybe this had led him to be callous about his time on the wire. He hoped that a realization that his walking days were finite would lead him to a place where he could stop, where he could step off the wire and know it was the last time and feel good about it. To honour this pledge was his resolution.

Salvo selected, from among many offers, a walk over the playing field between doubleheader Montreal Expos games. Although he had never actually seen a baseball game and didn't even think he would much enjoy watching one, he had liked Montreal on the one occasion he had visited the city. He also thought it might be nice to hear people speak in a language other than English.

He was nervous as the ninth inning of the first game began, not sure if he had done the right thing, not sure if he really wanted to walk for an audience again. As he prepared to climb to the wire he looked back at Anna, and for the first time since she had known him, her husband's eyes did not shine with the anticipation of walking; she saw fear, and only fear. "Don't worry," she said.

Salvo pulled himself together, for Anna's sake. "I am not worried. I will not fall."

"I know. If you were to fall, the world would fall with you, and I know the world will not fall."

Salvo smiled at these familiar words, then kissed Anna on the cheek. He climbed up to the platform, and when the third out came to end the ninth inning, he stepped onto the wire.

Immediately everything receded. All his fears, all his memories, all he loved and all he loathed. His daughters had not fallen; they had never existed. His life was only beginning, and it would end on the other end of the wire, and then it would begin again the next time he stepped out. Salvo smiled, breathed in hard and took another step.

EIGHT

S ix million years ago the Colorado River began to carve out what would eventually be named the Grand Canyon. Often forgotten is the fact that had this river not travelled through desert, there would have been no canyon. Rainfall would have washed away the canyon's steep slopes, preventing the feat of nature from forming. This was Salvo's favourite thing about the canyon, the requirement of desolation for wonder.

It had come quickly: 1975. After six years of skywalks across stadiums, over rivers, between buildings, and nearly everything a wire could be strung from, his sixty-fifth birthday was nearly upon him, and the time of his retirement had arrived. He had chosen his final walk carefully, and even though there were things about this walk he did not like, it was too good to pass up. Second to crossing between the Canadian and American sides of Niagara Falls, this was the most spectacular walk he could envision.

At this point the canyon was a quarter of a mile wide and one thousand feet deep. It had been difficult to secure an ungreased piece of cable long enough to stretch across the gorge. Because of the distance, the longest he had ever walked, the wire had to be unusually strong to support its own weight. It had taken crews a week to put the wire into place.

Salvo was hired to do the walk by a soft-drink company, on the condition that he stop in the middle and drink a bottle of their soda, and allow this picture to be used in advertisements. Salvo did not like this concession, but there was no other way for him to have the chance to walk the Grand Canyon, so he had agreed. He had waited for the day of the walk with growing impatience.

Anna viewed the day with more trepidation than Salvo. She was eager for him to retire, hoping against hope that he would finally be able to leave the wire on his own terms, and that their life would be returned to the ground for good this time. Mainly, though, she worried about him falling. Anyone could see that Salvo Ursari was not a young man.

Two years earlier András Ursari had died after an eighteen-month battle with cancer. His death had been a relief to his family; his final days contained more pain than his entire life had up to that point. There had been much debate as to how to conduct his funeral. András was most decidedly not a Christian, but on the other hand it could not be said that he did not believe in a God that resembled the Christian one in many ways. In the end they held a memorial service, then buried his cremated remains. Etel had not wanted to cremate him, but she remembered that he had once said that cremation was his wish, so she deferred to András's words. To her, it seemed sad that he had escaped so many fires in life only to willingly go to one once dead. When her time came, she wanted anything but the flame. Sometimes she daydreamed about burial at sea.

It was at this memorial service that Anna had noticed that none of them was young any more. She noticed for the first time the wrinkles on Salvo's face, the grey in his hair, the loose skin of his neck, and then she looked to Etel and saw the same. Examining her own hands she saw the hands of a woman far older than herself, and then she knew that somehow her life had gone into its retreat without her realizing it. For no good reason it instantly seemed colder out.

Since his accident, the feelings of invincibility János once entertained had evaporated. He had been working on the Ursari farm with far more success than Salvo had ever attained. Salvo had all but abandoned farm work since returning to the wire, and as he was now retiring he had no intention of returning to it. Following András's death, Etel and János sold their house and moved back into Salvo and Anna's home. It was clear to everyone that the farm would someday be János's. He was after all the only one who had ever grown anything on it.

Before leaving for this walk, Etel had confronted Salvo about the fire. "I forgive you," she told him, and he didn't have to ask to know what she was talking about.

"I am sorry," he said, clutching her shoulders.

"I know. It is forgiven."

"It was a horrible thing to think."

"Yes. But the past is the past. We are through it."

Salvo had embraced his sister, and he felt thirty years of guilt and shame peel off his back.

Though they never knew it, Daniel Ursari had seen Salvo walk on more than one occasion since he ran away from his adoptive family. He lived in Detroit, working as a parking-meter repair man, a job at which he excelled. Whenever he saw an advertisement for a walk of Salvo's, he would attempt to get the time off of work and travel the country to see Salvo perform. He was always careful to stay out of the way of anyone who might recognize him. He would arrive as the walk started and leave as soon as Salvo's foot hit the far platform. There was no point in hanging around any longer than necessary; he still had seizures, though he rarely had more than one a year.

Daniel was in the audience for the Grand Canyon walk, and though it never occurred to Salvo to look, if he had it is possible that he would have seen the boy whom he had pulled from the fire, sitting in the bottom row of bleachers constructed specifically for the walk. Salvo's mind was preoccupied anyway; this was a difficult walk, and his full attention was required to pull it off.

He checked his watch and, seeing that he would begin in only moments, took it off and gave it to Anna. She smiled and put it in her pocket.

"This is a long one," he said.

"This will be your last walk. Make sure to enjoy it." She did not say this with malice. It was a fact both of them knew, and she genuinely did want him to enjoy the walk, though she worried for his safety. These skywalks had been getting progressively dangerous, and she knew that this was by far the most perilous yet.

She did not know that only hours before, he had been asked to perform a skywalk between the towers of two of the world's tallest buildings. Because he was retiring, he saw no point in telling her what would only worry her further. He would turn them down when he returned home.

"I think I will enjoy it," he said. "It is a nice day." It was indeed a day to behold, the weather ideal for such a walk. It was sunny but uncharacteristically cool, and there was no wind to speak of.

It was time for him to begin. He picked up his balancing pole and checked to make sure that the bottle of soda was secure in its pouch hanging from his neck. "Wish me luck," he said.

"You don't need luck."

Salvo smiled and turned to the wire.

"I never hated you," Anna called to him.

He paused for a moment before looking at her. "I know."

He stepped onto the wire and it was all gone. He thought only of his feet moving forward, his hands on the balancing pole. For nearly three hundred steps he moved forward slowly, steadily, inexorably. He was not aware of the people who watched from the safety of solid ground. Then a thought began to form in his mind. It was small at first, almost a whisper of a whisper, but it grew louder and stronger until it was all there was.

This is your last walk.

It was plain, it was simple, and it would not go away. Salvo tried to clear his mind, knowing that a thought on the wire, even a simple one, was a very bad thing. Still it would not leave him.

He pushed on, head pounding, barely aware of himself. Finally he reached the centre of the wire, marked with a piece of red electrician's tape. It was here that he was to sit on the wire and drink the soda that was suspended from his neck. He sighed, thinking this a bad thing to do on the wire. Then, out of the corner of his eye, something floated into view, and his heart stopped dead.

The butterfly was blue and yellow and orange, quite large, and it fluttered past him, in no special hurry. For a moment it hesitated, then came to rest on the tip of Salvo's balancing pole.

Salvo clenched his teeth, waiting for panic to set in, but a strange thing happened: the fear that he expected never came. The butterfly sat, unmoving, and Salvo was not afraid. His balancing pole was weightless. He was calm as he watched the motionless insect for a long minute, and then it took flight, soon disappearing in the distance.

A smile wound its way onto Salvo's lips. Still standing, he took the bottle of soda from its cradle and dropped it, watching it fall until, like the butterfly, it was too small to see. He lowered his pole to the wire and raised his feet into the air. He held this handstand until his face turned hot with blood. Returning his feet to the wire, he reverted to a standing position.

All around him he saw the desert, a million shades of brown with points of green and red, and he felt warm air rising from below and smelled nothing but himself and open space. His bones were strong and his mouth was wet, and his eyes were clear as ever they had been.

Retirement receded from his mind as an idea that had never existed. He stood on the wire, and he knew that as long as he was standing, he would live forever.

ACKNOWLEDGMENTS

THOUGH THIS IS A WORK OF IMAGINATION, I have drawn in places from history and the experience of real wire walkers. Ron Morris's biography of Karl Wallenda, *Wallenda*; Paul Auster's translation of Phillip Petit's *On the High Wire*; *The Tightrope Walker* by Hermine Demoraine; Stewart O'Nan's *The Circus Fire*; *Budapest 1900* by John Lukacs; and *Big Top Boss: John Ringling North and the Circus* by D. L. Hammarstrom provided much of my picture of how things "actually" happened. Some of the Romany folk tales included are made up, and others are actual lore. The stories I have not made up myself can be found in a wide variety of incarnations, in books such as Diane Tong's *Gypsy Folktales*; *The Orange of Love*, compiled by Lars Gjerde, and *A Book of Gypsy Folk-Tales*, edited by Dora Yates. For some interesting descriptions of Romany life, Isabel Fonseca's *Bury Me Standing: The Gypsies and Their Journey* and Jan Yoors's *The Gypsies* were my favourites. However, being fiction, *Ascension* is mostly all lies.

I owe an enormous debt to Marita Dachsel, Lee Henderson, Rick Maddocks, Sioux Browning, George McWhirter, Madeleine Thien, Heather Frechette, Karoly Sándor, Lynda Milham, Chad Hunt, Gary Tayler, Mark Abbott, Timothy Taylor and Jason Willows for reading and providing suggestions, complaints and comments about the manuscript. Thanks also to Kevin Chong,

Tammy Armstrong, Anne Fleming, Annabel Lyon, Nancy Lee, Laisha Rosnau, Jennica Harper and Jeff Morris for their considerable lunching skills; to Isabel, George, Steve, Dina and everyone else at Helen's Grill for feeding and caffeinating me; to the Galloway, Tayler and Haslett families and their extensions for support and encouragement; and to the UBC Creative Writing Program for employment and enjoyment.

I am deeply grateful to my agent, Carolyn Swayze, and to Diane Martin, Noelle Zitzer, Louise Dennys, Astrid Otto, Deirdre Molina, Jennifer Shepherd, Gloria Goodman, Samantha Haywood and everyone else at Knopf/Random House of Canada for each of the million wonderful things they've done for me and this book.

I would like to acknowledge the financial assistance of the Canada Council for the Arts; without their aid I would have been up a creek in a big way.

Finally, thanks to my wife, Lara. Without her, none of this would be.

STEVEN GALLOWAY teaches creative writing at the University of British Columbia. His acclaimed fiction debut, *Finnie Walsh*, was nominated for the 2000 Amazon.com/*Books in Canada* First Novel Award. He lives in Vancouver.